Tangled Up in Love

HEIDI BETTS

St. Martin's Paperbacks

TANGLED UP IN LOVE

Copyright © 2009 by Heidi Betts.
Excerpt from *Loves Me, Loves Me Knot* copyright © 2009 by Heidi Betts.

Cover photo © Herman Estevez.

All rights reserved.

For information address St. Martin's Press, 175 Fifth Avenue, New York, NY 10010.

ISBN: 0-312-94671-6
EAN: 978-0-312-94671-5

Printed in the United States of America

St. Martin's Paperbacks edition / February 2009

St. Martin's Paperbacks are published by St. Martin's Press, 175 Fifth Avenue, New York, NY 10010.

10 9 8 7 6 5 4 3 2

Acknowledgments

Big steps and new endeavors are rarely accomplished alone. This one was no different, and I owe several people a rather large debt of gratitude:

My agent, Richard Curtis, who "had a feeling." God bless your gut, Richard. You've never steered me wrong, and this feeling turned out to be an exceptionally good one.

My delightful new editor at St. Martin's Press, Rose Hilliard, who loved this idea from the very beginning, has never faltered in her boundless enthusiasm, and has been an absolute dream to work with every step of the way.

My mom, Anne Betts, who taught me how to knit in the first place, and answered all those nagging little questions I had for this story and the others in the series.

My good friend and Pink Panty Plotting Partner (try saying that five times fast!), Karen Alarie, who acted as both my rock and sounding board as this entire trilogy was coming together. The next round's on me, babe!

My brother, Toby, who helped me with the research about Cleveland and didn't even complain when I e-mailed him a dozen times with last-minute questions that needed to be answered *right now*. Any mistakes are entirely my own—though I'd be happy to shift the blame, if he'd let me. *g*

And Elizabeth Berger for aiding me these past few years in more ways than I can count. (You know what I'm talking about, Elizabeth. *g*)

Thank you all so much for your help and support! I couldn't have done it without a single one of you.

Row 1

He wished she didn't have such a terrific ass.

If it were fat or saggy or flat as a board, or maybe one of those that jiggled when she walked, he would have no trouble ignoring her.

But it wasn't. Instead, it was world-class. A tight, round, delicious ass that looked good in pants and skirts and everything in between. And it definitely did not jiggle when she walked.

Oh, no, it sashayed. Swayed slowly from side to side like a hypnotist's watch, drawing appreciative, wolfish stares and sending every dick in the room pointing Due North.

Dylan Stone dragged his gaze away and took a long pull from his bottle of ice-cold Coors Light. Noise clattered around him from the football game playing on The Penalty Box's multiple television sets and the raised voices of its late-night customers. He was in his element, and this was his crowd.

All except for Miss Veronica Chasen, the bane of his existence and a huge, throbbing thorn in his side.

Of course, in addition to a butt that just wouldn't quit, she also amused him all to hell. She had a competitive streak a mile wide, and ever since he'd beaten her out of a prime columnist position at the *Cleveland Herald,* she'd kept him on his toes with the challenges she wrote in her columns every other month just for him.

It had started as a personal bitch session from her, which she'd taken public in one of her weekly columns for the *Cleveland Sentinel,* a smaller rival paper to the *Herald.* But since he'd known perfectly well she was talking about him and how he'd ruined her life by sweeping in with more in his pants than she possessed, he'd had no qualms about firing off a retort in *his* column the following week.

As best he could recall, he'd made a remark about men just being naturally more qualified for some jobs than women, and that if she couldn't hack it, maybe she should think about doing something more her speed—like needlepoint or working behind the makeup counter of a department store.

Not so surprisingly, she hadn't taken his suggestion well at all. The very next week, seething with barely suppressed rage, she'd basically announced that just because he filled out his jeans more in the front than she did didn't mean he knew how to use what God had given him, and she'd be willing to bet money she had bigger balls, anyway. She hadn't used those exact words, but he'd gotten the drift.

He took another sip of his beer, his mouth turning up at the memory. From there, it had been off to the races.

His response had been something along the lines of, *Oh, yeah? Let's see you go bungee jumping, then we'll talk about who's got the bigger set of balls.*

He hadn't actually expected her to do it, but just a couple of weeks later, there it was—a grainy black-and-white photograph of her hanging upside down beneath a bridge, connected only by a glorified rubber band around one ankle. Her eyes had been screwed so tightly closed, he was surprised she'd ever been able to open them again. And it had looked like she was screaming loudly enough to bust the eardrums of half the residents of the continental United States.

But she'd gone through with it, he had to give her credit for that.

And at the end of her column about her first experience at bungee jumping, she'd gotten him back by suggesting he prove his masculinity by going skydiving.

Boy, if she'd known how much he hated heights, she would have been cackling with glee. But he couldn't let her—or their readers—think he was a wuss, so he'd cowboyed up and jumped out of the freaking airplane. He'd just about pissed his pants doing it, too, but imagining her response to his challenge photo the following week had made it well worth walking around with undescended testicles for the next few days.

From that point on, they regularly sent each other off to do the wild, wacky, or dangerous.

He made her play goalie for a charity ice hockey event without telling anyone she was a girl.

She made him get his legs waxed.

He made her run a marathon.

She sent him mountain climbing.

He sent her white-water rafting.

In the latest round, she'd sent him into one of the meanest, nastiest biker bars on the outskirts of Cleveland wearing a hot pink Hawaiian shirt and gold lamé biker shorts to order some flaming pussy drink called a Pink Panty. He'd left with a black eye and bruised ribs, but had counted himself lucky not to have been made the girl-friend of one of the towering, unshaven, leather-clad, and personal-hygiene-deficient Hell's Angels, forced to ride around on the bitch seat of his bike the rest of the night.

To repay the favor, Dylan had dared Ronnie to get a tattoo. He was nonspecific as to where or what it should be, but thanks to him, she now sported a Chinese symbol somewhere on her anatomy.

Which brought his train of thought right back around to Ronnie's perfectly rounded ass, since that's where he suspected the tattoo was located.

He couldn't be sure, of course. A photograph of the actual symbol had accompanied her article that week, but it was a close-up and gave no hint as to what part of her body it was on. Since it was nowhere visible to the naked eye, however—and he should know; he'd spent enough time lately doggedly looking for it—and she'd made a reference in her column to it being in what she considered "a rather personal, private area," he chose to believe she'd gotten the tattoo on her ass.

His brand on her butt. He kind of liked that.

A round of female laughter from a table in the corner drew his attention, and he turned his head slightly to study the group of women seated there. His own friends were caught up in the Steelers–Patriots game playing on the giant television mounted above one corner of the bar, paying little attention to him or anything else going on around them.

Ronnie sat with her back to him, the long fall of her wavy chestnut hair reaching nearly to her hips.

He liked long hair on a woman. Too bad this partic-ular woman happened to be his sworn enemy.

She was bitter as a pill around him, but not for the

first time, he wondered if there was a softer side to Ronnie Chasen. A woman that beautiful shouldn't be a flaming bitch, and she seemed to get along well enough with her own friends.

The women laughed again, and Dylan had a sneaking suspicion they were having a jolly good time disparaging the shortcomings of men. Isn't that what women spent their time doing whenever two or more of them got together over a pitcher of margaritas?

He didn't know them all, but he was familiar with a few because they were intimately involved with his friends.

Ronnie, of course, his archnemesis.

Then there was Grace Fisher, Cleveland's hometown cross between Oprah Winfrey and Martha Stewart. She had her own cable talk show that covered everything from gripping emotional family dramas to making a cake in the shape of a porcupine. She'd even been nicknamed "Amazing Grace" because of her versatility and lack of any apparent faults whatsoever.

Grace was currently engaged to Dylan's friend, Zack, who played goalie for Cleveland's professional hockey team, the Rockets. The two had met at a charity hockey event where Zack first hit a puck over the protective Plexiglas shield straight into Grace's skull. Then after she'd been bandaged and examined by the team's physician, Zack had proceeded to fly off the ice and knock her flat on her rear.

What could have been touted as the most embarrassing moment of Zack's career had instead become his and Grace's answer to the question of how they first met. Dylan himself had heard the story going on about six thousand times now.

And Jenna Marshall was the ex-wife of another of Dylan's friends, undercover CPD detective Gage Marshall. He supposed Jenna was actually going by her maiden name, Langan, again, but he knew that didn't set well with Gage.

The others he recognized only because they seemed to come in every week or so with the rest of the group.

That in itself was an odd occurrence, seeing as how The Penalty Box was a sports bar, catering to hockey fans in general and Rockets fans in particular, with a primarily male clientele. The Box's TVs were always tuned to some sporting event or another . . . sometimes more than one at a time . . . and the walls were plastered with hockey memorabilia. Not exactly a chick-magnet kind of decor.

Zack's engagement to Grace had changed that, though. She'd started showing up to meet Zack's friends, spend more time with him, and learn the intricacies of the game. Then, like bunnies, they'd started to multiply until an entire back table was filled with women and the bartender was forced to make fruity pastel girlie drinks in a blender instead of simply pulling a tap or pouring out shots.

It was a shame, to Dylan's way of thinking. He also wasn't too happy that he had to see Ronnie on a regular basis at the one place he'd considered his estrogen-free escape from the world.

Dylan tipped back his bottle of Coors, draining the last remaining drops just as Ronnie pushed to her feet and headed toward the bar with the empty pitcher from their table. Well, shoot, looked like they both needed a refill.

The legs of his chair scraped across the floor as he

stood and headed in the same direction, meeting her at the bar and resting both his forearms on the scarred mahogany surface.

"Hey, there, Chasen. How's that tattoo of yours doing? Any pain or swelling I should know about?"

Ronnie cast him a withering glare, her lashes fluttering at half-mast over her coffee-brown eyes. "How would I be able to tell, Stone? You're such a pain in my ass, I'm not likely to feel anything else down there."

Ha! So he'd been right; the tattoo *was* on her butt. Now he just had to figure out where. Was it on the left cheek or the right? High up near her hip, or down lower on the soft spot?

"Good to know I've made an impression."

She muttered something beneath her breath as the bartender came toward them, and Dylan bit back a grin.

"We need another round of margaritas," she told Turk, handing him the empty plastic pitcher.

Turk was a tall black man with a shaved head, three silver hoops in one ear and two in the other, and a collection of tattoos that—unlike Ronnie's—were easily visible above the neck and below the arms of his tight white T-shirt. He wasn't the owner of the Box, but just about anytime the bar was open, Turk was there. And since he was roughly the size of a small redwood, he wasn't opposed to playing the part of bouncer if the crowd got a bit too rowdy.

When Turk returned with a full pitcher, Dylan slapped a couple of bucks on the counter and said, "I'll take another Coors." The man handed him an ice-cold bottle, collected the money, and walked away without ever altering his hard, blank expression.

"I've gotta tell you," Dylan continued, stopping Ronnie before she could escape back to her table with the fresh drinks, "I didn't expect you to go through with it. I mean, you're so uptight about your appearance, I never thought you'd mar your perfect skin with some big, ugly, permanent tattoo."

"What?" she asked, one dark brow arching while the corners of her mouth turned down in a frown. "You expected me to wimp out?"

She was wearing a fire-engine-red skirt that stopped well above her knees and a jacket to match. Beneath the tailored jacket was a white silk blouse that opened in a V over her high, ample breasts and gave him more than a glimpse of her generous cleavage.

Outfits like this were the very reason he'd felt confident she hadn't gotten the tattoo on one of her breasts. Because he'd have darn well spotted it by now if that had been the case.

He popped the cap on his new beer and took a slow draw before answering, his gaze landing on her full, ripe mouth. "Something like that."

"It will take more than a lousy tattoo to send me running, Stone. Anything you can do, I can do better, remember?"

She tossed her head to the side, sending all that long, dark hair back over one shoulder. Damn, how did women do that? *Why* did they do it? Didn't they know it sent every drop of blood straight from a guy's brain down to his package?

It took some doing, but he pulled his attention back to her face. Running splayed fingers through his own dark blond locks, he snorted and said, "Yeah, right. Let's see you write your name in the snow."

"Nice," she said, the word icicle-sharp and just as cold. "Not crude at all."

"Honey, in case you hadn't noticed, you're standing in the middle of a sports bar. If you want to avoid crude, you should go down the street to that coffeehouse where all the boring folks hang out."

"Thanks for the advice, but I'll manage. Besides, I think better with a couple of drinks in my system, and right now I'm working on your next challenge."

He took another sip of beer, his glance slipping to the pulse in her throat. Was her skin as soft as it looked? he wondered. If he leaned in and swiped his tongue over that very spot, would it taste salty like her mood or sweet like a woman should?

He took another, longer pull, trying to bring his imagination and his hormones under control. "Bring it on, babe."

She licked her lips, and his temperature shot up another fifty degrees.

"Are you sure you don't want to surrender now and save yourself the humiliation?"

"No way. I'm having a damn good time."

"So am I."

"Great."

"Good."

"Fine."

"Fine."

And with that, she stomped off, her tight, heart-shaped ass sashaying all the way.

"I hate that man with the flames of a thousand fiery Hells," Ronnie spat as she returned to her table of friends and started refilling glasses from the pitcher of slushy, pale green margarita that shook in her hand.

She said it. She meant it. So what was with the strange sense of exhilaration she always felt after one of their sparring matches? Even now, with adrenaline pumping through her system and rage burning in her brain, she almost wanted to dive back in for Round Two.

"What man?" one of them asked, glancing around the bar as though the offender would be standing under a spotlight.

"Who do you think?" Grace said. Blond and beautiful, she was the picture of calm, never a hair out of place, never an emotion left unchecked. Only her close friends knew she had a sharp wit and a tongue like a razor blade. "Only the same guy Ronnie's been bitching about for the past year—Dylan 'That Arrogant Jackass' Stone."

"Let's just call him 'The Jackass' for short," Ronnie clipped out, filling her own glass to the brim before plopping down on her chair with very little finesse.

"I don't get it," Grace said. "You're such a nice person otherwise, and get along with just about everyone you meet, but put you within a ten-mile radius of Dylan Stone and you turn into a slavering she-witch."

Ronnie's eyes narrowed as she finished filling glasses and set the pitcher aside. "Payback's a bitch," she quipped, "and you're looking at her."

"So what did he do this time?" the petite, short-haired Jenna inquired.

"He asked if my new tattoo was sore."

"Is it?"

"Of course it is," Ronnie grumbled, taking a long, fortifying drink of her deliciously frothy tequila-laced concoction. "It throbs like a suffering bastard and rubs against my clothes all day, every day."

"Did you tell him what it means?" one of the other girls asked. The rest of the group chuckled, because they knew. Ronnie had divulged that little secret at their first knitting meeting after having the body art done.

"No way. Let him wonder."

"Fuck him, right?" Grace teased.

A cocky, knowing grin spread across Ronnie's face, and she reached around to pat a spot high on her left buttock. She didn't even wince at the added sting it caused. "That's right."

"So it's your turn to send him out on a dare. What are you going to make him do?"

"I don't know. I haven't thought of anything yet that's adequately dangerous or embarrassing." Her brows knit in a scowl. "He's so obnoxious about thinking men are braver and more accomplished than women. I feel like daring him to walk into traffic blindfolded. A nice Greyhound bus to the temporal lobe would knock some of the smugness out of him."

She lifted her head and met the gaze of each of her friends around the table, her eyes conveying her desperation. "Any ideas?"

"You could figure out a way for him to go through simulated childbirth," Melanie, a mother of two, offered flatly. "That would shut him up and have him bowing down to every woman he met from now until the end of time."

"You could send him for a bikini wax."

Ronnie flinched slightly at that suggestion. "Don't remind me. I still have that landing strip in my panties that is in no way ready to wave in approaching air traffic.

Plus, I don't want to repeat myself, and I already made him get his legs waxed." She smirked. "Wonder if *his* hair has grown back yet."

"You could dare him to meet you at some no-tell motel for hot, sleazy sex, then leave him tied to the bed until the maid finds him the next day. And you could be there to capture his degradation on film."

Ronnie laughed with everyone else, but inside, her stomach had clenched, and picturing Dylan tied to the bedposts, beneath her and at her mercy, sent an odd fluttering through the rest of her body.

Which was ridiculous, because he was a jerk, and if she was going to be attracted to any man at the moment, it certainly wouldn't be Dylan Stone. She was only having this reaction because it had been so long since she'd had any type of sex that didn't require batteries. After such a long dry spell, it was completely natural to have a physiological response to anything even remotely suggestive.

"How about walking across hot coals or dressing in drag and going down to the red-light district?" one of the women asked, bringing her focus back to the matter at hand.

"If you really want to trip him up on the men-versus-women thing, then he should have to do something women do on a regular basis and are really good at," Melanie put in. "Like cleaning the house, getting a kid ready for school and to the bus stop on time, or making a Halloween costume from scratch."

Reaching under the table, she retrieved her purse, which was oversized and stuffed to the gills. She pulled the knitting needles and skein of yarn she'd been working with earlier that evening off the top and set them aside, then continued to remove items one at a time.

"Do you know any men who have to carry around the crap women do, especially ones with kids? They grab their wallets and keys and take off. The rest of us have to make sure we have tampons, tissues, makeup, and nail files. And if you have kids, then you have to walk around with a steady supply of Band-Aids, baby wipes, antibacterial lotion, snacks, toys . . ." Melanie punctuated her words by pulling every one of those things from her purse, including a couple of strawberry Fruit Roll-Ups and a tiny yellow dump truck that was missing one wheel.

"Yikes," Jenna commented, blanching at the pile of junk cluttering the tabletop.

"So what are you suggesting?" Ronnie asked. "That I challenge Dylan to carry an overstuffed lady's handbag everywhere he goes for a month?"

Melanie's mouth twisted as she started loading things back into the purse, making its seams stretch and bulge. "He's certainly welcome to carry mine. It's no wonder women end up with osteoporosis. Most days, I'd swear I'm going to be a hunchback by the time I'm forty."

She squinted an eye and twisted her mouth, lifting one shoulder much higher than the other in a near-perfect imitation of Quasimodo. "You guys will come visit me in the bell tower, won't you?" she inquired in one of the funniest voices they'd ever heard.

They all laughed, and Ronnie nearly choked on her ill-timed sip of margarita.

"If we're not already there with you," Jenna promised, deliberately straightening her spine and throwing her shoulders back, the model of perfect, chiropractor-approved posture.

A moment later Grace said, "I have a better idea," so quietly Ronnie almost didn't hear her.

Her attention was immediately drawn back to what had started this thread of the conversation—her ongoing feud with Dylan Stone. "What?"

One side of her friend's mouth quirked up in a sly, conspiratorial grin, and she inclined her head in Melanie's direction. Or more accurately, to the bag balanced on Melanie's lap, a tangle of pale yellow yarn and two shiny, metallic blue needles sticking out of the top.

Ronnie looked at the purse . . . then back at Grace . . . then back at the purse.

And finally comprehension dawned. A slow smile spread and lifted her lips until she was grinning like an idiot.

"Grace, I love you, I really do. That's it! It's perfect. Not only will he *hate* it, but there's no way he'll ever manage it in only a month's time."

She sat back, the discomfort of the tattoo on her rear end forgotten as she laughed and began to mentally plan the text of her upcoming column, where she would stump Dylan but good.

"The next round's on me, girls," she announced, reaching for the near-empty pitcher and raising it over her head. "To my partners in crime. And The Jackass's crushing defeat."

Row 2

Anticipation coiled in Dylan's stomach as he sat back in his creaky old metal chair, crossed his feet on the corner of his desk, and opened the latest edition of the *Sentinel* to page six.

It was late Friday afternoon, which meant another one of Ronnie's columns and another challenge doled out for him to complete. He wondered what she'd come up with this time. Fire eating? Firefighting? Cosmetology school?

The sounds of the newsroom buzzed around him, but he blocked them out. The ringing phones, raised voices, clicking keys of computers and ancient typewriters alike.

He'd been hoping for his own office by now, but instead he was stuck inside this ugly blue cubicle the size of a postage stamp, with enough noise to drive the sanest man stark raving mad. It was a wonder any of them could think straight, let alone manage to get any writing done.

Now, at a game—football, baseball, basketball, hockey, it didn't matter—the noise and chaos were exhilarating. If he were writing about sports and reporting about the play-offs or the latest team trades, he'd be in his element. But instead he was stuck here, hiding out inside four five-foot-high, paper-thin walls just to read one lousy column in a rival paper.

Though the art of knitting has been around for hundreds of years, he read, finally getting down to Ronnie's article, *it seems to have made a comeback recently.*

Huh? Her column this week was about *knitting*? What happened to daring him to eat glass or stand on his head while eating a bowl of soup?

Brows crossed, he continued to read. She talked about the number of books, fiction and nonfiction alike, cropping up lately about knitting. About the celebrities who seemed to be taking it up as the hobby *du jour*. About Julia Roberts's role in turning one of the aforementioned books into a major motion picture.

Jeez, this was a complete snooze, Dylan thought, his eyes moving faster and faster over the tiny print as his patience wore thin. Ronnie must have run out of ideas for challenges and decided to ignore the topic entirely, hoping their little competition would simply fade away.

Not that he'd let her get away with it. If she wanted the dares to stop, then she'd have to come out with a public admission via her column that women just weren't cut out to do all the things men could.

He didn't actually believe that; as far as he was concerned, men and women were equals, and if women had the balls to fly jumbo jets or charge into battle in the armed forces, more power to them. There were some things even he, being a guy, had no interest in experiencing. And yeah, maybe not the balls for, either.

But Ronnie had started this, putting him on the men-are-better-than-women side of the debate, and truth be told he enjoyed baiting her. So in order to put this whole game to rest, *she* would have to be the one to admit defeat.

And that's why, he read on, near the bottom of the article, *women make better knitters than men. Men don't have the . . .* needles *for such intricate work, and I challenge one of them—one of them in particular—to prove me wrong.*

Oh, shit. It *was* her challenge column. His eyes had been so glazed over with the history of knitting by paragraph three that he'd failed to spot the trap and she'd gotten the drop on him.

He went back to the top and read the article again. Every word, every punctuation mark, every stylistic point and personal nuance.

Sneaky, very sneaky. Like the perfect bowling score, Ronnie had set him up and knocked him down. And now he had just one month to not only learn to knit, but do it well enough to produce some knitted item that would prove his skills.

He thought he'd rather do the upside-down-soup-eating thing. At least then he wouldn't end up with egg on his face . . . maybe just a little split pea.

With a thumb and index finger digging roughly into his eye sockets, he took a breath and started to consider his options. There was no backing out or wiggling his way around it, so he'd have to approach Ronnie's latest challenge the same as he had all the rest—figure out where to start and how to follow through.

Kicking his feet off the desk, he swung his chair around and began tapping his keyboard to log on to the Internet and do a search for all things knitting. The number of results at the bottom of the first Google page made him groan, and he quickly realized he was going to have to narrow his scope.

He typed in "knitting for beginners" and "learning to knit," then went to Amazon and did the same. It didn't exactly raise his spirits to find a book called *Knitting for Dummies* and realize his weekend was going to be spent reading the stupid thing, but if that's what it took to make Ronnie eat her words, then so be it.

Grabbing a phone book out of a bottom drawer, he looked up the number of a bookstore that was on his way home and dialed with the receiver pressed between his ear and shoulder while he continued to surf the 'Net for knitting information. When a woman answered, he asked if they had a copy of the *Dummies* title in stock, then waited for her to check. When she assured him they did, he asked her to hold it until he could pick it up.

He shut down his computer, shrugged into his jacket, and grabbed up a few things to work on at home. Heading out of the *Herald* office building and toward the parking lot, he decided he had this competition in the bag.

He'd pick up the how-to book on the way home, as well as some yarn and a couple of needles, and spend the weekend reading up and practicing. Millions of people knew how to knit. He even thought he remembered his own grandmother sitting around, needles clacking together as she made something or other. And if his little old arthritic grandmother could do it, how hard could this knitting business be?

Dylan scowled, wishing his friends into the deepest, darkest bowels of Hell. They were seated at their usual table at the Box, tossing back a couple of brewskis, but Zack and Gage were more interested in howling like monkeys than keeping track of whose turn it was to buy.

So much for support in the face of adversity. So much for a little freaking loyalty.

Zack swiped a thumb under one eye. "Oh, man, that's priceless. She's really got you by the short hairs this time, doesn't she?"

Narrowing his eyes to slits, Dylan took a drink and refused to answer.

His friends might find this situation amusing, but he sure didn't. He'd spent the weekend reading that stupid-ass knitting book that hadn't made a lick of sense or helped him one whit toward figuring out how to use the bloody needles and yarn he'd also picked up.

Cast on, bind off, knit, purl, yarn over, slip stitch . . . Jesus, it was like a whole other language. Some alien dialect you couldn't understand unless you'd undergone an anal probe.

He was a guy. He had a zillion sports statistics swimming around in his head and could rattle them off at the drop of a hat, but damned if he could figure out how to make a flipping slipknot without wanting to blow his brains out.

And the illustrations were even worse. They were like those Magic Eye 3D pictures that he'd never been able to figure out. After staring at the knitting diagrams for hours on end, he'd gone cross-eyed and seriously considered blinding himself with one of the needles. They seemed sharp enough to do the job.

The book had made a satisfying thud as it hit the wall the first three or four times, though.

Then he'd decided to just dive in and figure it out the

old-fashioned way. What he'd ended up with was a knot of yarn as big as his fist that he didn't think he'd ever get untangled. And worse, he couldn't seem to get it loose from the needles to start over.

So now he was back at square one, with no clue what he was doing or how he'd figure it out, and though only a few days had passed since Ronnie had issued her challenge, time was ticking away.

"This might be the one that sends you down in flames," Gage added. Though he'd gotten a good chuckle out of Dylan's predicament, he didn't seem to be quite as amused as Zack, who was still snorting.

"Over my dead body," Dylan grumbled. "I don't care if I have to hire an army of little old ladies to teach me how to use those damn sticks, Ronnie is not going to beat me on this one."

Zack leaned his long, solid, six-six frame back in his chair, taking his bottle of beer with him. "I still say the only sticks a guy can be expected to know anything about are a hockey stick and the one between his legs."

"Brave words coming from a professional hockey player and a guy who's getting laid on a regular basis."

His friend shot him a shit-eating grin before lifting the bottle to his lips.

"You could try finding a knitting group." This from the more stoic Gage. His thick bicep twitched as he raised his own drink, causing the tribal vine tattoo visible below the arm of his tight black T-shirt to bunch and release.

The noise in the bar around them seemed to fade away as Dylan perked up, leaning his elbows on the table to study his friend. "What's a knitting group?"

"You know, a group of women who get together once

a week or once a month to knit and talk about whatever." He shrugged. "I'm guessing new patterns, new yarns, and eventually men."

"And just how do you know so much about these groups?" Zack asked, waggling his brows suggestively.

Gage shrugged, avoiding both his friends' gazes to stare at the flat tabletop instead. "I heard Jenna mention it."

His ex-wife was never a pleasant topic for Gage, and a stoniness came over his face the minute Jenna's name passed his lips. They'd been divorced for almost a year now, and Dylan still wasn't sure exactly what had caused the breakup. All his friend would say was that Jenna couldn't handle him being a cop and they'd decided it would be better to go their separate ways.

Dylan suspected there was more to the story than that, but didn't press. As close as they were, they each had their own secrets and valued their privacy. And when he was ready, Gage would tell them what he wanted them to know.

"That's right," Zack said, sitting up as he warmed to the subject. "I've heard Grace talk about it, too. I think she might even belong to one of those things. God knows she's got enough yarn and shit lying around her apartment."

"You don't know whether your girlfriend is in a knitting group or not?" Dylan asked.

Zack rolled his eyes. "That woman has more going on than six normal girlfriends. Book clubs, craft groups, cooking classes . . . I have to sit down sometimes just to catch my breath from *watching* her work."

"So when do you find time to have all this hot sex you keep bragging about?" Gage wanted to know.

Zack took a swig of beer before smiling slyly. "Where there's a will, there's a way, brother. Where there's a will, there's a way."

While Dylan's mind would normally be more than willing to follow the string of the conversation straight into the gutter, at this point he was much more interested in getting back to the knitting thing.

"How do I find one of these groups?" he asked of no one in particular.

"I don't know," Gage said. "Phone book, Internet, maybe call around to local craft stores."

"I could ask Grace about hers," Zack offered. "Maybe she'd even take you along with her."

"No way!" Dylan slammed his bottle down on the table, making the rest of the empties jump and rattle. "Are you kidding me? I don't want Grace or any of Chasen's other friends knowing anything about this, got it? Christ, it's bad enough all of Cleveland is going to be witness to my humiliation if I can't pull this off. I sure as hell don't need anybody who can report back to Ronnie knowing I don't already have this in the bag."

"Okay, okay." Zack held up both hands, warding off another outburst. "Take it easy, I won't say a word." He held up three fingers. "Scout's honor."

Since Zack had never been a Boy Scout, and Dylan was only too familiar with his friend's so-called honor, he didn't put much stock in the vow. But he also had more important things on his mind . . . like getting the show on the road with Ronnie's latest dare.

"Good." Dylan pushed his empty Coors bottle into the center of the table and said, "Now order another round while I find a phone book, then get out your cell phones. You bozos are going to help me track down a knitting group where I can pay somebody's granny for some private tutoring."

Wind whipped through Ronnie's hair and tugged at her leopard-print raincoat as she sprinted across the parking lot of the small strip mall and into The Yarn Barn. Like most of the other items in her wardrobe, she'd bought the coat at a secondhand shop, but she knew no one would ever guess it was used. She was very careful about that sort of thing, and never purchased anything that looked faded or worn unless she thought she could fix it herself and make it look brand new.

Her heels clicked on the hard tiled floor as she shook off tiny droplets of rain and brushed the hair out of her face, loosening the belt of her jacket as she headed for the back of the store. She was running late, but not too late.

The Yarn Barn had set up a lovely, homey alcove for groups just like this one, with soft brick-colored carpeting and big, comfortable chairs arranged in a circle. Off to the side was a small refreshment area where they could make coffee or cocoa or tea, and in the center of the chairs was a low cherrywood table with a few assorted craft magazines spread out, where group members could set their drinks.

Everyone else was already seated, drinks poured and needles out. She greeted them all with a wide smile, shedding her jacket and carrying her small tote with her to one of the empty chairs.

"Looks like you're in a good mood tonight," Grace commented from the other side of the circle. She was working with a pair of tiny needles and thin, delicate white thread, determined to knit her own gown for her upcoming wedding to Cleveland Rockets goalie Zack "Hot Legs" Hoolihan.

"I'm in an excellent mood," Ronnie replied.

"Would this have anything to do with last week's column, in which you challenged Mr. Stone to something you're sure he'll never pull off?"

Ronnie couldn't restrain the grin that spread across her face. "I haven't stopped smiling since I turned the article in," she admitted. "I keep picturing Dylan's reaction when he read it, and it makes me feel all warm and tingly inside."

"A few more columns like that and you can get rid of your vibrator," Grace quipped. "I suggest you give it to Jenna. It's been entirely too long since that girl had an orgasm."

Everyone tittered, and though Jenna laughed along with them, a slight blush colored her cheeks.

"The next time I have an orgasm," Jenna said, "I'm hoping it will get me pregnant, so a vibrator would sort of defeat the purpose."

"How do you expect to get pregnant when you aren't even seeing anyone with the equipment to accomplish that goal?" Grace asked. "Not since you and Gage broke up, anyway. Or is there something you'd like to share with the group?"

"No, nothing to share," Jenna admitted, keeping her eyes on the long, bright-pink boa she was knitting from a slinky, feathered type of yarn.

It was a testament to her slow-but-sure recovery that she was finally back to knitting and occasionally even wearing the long, colorful scarves that had practically been a trademark for her before the divorce. Ronnie and Grace often commented that they could determine

Jenna's moods by the presence or absence of a boa around her neck, and by its color if she was wearing one.

"Unfortunately. But I'm remaining optimistic, and even considering my options. I mean, I can get pregnant without the orgasm, know what I mean?"

Ronnie dug into her homemade tote for her own thick, variegated wool yarn, which she was using to make a rather complicated cable-knit cardigan. She pulled out the pattern book she was following and removed from her needles the plastic caps that kept her from losing stitches, then picked up where she'd left off at their last meeting.

"Good for you," she told Jenna.

She'd been as sorry as the rest of them when Jenna and Gage had gotten divorced. That had been an ugly time, with Jenna arriving for their Wednesday night knitting circle in tears more often than not, and the bulk of their time being spent comforting her—and disparaging Gage—rather than actually knitting.

It had taken nearly a year of ups and downs, but Jenna was finally beginning to return to her old self. She seemed happier, more confident, and ready to do whatever it took to get what she wanted.

And what she wanted—they all knew, since she'd never made any secret of the fact—was a baby. It had been the impetus behind the split with her husband (she'd wanted one, he hadn't) and had now become almost an obsession.

"You don't need a man to have a baby," Ronnie continued, sending her needles clicking as she looped stitch after stitch. "They may possess half the DNA necessary, but you can *buy* that, and then you don't have to put up with a guy's crap for the rest of your life. They never help with midnight feedings or diaper changes, anyway."

"It won't be nearly as fun as getting knocked up the old-fashioned way, though," Melanie put in with a wicked grin. And she should know; she had two rugrats of her own.

"Poor Charlotte," Grace said, slanting a glance at the oldest woman in the group, who just happened to be Jenna's aunt on her father's side. "You probably hate it when we start with all the dirty talk, don't you?"

Charlotte had a mop of curls on top of her head in Lucille Ball orange that were sprayed so heavily, a Category Four gale-force wind couldn't dream of budging them. Short and pudgy with a round, smiling face, she always wore some form of polyester pants stretched tight across her wide behind and a floral-design top that drew attention to her ample breasts and lack of discernable waist.

But Charlotte was a hoot, and they all adored her. Though she had to be at least sixty, maybe even seventy—they really ought to ask Jenna sometime—she was the sole owner of an alpaca farm, and ran it practically single-handedly. She sheared the llama-like creatures, cleaned and spun the fiber into yarn, then sold both the yarns and her own knitted and crocheted items at a booth she kept at a local indoor, year-round flea market. And if any of the girls from the group wanted to sell the items they made, Charlotte was only too happy to display those, as well, and give the women 100 percent of whatever she got for them.

Ronnie took regular advantage of the woman's kind offer, and while the money it brought in was nothing to write home about, every little bit helped.

Charlotte may have been Jenna's aunt by blood, but they all considered her a mother figure, and Ronnie often thought the majority of the women who attended the Wednesday night knitting circle came as much to see the older woman as to knit or chat with the younger ones.

"Oh, no, dear," Charlotte answered without lifting her gaze from her knitting, "I love listening to you girls go on about your jobs and your men and your lives. It keeps me young. And I may not be married, but I have had my share of beaus, so I know a thing or two about men myself."

Ronnie noticed that Charlotte straightened at that last part, raising her chin and thrusting her chest out just a bit.

"You're not telling us that you own a vibrator, are you, Charlotte?" Grace teased.

If she was hoping to make the woman blush, she was destined for disappointment. Charlotte's hands barely slowed as she cocked a brow and looked Grace straight in the eye. "You have to remember that I'm from a different generation, dear. One that learned not to rely on batteries for every little thing."

That caused a burst of raucous laughter. Nothing new for this group, really, but they were lucky other store customers didn't complain to the manager and get them kicked out. Then again, if they were going to get the boot, it probably would have happened long ago.

"Ronnie, dear, you should invite your young man to visit our group sometime," Charlotte said. "We could show him a thing or two about knitting."

"Aunt Charlotte, the idea is for him *not* to learn how to knit. If he learns and does a good enough job to make a scarf or dishcloth or something, then he wins the bet and Ronnie loses."

"And Ronnie does not want to lose," Ronnie mumbled.

"Well, I can't say I understand the point of the little competition you have going with that Dylan Stone fellow, but I do think it would be nice if more men learned to knit. It would do them a world of good—teach them to relax and maybe even appreciate something that we've been doing for years."

"Yeah, that would be great," Grace agreed, but even Ronnie couldn't tell if she was being serious or sarcastic. "But in this man's case, we're rooting for him to fail."

"Miserably," Ronnie added.

"Miserably," Grace repeated dutifully. "You get to keep the trophy if he loses, right?"

Ronnie grinned, picturing Dylan's beloved Harrison Award that he'd won for some piece or another, all silver and gold and sparkling. She kept it on the dresser in her bedroom both as motivation and to remind her that she'd whipped his butt on the last task he'd put her on. Whipped his butt and gotten a tattoo on hers, but that was beside the point.

He loved that stupid award, and she knew it galled him to no end that she kept taking it away from him. And this time around, she meant to keep it.

"Oh, yeah. And as soon as he loses this stupid competition altogether, I'm going to have his name removed and replace it with mine. That'll really kill him."

"Good to know you've got your priorities straight," Grace quipped, setting aside her knitting and grabbing her now empty mug.

"Isn't it, though?"

The conversation branched off into other topics as Grace moved to the sideboard to make more hot tea, Jenna close on her heels. Ronnie hadn't gotten a drink yet, mostly because she was looking forward to a cocktail or two at The Penalty Box later. But maybe after a couple more rows, she'd grab a bottle of water.

"Excuse me," a voice broke in, and Ronnie froze in midstitch.

She was sitting with her back to the store, so she hadn't seen anyone come up, but she knew that voice. It was male, deep, and rumbling, and she knew, just *knew* who it belonged to.

To six feet of rugged, well-built male. One with sandy blond hair and eyes the same blue as a patch of bachelor's buttons blowing in the breeze.

A heavy, lead weight settled at the bottom of her stomach as she swallowed hard and waited. Maybe if she didn't move, he wouldn't realize she was there. Maybe if she let someone else respond to his question, he would get the answer he wanted and be on his merry way.

Rolling only her eyes as far to the left as they would go, she glanced at Grace and Jenna, noticing that both women were standing stock-still at the refreshment counter, matching expressions of shocked horror etched on their faces.

Oh, God.

But of course Charlotte had never met a person she didn't immediately take a liking to, and she was the first to pipe up.

"Yes?"

"Is this the Wednesday night knitting group?"

It was definitely Dylan. She'd recognize his voice anywhere, especially since he seemed to be standing directly behind her, towering over her armchair, so close she was surprised she couldn't feel his breath on the back of her neck.

God bless Melanie for having the chutzpah to say what she couldn't at the moment.

"No, honey," her friend deadpanned, lifting her knitting a few inches higher, "these are golf clubs and we were just about to tee off. Care to join us?"

Ronnie bit her tongue, sinking lower in the cushions of her chair as she covered her mouth with both hands to keep from snickering. If it was anybody else on the receiving end of that remark, she'd have felt sorry for the poor bastard. But since the current recipient happened to be her sworn enemy, and it was no less than Dylan deserved . . .

Behind her, she heard him shuffle his feet. She could picture him standing there, looking infinitely hot in some snug tee or button-up shirt, with a jacket over top in deference to the rainy weather. And he would of course be wearing his typical faded blue jeans, since he'd never met a pair of Levi's that didn't frame his pinchable ass to perfection.

Not that she'd ever paid all that much attention to his appearance.

Remaining perfectly still and silent, Ronnie prayed that Dylan had gotten his answer and was turning to leave.

Is this the Wednesday night knitting group? Yes. *Thank you very much, I'll be on my way.*

It could happen.

A few chairs away, Charlotte made a *tsk*ing sound

and sent Melanie a disapproving frown. "Pay no attention to her, dear. If you're looking for the Knit Wits, then you've come to the right place. Can we help you with something?"

"I sure hope so," he replied, *not* leaving, as Ronnie had so desperately wished he would. "I'm in need of a bit of instruction about learning to knit. Would anyone here be willing to teach me, at least the basics?"

Yep, that was about right. Of all the craft stores and all the knitting groups in the city, of course he would walk into hers.

Damn Murphy and his law straight to Hell.

Ronnie's lips parted, her mind screaming *nooooo-oooooo* at the top of her lungs while in reality her mouth worked like a fish's and no sound beyond a tiny squeak came out. Then, before her motor functions could return to normal, Charlotte . . . dear, sweet, benevolent, soon-to-be-strangled-with-her-own-yarn Charlotte . . . beat her to the punch.

"Of course, dear. I'm sure someone here would be delighted to teach you to knit."

And damned if that old woman's cagey gaze wasn't aimed directly at Ronnie.

Row 3

"Great," he breathed, and Ronnie could hear the relief in his voice. "Because I seem to be having a bit of trouble trying to figure this out on my own."

Before the words were completely out of his mouth, a blur of something dropped in front of her and landed with a light bounce in her lap. She jumped in surprise, then glanced down to see an ungodly tangle of baby-blue yarn knotted around two size ten needles.

"Oh, sorry," Dylan said, reaching around to retrieve the mangled mess. "I didn't mean to—"

He broke off as his head came level with hers and their eyes met.

So much for melting into the seat of the faux leather armchair.

"Chasen," he muttered, making her name sound like a curse.

Ignoring the erratic pounding in her chest and the spark in his clear blue eyes, she returned the favor. "Stone."

She curled her fingers, with their long, blood-red tips, around the sad proof of his colossal first attempt at knitting and held it out to him, her lips curved in an amused sneer. "I believe this is yours."

He took the ball of yarn—if it could be called that by any stretch of the imagination—and tucked his arm behind his back. "I didn't know you'd be here."

"Are things not going well with your latest challenge?" she asked sweetly.

The corner of his eye twitched; a tiny, involuntary movement, no doubt brought about by an overload of stress.

Deep down, Ronnie knew she should feel guilty for that, for being the one to have caused a facial tic in another human being. But even deeper down, she was giggling like a four-year-old who'd just discovered the Teletubbies at her birthday party.

"I've got a month," he reminded her. "Don't count me out yet."

"Whatever you say." She turned her attention away from him and back to her knitting. "That Harrison Award looks lovely on my dresser, and I'm in no hurry to give it up. I'm even thinking of building a little display case for it and any other awards I win from you in the future."

Though she wasn't looking directly at him any longer, she imagined his eye was twitching again. He really loved his Harrison Award for excellence in journalism, which she grudgingly acknowledged he deserved, since she'd read the article that gained him the coveted prize. Not that she would ever admit such a thing to him or anyone else. Not even under threat of death . . . or a really bad perm.

It galled him to no end that she maintained possession

of it, and that only made the attainment that much sweeter.

His reply, when it came, was low and tight and edged with more than a hint of bitterness. "Like I said, don't count me out yet. It might hurt too much when I take my award back and make you eat your words."

Ronnie gave a snort and increased the speed of her stitches, making sure he heard the rapid-fire clack of her needles. "Bring it on, Stone."

Like a tiny, red-haired Mother Teresa, Charlotte waddled across the space inside the circle of chairs and reached behind Dylan for his tangled ball of yarn.

"Why don't you have a seat and we'll see what we can do about this. I'm Charlotte, by the way. You already know our Ronnie, I take it, but this is Melanie and Susan and Louella and Grace, and my darling niece, Jenna."

She went around the group, introducing everyone, and Ronnie was pleased to note that none of her friends offered more than narrowed eyes and semi-polite nods in response. Even Jenna and Grace, who already knew Dylan and were (or had been) involved with two of his best friends, remained stoically silent.

God, she loved female loyalty. Dylan might think he was going to get some help with his knitting here, but she suspected they'd succeed in driving him away in a matter of hours. Two meetings tops.

"Dylan Stone," he offered, moving to take a seat right beside her.

Of course.

She ignored him completely, concentrating on the arm of her sweater, needles and yarn blurring together, fingers dancing. Charlotte's voice droned in her ears, going on about the Knit Wits and knitting in general, while in her head, Ronnie imagined losing control of her needles and sending one flying in Dylan's direction. With her luck, though, it would probably just bounce off his thick skull or his firm bicep.

She dragged her attention back to the real world in time to hear Charlotte say, ". . . why I think you'd do well with a bit of one-on-one instruction."

Hmph. She'd have to have a little talk with Charlotte about being *too* friendly, especially to the enemy. Not that he'd have any luck finding private tutoring from this group. They all knew who he was, knew about the columns and competition, and would rather chew glass than help Dylan win a wager against her.

Even if he did manage to find someone else to help him learn to knit—thanks to Charlotte and her big mouth (second only to her big heart)—Ronnie still wasn't worried. There was no way he'd learn to knit well enough in only a month to complete a decent project, no matter how simple.

And if he started to get close enough to make her nervous, there was always lighter fluid and a match.

"There!" Charlotte announced, finally getting to the end of the ball of mangled yarn. A pile of the loose blue strands lay on the floor at her feet, and she quickly began to coil it back up.

"Now, which one of you ladies would like to get this young man started again? I'm afraid my hands are starting to bother me. Arthritis, you know." Without waiting for an answer, she said, "Ronnie, how about you, dear? You're nearly finished with that row, and you're so very talented with the needles."

Ronnie's fingers stilled and her jaw nearly dropped

to the floor. Was Charlotte insane? Was the old woman finally losing her marbles? What was she thinking, not only *helping* Dylan, but now trying to get *Ronnie* to help him, too?

And if Charlotte had arthritis in even one of her pudgy knuckles, Ronnie was a duck-billed platypus.

The woman was up to something, and Ronnie didn't like it. She gave Charlotte her meanest glare, but the evil, mop-headed little troll merely smiled, dropped the ball of yarn into Ronnie's lap, and returned to her chair on the other side of the circle.

Ronnie knew she looked like a crazy person. Her lips were moving as she muttered beneath her breath— every garbled thought and vile curse that came to mind.

"What's the matter?" Dylan asked after several long seconds when she neither responded to Charlotte's suggestion nor jumped up to give him a hand. "Afraid I'll bite? Or afraid I won't?"

His grin, and the whiskey-smooth tone of his voice, might have affected other women, but the pump of her blood and pound of her heart were signs of her annoyance, *not* signs that he was in any way attractive or charming. Please!

"Only in your wildest imaginings, Stone."

His smile widened, flashing rows of gleaming white teeth. "How did you know, Chasen?"

Rolling her eyes, she made a sound between a gag and a groan and pushed to her feet.

"Fine." She stabbed the caps back on the points of her needles and shoved everything back into her bag. "Don't expect me to be too accommodating, though. After all, I'm the one who wants you to fall flat on your face."

"Huh. In my dreams, you always seem to want me flat on my back."

It was her turn to twitch, and she quickly slapped a hand over her right eye to keep him from noticing. With the other hand, she grabbed his needles from his lap and held the pointy ends to his jugular.

"Do not tempt me," she bit out, enjoying the image of using his own knitting needles to make Dylan-kabobs.

For long seconds, he held his tongue, waiting until his life no longer hung in the balance. But the minute she lowered the needles from his throat and took a seat closer to him on his other side, he couldn't seem to resist muttering, "That's not what you said in the dream, either."

The rest of the group may not have heard his remark, but they certainly heard his yelp when she drove the needles sharply into the side of his thigh. All heads turned in their direction—if they hadn't been already—but Ronnie merely smiled sweetly and played dumb. As dumb as she could, anyway, with everyone in the room already aware of the animosity she held toward Dylan.

For the next half hour, without leaning into it very much at all, she worked with Dylan to teach him the basics of knitting. Casting on and the simple knit stitch, but that was about it. She wasn't about to help him learn anything to aid his success in this latest challenge.

And it delighted her to see that he wasn't doing so well at catching on to even the easiest steps. He would either pull the yarn too tight or leave it too loose; yarn under when he should yarn over; purl when he should knit. She didn't always correct his mistakes, either, because . . . well, that would defeat the purpose of their competition, now, wouldn't it?

But she'd been as nice as could be expected under the circumstances and had gotten through the evening without any more sideways glances or chastisements from Charlotte. The woman was positively gifted at making her feel like a misbehaving six-year-old, even if her actions and attitude were entirely warranted.

When, though, had Dylan started smelling so darn good? Like fresh pine needles and woodsy musk and sex on a stick.

She'd also never noticed before how big and rough his hands were—in an extremely attractive way. They looked as though they could make a layup shot or stroke a woman to orgasm with equal finesse.

It was disturbing, to say the least. Especially when she found herself leaning closer and closer to "guide" him along, taking deep, lung-filling sniffs of him in the process.

Of course, it wasn't him, not really. Just whatever aftershave or cologne he'd chosen to wear today. That was the only explanation she could think of for the little zing of electricity that seemed to pass between them whenever they touched.

If she could find out what brand it was, then she could pick up a bottle for herself and whiff her way to sensual pleasure all by herself, without ever again getting within ten feet of Dylan Stone.

Yes, that's what she would do. Because any cologne that could make a woman's nipples go hard beneath her top and have her squirming in her seat was definitely worth the twenty bucks, whether she had a man to wear it for her or not.

About ten minutes after their meetings usually broke up, Melanie stuffed her knitting on top of her overloaded handbag and stood. "Well, I wish I could stick around, but I've got to get home and pack lunches for my kids' field trip tomorrow."

"You're not going to the Box with us?" Grace asked, following Melanie's lead and beginning to gather her things.

"Not this time," Melanie said, sounding genuinely sorry. "Next week, though, God willing."

The light drizzle from earlier had let up by the time they all made their way out of The Yarn Barn, leaving behind only a few puddles and a dampness to the air. As though by tacit agreement, they ignored Dylan completely on their way out, leaving him at the curb as they headed for their cars.

It was too much to hope that she could be done with him for the night. Two seconds after she walked into The Penalty Box with Grace and Jenna, Dylan showed up, too, making his way to the table Zack and Gage already occupied.

Grace made a beeline for the same table, throwing her arms around Zack's neck for a long, slow kiss. He pulled her onto his knee and they talked in low whispers for a few minutes.

They looked like Get-a-Room Barbie and Ken, blond heads bent close, long limbs twined together like vines of climbing ivy.

Normally, public displays of affection didn't bother Ronnie; she'd been known to participate in them a time or two herself. But she wasn't in the mood to watch the lovey-dovey, ooey-gooey stuff at the moment. Not when the only man in her life was giving her both a bleeding ulcer and an all-over body rash.

Jenna, she noticed, was equally uncomfortable. She turned away from the guys' table almost immediately and headed for an empty booth at the back of the room. But then, that could have been less because of Zack and Grace and more because of Gage.

It wasn't easy being part of a group where two of the members used to be a happy, loving couple, but were now divorced. Anytime they were together, the room filled with tension and Ronnie felt as if she were walking through shards of broken glass in open-toed shoes.

For all that, though, she imagined it had to be a hundred times worse for Jenna. Yes, her friend had been the one to initiate the divorce proceedings, but Ronnie got the distinct feeling leaving Gage hadn't been what she'd wanted at all—and that she was still in love with him. She didn't talk about it, tried not to show it, but some things a woman just wasn't able to hide.

The one time Gage had come into the bar with another woman while they were there . . . a bleached-blond, silicone-boobed tramp, no less . . . Jenna had turned green around the gills and taken off like her hair was on fire.

Ronnie didn't think Gage was entirely indifferent, either. He'd never been the most exuberant man she'd ever met—more the strong-and-silent or walk-softly-and-carry-a-big-gun type—but he'd definitely become more quiet and subdued since the breakup. When he didn't think anyone else was looking, she'd caught him staring more than once in his ex-wife's direction with an expression of longing and regret on his chiseled face.

With a sigh, Ronnie followed Jenna to the rear of the bar and slid into the booth beside her. She might have asked her friend how she was doing, if she maybe wanted to go somewhere else for drinks instead of sitting here within spitting distance of her ex . . . but she knew the response she would get, since they'd had that conversation before.

To Jenna, going somewhere else and avoiding Gage would be the same as acknowledging she still had feelings for him or that she was still smarting from the divorce. And quiet, even-tempered Jenna would rather walk naked through Metro Park than admit to either.

"What do you feel like drinking tonight?" Ronnie asked. "Margaritas again, or just beer?"

"How about a couple of Cosmopolitans?" Grace suggested, sweeping up with a wide smile on her face. "I could go for something sexy and fruity."

Jenna nodded, sending her short, black pixie cut flying. "That sounds good. I'll take two."

Grace flopped down on the bench seat on the other side of Jenna. "Me, too."

Ronnie laughed. "I'll go place our orders, but let's go slowly, ladies. I'm not up for being a designated driver tonight, and I don't feel like calling cabs for everyone."

Getting to her feet, she made her way around tables and chairs to the bar. The place was crowded and loud, much like every other night, keeping Turk busy behind the bar.

A Rob Thomas song was playing on the digital jukebox in the far corner, and she found herself tapping a toe and humming along while she studied the assortment of liquor bottles lining the mirrored shelves in front of her.

They could have flagged down a server and waited for her to bring their drinks, but Ronnie didn't mind squeezing in at the bar and waiting to catch Turk's attention. He was a good-looking man, and though flirting had never gotten her anywhere—honest to God, she didn't think the man's expression would change if she lit his crotch on fire—she enjoyed taking a few seconds to get a nice eyeful.

It was that ass again. Son of a bitch.

Dylan swallowed hard, wishing the waitress would come with his beer already. He could use a tall, cold one to wet his dry throat and lower his internal temperature a few degrees.

On either side of him at the wide round table, Gage and Zack were arguing about the Rockets' last game. It hadn't gone well, and Gage was giving Zack some pointers on how the team might win next time around. To which Zack was suggesting Gage do one of two things— get out on the ice and put his stick where his mouth was, or do something to himself that Dylan was pretty sure was anatomically impossible.

Dylan had watched Monday night's game and was as disappointed in the loss as the others, but at the moment his full attention was locked on Ronnie's hips and rear and long, long legs where she stood at the bar, shimmying in time with the music that filled the room.

No matter where he went, he couldn't seem to get away from her tight, heart-shaped ass. It was beginning to haunt his dreams, and that was just downright scary.

He shifted in his seat, aware of the sudden tightening of his jeans in the area of his zipper.

Along with Ronnie's behind dancing through his dreams on a regular basis these days, the other thing he did not need was to start getting turned on by his archrival. She was a ball-busting shrew who shouldn't be able to attract any man unless he lived under a bridge somewhere, threatening to eat little billy goats as they passed.

But erections didn't lie, and his was like a divining rod pointing straight in Ronnie Chasen's direction.

Tired of waiting for his beer to arrive, he pushed away from the table and stood. "I'll be back," he said by way of explanation to his two friends, who were still arguing heatedly over Monday night's game and getting no closer to a truce.

He sidled up beside Ronnie, bumping into her as he made room for himself at the crowded bar. She turned to see who'd jostled her and her expression transformed from calm and unlined, almost happy, to scowling.

"Can't you find anyone else to annoy, Stone?"

"Do I annoy you, Chasen?"

"Only as much as a pebble in my shoe, a thorn in my side, a boil on my butt . . ."

He let his gaze slide down, figuring her mention of that portion of her curvaceous anatomy was as good as an invitation to look his fill.

"And a nice butt it is, too. If you've got any boils on it at the moment, I hope you get them lanced before they scar an otherwise perfect canvas."

While he was preoccupied ogling her behind, she placed three fingers of her right hand flat to the side of his jaw and applied just enough pressure to pull his gaze upward again. The heat of that touch burned against his skin and made his chest go tight.

"Don't you worry about my butt," she told him in a tone just this side of arctic. "And keep your eyes up, or I'll be tempted to poke them out."

As much as he knew it would piss her off, he couldn't help the grin that spread across his face. Only Ronnie could dress him down like a parochial school nun and still send blood pumping hot and thick to his groin. Coming from any other woman, those words, in that cold, sharp tone of voice, would have shut him down in an instant and threatened to shrivel his tea bags.

"You gonna do that poking with your knitting needles?" he asked, thinking back to earlier when she'd both held a pair to his throat and stabbed him in the thigh. The two spots on his upper leg still throbbed.

"With whatever's handy," she murmured distractedly, catching the bartender's attention and waving him over to take her order. When Turk approached, she ordered a round of Cosmos and pointed to the back booth where her friends were waiting.

She turned to leave, but before she could move away, Dylan caught her arm. Her dark brows arched, and she looked pointedly at where his fingers curled around her elbow.

Risking another poke with whatever she might be able to find near the bar, he didn't let go. "I've been thinking . . ."

"Did it hurt?"

He made a face, one side of his mouth lifting in an unamused quirk. "Ha ha. Seriously, though, I think your friend Charlotte is right. I could use some one-on-one tutoring for this knitting thing."

"So what do you want me to do?" she asked on a half laugh. "Recommend somebody?"

"No, I thought maybe you'd be willing to do it."

At that, her eyes went wide and the tension drained out of the arm he was holding. "You're joking, right? Why in God's name would I be willing to help you learn to knit *at all,* let alone one-on-one? In case you've forgotten, this is a competition. You challenge me to something, then I challenge you to something, and we both sit back and pray the other will fail miserably and crawl away to a cave somewhere to die of shame."

She had a point, and until she'd touched his face, sending spear-points of awareness rocketing through his system, the idea had never even occurred to him. Until he'd grabbed her arm and gotten a second dose of that electricity, he hadn't known what he planned to say, let alone this.

It didn't make a lot of sense, and there was certainly nothing in it for her, but the more he thought about it, the more he liked it. The more determined he was to convince her to go along with it.

"Oh, I don't know, I thought maybe you'd consider it a challenge within a challenge. We can make a little side bet."

Her full red lips, shiny with a layer of gloss, pursed doubtfully. "Such as?"

"You believe there's no way I'll ever learn to knit, otherwise you wouldn't have made it part of the competition, right? Well, I think I *can* learn, though I admit to needing a bit more help getting started than I first expected. So I'll bet you . . . I don't know, another one of my trophies that you can't teach me to knit. You don't have to do a great job, and you don't have to stick with it long. And provided I don't complete a full knitting project in the month's time, you'll still win the original challenge."

For a moment, she seemed to consider his offer, but just as quickly, a flickering change in her expression signaled she was about to turn him down.

"I'll even sweeten the pot by paying you outright for your time," he rushed to add, feeling almost desperate now. "Say, a hundred bucks?"

"A hundred bucks?" she retorted. "Hardly worth it. I'd much rather see you crash and burn."

She tugged her arm free and took another step toward the booth where her friends' drinks had just been delivered.

"All right, then," he called after her, raising his voice enough to be heard over both the music from the jukebox and the distance she'd put between them. "How about a thousand?"

Row 4

All the way home from her knitting group, Charlotte Langan's mind raced. She kept thinking about every look and every word that had been exchanged between Ronnie and that nice boy, Dylan Stone.

They purported to be mortal enemies—or at least that's what Ronnie would have people believe. But Charlotte had been around for a lot of years and had seen a lot of things.

Her hair might be gray . . . not that anyone would know her natural red had long ago faded away, thanks to Nice 'n Easy Morning Sunrise Number 86 . . . her eyesight might be waning, and her hearing might not be what it used to be, but she could still spot sparks when they shot ten feet into the air over her head.

Ronnie and Dylan might claim to hate each other, but Charlotte suspected there was more to the situation than that.

Oh, yes, there was something there. She just had to find a way to bring it out . . . and to get two people who were possibly the most stubborn and obstinate in the world to stop fighting long enough to realize that all the bitterness and vitriol they were busy tossing back and forth was really just an overabundance of pent-up desire.

Easier said than done, of course. It wasn't as if two young people like Ronnie and Dylan were going to listen to an old woman they probably thought was half senile already. They may love her and think of her as an aunt or mother figure, but that didn't mean they were going to let her give them advice about their love lives. And, frankly, she was afraid that if she so much as hinted to Ronnie that her feelings for Dylan could be more intimate than she realized, Ronnie's head might just explode.

There had to be some other way, then. Something subtle and sneaky.

A smile curved the pink of Charlotte's heavily lipsticked mouth as she put on her turn signal to turn into her driveway, even though the long dirt road she was currently on was rarely traveled by anyone but herself, and there were no other cars behind her.

Sneaky could be good, she thought, cutting the engine and stuffing her keys into her purse as she got out and headed for the front door of her small white farmhouse. Sneaky was possibly her very favorite thing.

The house, along with several acres of land, had been in the Langan family for years. It was only five years ago that Charlotte had decided to have the barns rebuilt and turn what used to be a small horse-and-cattle spread into an alpaca farm.

The little critters could spit and kick like the dickens when they got their dander up, but the rest of the time they were downright adorable. They had also provided her with enough fiber to maintain a tidy income.

Most of the time, she cared for the small herd herself. It was nothing she couldn't handle, and when she did need help with heavy lifting or more difficult aspects of the job—especially once a year at shearing time—she simply hired a few extra folks to come in.

The annual shearing left her with enough fleece to keep her busy, that was for sure. She cleaned, dyed, and spun the fiber herself into soft, wonderful yarns. From there, she both sold a good portion of the yarn and kept some of it for herself. What she kept, she used to knit any number of beautiful items to sell at the booth she kept at the local, year-round craft and antiques mall.

Most people didn't realize that alpaca fur was five times warmer than wool and five times finer than cashmere . . . but once they discovered those facts for themselves, they often became addicted to the feel of alpaca sweaters and scarves against their skin.

Stepping inside the house, she flipped off the porch light and locked the door behind her. It probably wasn't necessary, living out here on the rural outskirts of the city with her nearest neighbor a mile away, but being an elderly woman who lived alone, she was taking no chances.

She hung her purse on a hook beside the door and covered it with her jacket before strolling into the kitchen. Filling her chicken-shaped teapot with water, she set it on the stove to heat, then made her way upstairs to change into a long floral nightgown.

Padding back downstairs in her robe and slippers, she poured hot water over an orange spice tea bag and let it steep, unconsciously tugging up and down on the thin string while she gazed out the window above the sink. Everything was dark, only a thin sliver of moon making the outbuildings beyond visible. The alpacas were fed, watered, and taken care of for the night, and all Charlotte had to occupy her mind was Miss Prickly Pear and Mr. Cute as a Bug in a Rug.

She hoped Dylan would attend their knitting group again. Maybe then she could find a way to force the two of them to spend even more time together. But the next meeting was a week away, and that seemed somehow too long to wait.

Her drawn-on dark brown brows crossed as she removed the tea bag from the cup and set it aside. Carrying the steaming mug into the living room, she took a seat in her favorite armchair and propped her feet on the matching ottoman.

She'd never played at matchmaking before, and had to admit she was at a loss. If only there was some way to throw Ronnie and Dylan together, some situation that could be created to force them to recognize the attraction zinging between them.

Sipping her tea, she stared at the spinning wheel off to one side of the room and considered working a bit before going to bed. She was tired, and normally turned in after a nice, relaxing cup of herbal tea, but spinning often helped her to think, and that's exactly what she needed to do tonight.

Though she enjoyed each part of the process of raising alpacas and preparing their fur, including selling her wares, the actual spinning was one of her greatest pleasures. It was an art, really—not to mention extremely soothing—and she was very good at it.

She supposed one could even say spinning was in her blood, a skill passed down from generation to generation in her family. Her mother had taught Charlotte to both spin and knit, as her mother had taught her, and so on and so on through the years.

There was even—

Charlotte sat up straighter, knuckles going white on the handle of her mug as tea sloshed dangerously close to spilling over.

There was even an old spinning wheel that had been passed down through the family, said to be enchanted and to bring true love to those who used the yarn it created.

Good Lord, how could she have forgotten? It was perfect!

Abandoning her cup on the small table beside the chair, she pushed to her feet and hurried up the stairs to the second floor. The door to the attic was located in one of the guest rooms, and she hurried inside and up the steep, unfinished steps. A single bare lightbulb hung in the center of the attic, not terribly bright, but illuminating enough that Charlotte could make out the shapes of boxes and trunks littering the floor.

In the far corner, beneath a white sheet turned gray with age and covered in a fine layer of dust, was exactly what she was looking for. Slippers shuffling as she crossed the coarse plank floor, she carefully pulled back the sheet.

Charlotte stared in awe at the beautiful, carved wood spinning wheel. It was probably hundreds of years old and needed a good polishing, but otherwise looked to be in perfect condition. She ran her hand over the top of the wheel and was delighted to feel it move smoothly, see the foot pedal bob slowly up and down. Not a single squeak, and if that wasn't enchantment after being stored away for so many years, she didn't know what was.

She hadn't seen the wheel in ages, had never used it. She'd almost completely forgotten that it was in the attic at all.

Her only clear memories of the wheel were seeing her grandmother use it once, seeing it a time or two in this very house as she was growing up, and hearing the stories of its powers to create luxurious yarns that brought true love.

It took some doing, but Charlotte managed to pick up the ancient spinning wheel and carry it down the narrow attic steps. Rather than taking it downstairs to join her other wheel in the living room, where she normally did her spinning, she put this one in her bedroom.

She didn't get many visitors, but just in case, she didn't want this wheel to be out in the open, where someone might see it. And since what she was planning to do was a bit odd, perhaps a bit fanciful, she preferred to keep the activity a secret.

Once the wheel was situated where she wanted it, Charlotte stood back and wiped the back of one hand across her damp brow. There was no guarantee this would actually work, but according to her mother and grandmother both . . . and probably her great-grandmother and great-great grandmother before them . . . the yarn created by this spinning wheel had never failed to bring two lovers together, star-crossed or otherwise.

Of course, the wheel had probably never come up against two people as mulish, pigheaded, and determined to avoid emotional entanglement as Ronnie

Chasen and Dylan Stone, but she had faith. She believed in the power and enchantment of the spinning wheel.

And if all else failed, at least they'd have a nice knitted something-or-other to show for her efforts.

Row 5

A thousand dollars.

A thousand dollars.

A thousand dollars.

Maybe if she kept saying it to herself, over and over, she would eventually stop feeling like a pathetic, weak-willed sellout.

She didn't particularly care about winning another one of Dylan's trophies. She had the Harrison already, which was the best of the best and the one he valued most.

Plus, in order to take possession of a second award from his collection, she would have to help him enough to ensure that he actually *did* learn to knit and would most likely win the challenge, and that was just *not* gonna happen. Not if she had anything to say about it.

But the money . . .

A thousand dollars was a lot of dough, and God knew she could use it. It would make a nice addition to her savings, to the cushion she liked to keep between herself and the poverty line.

But why, oh, why did the windfall have to come from The Jackass?

She should have walked away. She had, actually, just not very far.

Over the loud music thrumming through The Penalty Box, he'd called out that ridiculous figure, but she'd just kept going, returning to the booth where her friends—and drinks—were waiting. She'd sat down, sipped her Cosmo, and carried on a perfectly normal conversation for the next hour or so.

And then, as she'd passed his table on her way out, she'd stopped, leaned close to his ear, and given him an answer to his generous—and, she was beginning to suspect, evil—offer.

"Okay," she'd whispered so that no one else would overhear her shame. "We'll start next week, after knitting group."

She hadn't waited for a response. Had actually dashed out of the bar as fast as her Dolce & Gabbana knockoff platform wedges could carry her. Because she didn't want to see his reaction, didn't want to see him gloat or hear his loud guffaws as he shared the details of her humiliating capitulation with his friends.

Now she was simply waiting for the moment he would walk into The Yarn Barn, into her circle of friends who were all busy knitting their little hearts out, and announce that she'd caved to cash bribery like a house of cards.

Cursing under her breath as she lost another stitch on the sleeve of the sweater she was knitting, Ronnie checked her watch for the fifth or sixth time in less than an hour. Only ten minutes left before the meeting would end, which meant that Dylan was either running extremely late or he'd decided not to take her up on the tutoring sessions, after all.

A part of her was relieved. She didn't *want* to help him, so she would be just as happy if he changed his mind and went off to fail this particular challenge on his own.

She would miss that thousand dollars, though. It wasn't even in her bank account yet, but she'd already imagined it there, happily increasing the amount of her balance.

When the meeting broke up, for the first time in as long as she could remember, Ronnie begged off going for drinks at The Penalty Box. Grace and Jenna both looked at her like she'd gone berserk, but she merely shook her head and promised to talk to them later.

Tucking the lapels of her leopard-print raincoat tighter around her throat, she prepared to step off the sidewalk and head for her car, but Charlotte's voice stopped her.

"Ronnie, dear," the older woman called, still standing in front of the craft store doors.

Ronnie forced a smile she didn't quite feel and turned back around. "Hey, Charlotte. Are you going over to The Penalty Box with the girls?"

"Oh, no," she said with a deep chuckle. "One glass of wine a week is my limit, and I like to drink that on Friday evening while watching my programs."

Ronnie smiled indulgently while Charlotte dug around in her tote.

"I spun this just for you," Charlotte said, handing her a soft, thick skein of black yarn. "I hope you'll use it."

"Of course I will." Ronnie smiled and gave Charlotte a tight hug. "You know your yarns are my very favorite to work with. Thank you."

Charlotte's smile was wide and pleased. "I'm glad

to hear it. Maybe you can even use it to help that Dylan fellow learn to knit."

Ronnie pulled back, studying Charlotte's face. Was she blushing? And why wouldn't the woman look her in the eye?

"I'm not sure that's going to happen," she said slowly, "but thank you all the same. I really will put this to good use."

Tucking the yarn into her brightly checkered bag, she started toward the curb again. "Drive carefully, Charlotte. I'll see you next week."

It wasn't unusual for Charlotte to give skeins of her homemade yarn to the ladies in the knitting group. Usually, though, she brought enough for everyone and handed them out during their meetings. And she'd never before handed one to Ronnie with such an odd expression on her face.

Maybe it was the weather, or the time of night, or even the amount of pressure Ronnie felt pressing down on her from every direction these days that had her forming conspiracy theories about a dear old woman who was only being nice. She was tired and annoyed and reading too much into the situation.

But when she drove past The Yarn Barn on her way out of the parking lot and found Charlotte standing exactly where she'd left her in front of the double glass doors, her suspicions sprang to life all over again.

Honestly, what was *with* people these days? Charlotte acting strangely, her archnemesis asking her to help him . . . As she drove home, she let herself remember and long for the days when those around her acted normal and didn't intentionally try to drive her into the wacko ward of the nearest mental health facility.

Though she probably could have afforded better, she lived in a modest downtown apartment complex overlooking Lake Erie. The wind blew a bit stronger and colder this close to the lake, but then all of Cleveland was positively frigid during the winter months, so she couldn't see that it mattered much one way or the other.

She let herself into the building, then took the elevator up to the third floor and walked down the short hall to her apartment door. Inside, she shrugged out of her coat, kicked off her shoes, and unzipped her skirt on the way to her bedroom.

Stripping out of her work clothes, she padded naked into the bathroom to remove her makeup, wash her face, and take a nice hot shower. With her hair still wet and falling loose around her shoulders, she put on a pair of cotton lounge pants and matching top, then made her way back to the living room.

She set up her laptop on the low coffee table before running to the kitchen for a glass of water. Drink in hand, she returned to her computer and sat cross-legged on the floor with her back to the sofa to work on her latest column.

It should have been written already. Would have been, except that she'd been putting it off. She couldn't seem to land on a decent topic and had been distracted by Dylan's latest proposition.

Her brows knit as she admitted the last, hating that he had any effect on her at all, especially if it meant muddling her brain when it came to her job.

In the past, she'd covered issues ranging from those as serious as safe sex and self-defense for women to those as inconsequential as nail polish brand comparisons and popular cocktail recipes.

This week, she was torn between writing about how to get rid of a guy you weren't interested in—but who always seemed to be around, becoming a complete pain in the ass—or warning readers about a popular downtown eatery that was rumored to be bribing health inspectors to stay in business. The idea of venting her frustrations with The Jackass was tempting, but honor—and a fair share of potential guilt—dictated that she alert the citizens of Cleveland that there might be rat droppings in their sandwiches or roaches in their salads.

Reaching for the remote control, Ronnie flipped through channels until she found something with decent background music, then started tapping away. Since everything she'd heard about the restaurant in question was merely rumor and speculation, she didn't mention it by name, but she gave enough hints that she thought anyone who was familiar with the businesses downtown would put two and two together and choose to dine elsewhere in the future.

Her fingers danced across the keyboard as she hit her stride and was typing out words almost faster than she could read them. She no longer heard the noise of the television, wouldn't have known if she was in the middle of her living room or Grand Central Station. It was The Zone, one of her favorite places to be.

But while The Zone was great, almost like being inside a bubble that kept minor irritations at bay, it didn't render her entirely deaf and dumb. Over the clicking of the keys and the humming of the laptop's fan came an insistent, bothersome knocking.

Ronnie's fingers slowed, her mouth pulling down in a frown as she was yanked out of her nice focused cocoon and forced to identify the annoying noise. It took her a second, but she finally realized that someone was at the door.

Muttering a creative curse, she saved her work, muted the television, and climbed to her feet, crossing the carpeted floor to peer through the peephole.

Oh, God in Heaven, it was *him*.

Glancing into the kitchen, she checked the time on the stove's digital clock.

What the heck was The Jackass doing outside her door at ten o'clock at night?

She rested her head against the flat wooden panel and tried to slow her erratic breathing. Maybe he would go away, maybe . . .

He pounded again, louder and longer this time.

He wasn't going away.

All right, Veronica, you can handle this. Take a deep breath, open the door, and show this man you aren't intimidated by having him show up at your apartment unexpectedly.

Following her own advice, she steeled her nerves, twisting the dead bolt and slipping the chain loose. Dylan stood in the hallway, a dopey half smile on his face, blue eyes sparkling with mischief. Ronnie kept her own expression stoically blank.

"What are you doing here, Stone?"

He leaned a shoulder against the doorjamb, careless and nonchalant. "I expected you to show up at The Box after your knitting group. Where were you?"

"I had things to do," she answered shortly. "Why do you care?"

From behind his back, he produced his needles, yarn, and the portion of knitting he'd gotten done the week before with her guiding him every step of the way. "Our lesson, remember? You said we'd start after tonight's meeting."

For several long seconds, she stared. Yes, she'd told him she would tutor him in the art of knitting. Yes, she'd told him they'd start after this week's knitting group. But when he hadn't shown up, she'd decided he'd had a change of heart and put him completely out of her mind.

"You want to start the lessons *now*?"

He shrugged, continuing to grin at her with those crystal blue, spine-melting eyes. "Why not?"

Because it was ten o'clock at night.

Because she hadn't agreed to work with him at her apartment.

Because she wanted to finish her article and go to bed without being plagued by his exasperating presence.

But what came out of her mouth was a deep sigh and then, "Fine." She stepped back and let him in, shutting the door behind him with a click.

"I like your jammies," he said when she turned back around.

Yet another reason she would never have invited him anywhere near her home. She didn't want him seeing her in her pink basset hound lounge pants and matching top. She didn't want him invading her space, seeing how she lived, knowing things about her that she let very few others become privy to.

Some might say she was secretive, but she liked to think she merely valued her privacy and chose to reflect a certain image in public that she didn't necessarily maintain when she was alone.

And she would sincerely prefer Dylan only ever see her in her perfectly tailored power suits without knowing she came home and climbed into pink puppy-dog pajamas.

As far as small favors were concerned, she supposed she should be relieved that she hadn't opted for her pair of Austin Powers *Do I make you horny, baby? Do I?* shorty pajamas.

There were some questions in life she *really* did not want Dylan to give her an answer for.

"Would you like something to drink?" she asked, however reluctantly, ignoring his comment.

He moved into the living area, making himself comfortable without an invitation to do so. "What have you got?"

She thought a minute, picturing the contents of her refrigerator. "Milk, juice, water . . ." A bottle of wine in one of the cupboards, but she didn't mention that. She wasn't going to waste good alcohol on him.

"No beer?" he asked.

"No, sorry."

He glanced at the muted television screen as though checking to see what was on, then turned again to face her, towering over her low coffee table and small, over-stuffed sofa.

"Guess I'll take some juice, then." His lips quirked as he shot her a relaxed smile. "Although, if you had a little vodka to spill in the glass, I wouldn't complain."

"Sorry, no vodka, either."

"Spoilsport."

Not bothering to reply, Ronnie turned on her heel and moved into the kitchenette to pour a glass of orange juice. When she returned to the living room, she found Dylan perched on the edge of the sofa, elbows on his knees, studying the open screen of her laptop.

"What are you doing?" she snapped, more sharply than she'd actually intended.

Lifting his head, he met her eyes and without a shred of remorse said, "Reading your column."

As she moved forward, he slid over on the couch, making room for her and reaching for his drink. "It's good. But the deli you're talking about isn't Sardowski's on East Ninth, is it? Because I stop there a lot for take-out, and I don't even want to think about what I've been eating if all this is true."

The corner of her mouth twitched as she fought not to laugh. "You might want to consider finding some-where else to pick up lunch," she said by way of an answer, taking a seat on the cushion beside him.

With an overly dramatic groan, he threw himself back against the arm of the couch. "Oh, man, I feel sick. Maybe you should drive me to the hospital so I can have my stomach pumped."

She chuckled, sipping from her own glass of water. "I think you'll be all right. Though you may want to consider starting a course of heavy-duty antibiotics, just to be safe."

Dylan groaned again and clutched his midsection, making Ronnie laugh even harder. He listened to the sound, feeling it slide down his spine and warm him to the soles of his feet.

A second later, she noticed him studying her and sobered. "What?" she asked, that same wariness that he noticed much too often creeping into her gaze.

"That's a nice sound, your laughter."

She rolled her eyes and pulled her shoulders back a fraction. "Don't get used to it," she told him, the words lacking any signs of warmth.

"Don't worry," he said, fighting the urge to grin, "I won't."

Sitting up straighter, he produced the yarn and needles he'd brought along . . . hell, the yarn and needles he'd been carrying everywhere with him, hoping for some miracle to occur and his fingers to suddenly get the hang of the sticks and stitches.

With an exaggerated sigh, she reached for the jumble of yarn and slid closer to him. Intentionally. Voluntarily. Without baring claws and teeth.

Dylan felt like calling Ripley's and reporting a truly astounding event. It should be documented, investigated . . . duplicated, if at all possible.

"All right," she said, "the first thing I think we should do is pull this out and start over."

She yanked the entire collection of loops he'd worked so hard on off its needle and started tugging at the yarn until the stitches began to unravel. He wasn't sure, but he thought he might have whimpered.

"Watch carefully," she told him, and proceeded to cast on several stitches. "See what I'm doing here?"

"Uh-huh." He saw. He'd seen this part before. He'd even tried it a time or two himself. It looked simple, but he might as well have been a giant playing with the individual strands of a spider's web.

She paused and held the needles out to him. "Now you try."

It was embarrassing for a grown man to break out in a cold sweat at the prospect of dealing with a couple of tiny metal sticks and some blue yarn—*baby* blue, no less—but that's exactly what he did.

Holding his breath, he took over and very slowly tried to mimic the movements she'd shown him. The yarn got stuck around his big fingertips, and he kept fumbling the needles. He knew almost immediately that he was screwing it up again.

"Wait a minute," Ronnie said, obviously noticing his awkwardness.

She sat for a minute, tapping the palm of her hand against the side of her leg. Then she bounced up and paced across the carpeted room.

"I think you're having trouble because the needles are so small and the yarn is so thin."

She came back with a bright turquoise faux leather tote in one hand and a woven basket in the other. The basket was filled with a multitude of yarns and needles, and she began sorting through them, searching for exactly what she wanted.

"Here you go," she said, handing him a set of white plastic needles a couple of sizes larger than the ones he'd been using.

Then she dug into the bag and drew out a small, fat skein of soft black yarn. "Charlotte gave this to me tonight. She spun it herself from fiber sheared from the alpacas she raises. I really think you'll like it. Feel how soft it is, even though the strands are nice and thick."

He ran his fingers over the yarn, feeling the texture. He didn't know jack shit about yarn, but it was definitely softer than what he'd bought at the craft store, even though the other stuff looked stronger.

"Okay, let's try again."

This time, when she plopped down beside him, their thighs touched from knee to hip, and the sensation shot straight to his groin.

Great. Just what he needed was to be sitting flush against the woman who'd made his life a misery this past year, and whom he'd endeavored to make just as miserable, with a stiffy straining against his fly.

She arranged the larger needles in his hands, then showed him how to start the yarn. He followed her instructions to the letter, trying to do exactly what she was doing, exactly how she was doing it.

And he had to admit, the thicker needles and yarn did seem to make the task easier. He felt less clumsy, less like his fingers were fat sausages working to balance a couple of tiny toothpicks.

"Good," Ronnie said after he'd managed to cast on a good number of stitches. "See, size really does matter. I knew the bigger needles and thicker yarn would work better for you. Now we can start to actually knit."

"You mean we aren't knitting yet?" he asked, jaw clenched in concentration.

She chuckled, rearranging herself on the sofa cushions. "Not yet. That was just the setup."

Folding her legs beneath her, she leaned against him, hovering above him to observe his progress. Her arm rested on his back and shoulder, the side of her breast rubbing his bicep. The heat of her body burned through the material of his tan buttondown shirt, and they might as well have both been naked.

Now he was thinking about her naked. Crap.

He could picture her, too. All sleek, glowing ivory skin. Nice, firm breasts, full enough to fill a man's hands and pert enough to make his mouth water. Her long, wavy brown hair falling down around her shoulders, a few stray curls framing those amazing breasts with their tight raspberry nipples, and drawing his gaze to her flat stomach, then lower . . .

He swallowed hard, his nostrils flaring and vision

going fuzzy at the edges. As if the snugness at his crotch wasn't bad enough, now his diaphragm was growing tight, his palms turning damp, and his heart beginning to pulse beneath his rib cage.

He needed a drink, a cold shower, to put about a hundred miles between him and Ronnie's hot, luscious body. Those pajamas, with their funny-looking dogs on them, might have been more-than-adequate covering when he'd first arrived, but now the only thing he could think about was ripping them off to see if the reality of her naked body was as good as his imagination painted it to be.

Oblivious to his inner turmoil or how close he was to spontaneously combusting, Ronnie remained pressed close to him, counting the number of stitches already lined up on one of the needles. She wiggled a bit more, ratcheting his temperature up another ten or twenty degrees, before covering his hands with her own.

She was practically in his lap . . . crap, crap, crap . . . ready to show him the next part of the knitting process. Only he couldn't follow her instructions because every time he took a deep breath in an attempt to calm his raging libido, all he smelled was Ronnie.

She smelled fresh and clean from her shower, with a hint of sharp, sweet citrus, probably from whatever soap or shampoo she'd used.

His fingers clenched around the needles, so tight, he was surprised they didn't snap. He wanted to inhale her. Wanted to turn his head just a few degrees and lick the column of her throat like a cat licking cream.

Admit it, Stone, you want to do a hell of a lot more than that.

Yeah, he did. Way more.

Slow things. Fast things. Hot, slurpy, sexy things.

"Are you watching?"

Blinking, Dylan raised his head to find Ronnie frowning at him. He shifted slightly, trying to find a more comfortable position for his trapped, straining boner, and hoping she didn't notice his predicament.

"Yeah, I'm watching." Watching, fantasizing, salivating.

"Oh, really?"

One of her dark, perfectly sculpted brows arched higher than the other, making him feel like a grade school student being singled out by the teacher.

"Then what did I just show you how to do?"

Damned if he knew. He was still trying to get the image of her long legs wrapped around his waist as he pounded his way to glory out of his brain.

"Um . . . I forget. Can you show me again?"

Row 6

Counting to ten, she concentrated on her breathing and reminded herself that she didn't *care* if he listened to her or not. Didn't *care* if he learned to knit or not. In fact, for the sake of their competition, she preferred he didn't. And either way, she was going to get her thousand dollars just for pretending to help him.

The thought of that amount of money sitting all safe and sound in her bank account washed the tension from her body and relaxed her from the crown of her head to her polished toenails.

She inhaled and exhaled once more, then leaned back in to wrap her fingers around his and guide his movements.

"Try to keep up, Stone. You don't want me telling folks you're a slow learner, do you?"

That seemed to snap him out of whatever haze he'd been in. He made a scoffing sound and replied, "I'm only a slow learner when it comes to certain subjects. With others, I catch on real quick."

His voice was low and husky and carried a hint of suggestiveness. Slanting a glance in his direction, she noticed a heat in his gaze she'd never seen before.

Other men had looked at her that way, with lust and longing, but never Dylan.

She licked her lips and swallowed, quickly returning her gaze to the needles and yarn in front of them before he caught her watching him.

Having Dylan think of her in sexual terms wouldn't have been so bad. He was a man, she was a woman, and that's what men did around any woman who didn't look like she'd just climbed out of the primordial ooze. They were horny bastards who could get turned on watching paint dry.

That was fine. *His* lust she could handle.

The problem was that she very much feared a similar desire would be visible in her own eyes if she let him meet her gaze. She was pressed up against him—how in God's name had that happened? She didn't even like him, didn't think she'd ever touched him willingly before, but suddenly she was draped along his side like she was trying to share his skin. Gads!

And she was suddenly warm, warmer than she suspected the temperature in the apartment called for. She could feel the flush of her cheeks, the blood pulsing in her veins, the shakiness in her limbs.

That wasn't the worst of it, though. The worst was that in addition to being warm all over, she was wet. Down there, between her legs, where arousal couldn't be denied no matter how vehemently she tried.

Oh, God. Oh, god, oh, god, oh, god. This couldn't be happening. She *could not* be sexually attracted to Dylan Stone. She would rather eat glass . . . walk across hot coals . . . cover her body in paper cuts and jump naked into a vat of lemon juice . . .

Panic pressed in on her from all sides. She tried to

breathe, but her lungs refused to expand. Her head began to spin as she fought for oxygen, but the seconds ticked by with little success. She had to get out of there and away from him, before she freaked out.

"Water," she croaked, jumping to her feet.

Dylan leaned back slightly, cocking his head to stare up at her. He looked as confused as she felt. "What?"

"Water. I need a drink of water." She plucked her glass from the coffee table before he could notice it was still half full, sloshing water over her fingers in the process. "Do you want anything?" she asked, making a beeline for the kitchen.

She was already at the sink, splashing cold water on her face and, unfortunately, down the front of her shirt, when he answered from the living room.

"Only that beer, if you find one."

She didn't have beer, but she did have wine, and suddenly keeping it for a special occasion didn't seem nearly as important as it had an hour ago.

Shutting off the spigot, she dug in the cupboard for the hidden bottle of Pinot Grigio in the back. It wasn't an expensive brand, but it was tasty—one of the best she'd found within her price range—and would do the trick.

"How about a glass of wine instead?" she called back.

"If that's the best you've got, I'll take it."

She already had the cork out and was pouring herself a glass, draining it in one long gulp. Feeling the smooth, slightly fruity, pale liquid rolling down her throat and into her belly fortified her and steadied her nerves.

"Mind if I use your computer to check my e-mail?"

Even from a distance, his voice rolled over her like a

warm ocean wave. Closing her eyes, she leaned against the edge of the counter and tried to slow her out-of-control heartbeat.

"No, go ahead," she told him, mortified when the words came out weak and squeaky.

What was wrong with her? Where was her strong-as-nails, steel-heeled personality? Her fuck-you-and-the-horse-you-rode-in-on attitude?

Her world was tilting off its axis, and she didn't like it one bit.

Pressing the heels of her hands into her eye sockets, she concentrated on her breathing and struggled to regain her equilibrium.

A little misdirected sexual frustration, that's all it was. Dylan was a man, she was a woman, and she supposed women could be as indiscriminate as the male of the species. That had never been her practice, but after a while, when a dry spell dragged on a bit too long and things below the equator started to thrum, apparently any guy in close proximity would do.

That wasn't exactly a comforting thought, but she had no intention of letting her errant hormones overrule her more prudent sensibilities, no matter how loudly they sat up and begged.

Pouring a few more inches of wine, she took another hearty swallow, then topped off her glass before filling his and carrying both into the living room.

He was seated on the floor now, the same as she'd been before his arrival. His long, denim-covered legs were stretched out beneath the table, crossed at ankles that stuck out from the other side. He tapped a couple of keys on the laptop, then sat back and took the glass of wine she offered.

She moved to the far end of the sofa, putting as much distance between them as possible. Where she'd been feeling loose and comfortable before, she now held herself stiff and rigid. Even though a couple of feet of empty space separated them, she still leaned into the arm of the couch, away from him, and crossed her legs primly.

Dylan took a sip of his wine . . . a small sip that didn't even remotely catch him up to her . . . and shifted to face her, resting his free arm on the cushion of the sofa.

"So," he said casually, his tone light, "who's Domiknitrix?"

Her eyes widened in surprise, and the mouthful of Pinot Grigio she'd been in the process of swallowing threatened to go down the wrong pipe.

How had he found out about that?

Of course, since her luck seemed to be in the toilet already, it was only logical that things would continue on that track. Instead of keeping his distance, Dylan popped up off the floor to come to her rescue. He slid onto the sofa beside her and patted her on the back until her coughing fit subsided.

"You okay?" he asked. His wide, strong hand made rhythmic taps and circles on her back, sending shivers out in every direction from where he touched.

She nodded, despite the fact that her face was hot with embarrassment. Lower, though, and deep down inside, everything hummed in sensual, sizzling awareness of the man beside her.

Showing no concern whatsoever for her ability to breathe, he leaned back, adopting a slouched posture in the center of her overstuffed sofa, and murmured, "I have to admit, I'm intrigued. It's not just any woman who would have the *cojones* to use Domiknitrix as her onscreen user name. That's kind of . . . kinky, don't you think?"

Prior to her anxiety attack, her glass had been nearly empty, so none of her wine had spilled. But why take chances? Raising the wine to her lips, she drained the last of her own, then grabbed Dylan's right out of his hand and drained that, too.

"I don't know why you're surprised, Stone. We've already established that my balls are at least as big as yours."

He chuckled, moving to relieve her of both wine-glasses and set them aside on the coffee table.

"True—figuratively speaking, at least." He cast her a pointed glance. "I hope."

"Don't worry, Stone, I'm not packing anything other than the average, everyday female parts. But I can still kick your ass at anything you claim men do better than women."

He studied her for a moment, and when he spoke again, his voice was lower, gentler. "Don't you think it's about time you started calling me Dylan?"

She blinked, taken aback by the question. She'd just been working up a good head of steam, feeling fully in control of herself for the first time that evening and back on the solid ground.

And then he'd pulled a 180, yanking the rug out from under her with a completely unrelated—not to mention civil—request.

She hated when he did that.

"Do you really think it's a good idea to be on a first-name basis?"

He threw his head back and laughed.

"Ronnie, Ronnie, Ronnie," he said after he'd recovered from whatever he found so amusing. "You really are a treat. You're the only woman I know who would invite a man into her apartment while she's in her jammies, do her best to teach him to knit, and still refuse to call him by his first name."

"It's late. What did you expect me to be wearing?" As comebacks went, she knew that was lame, but it was all she could come up with at this time of night, with three glasses of wine in her, and feelings cropping up inside that she'd never expected to have to deal with, *ever*.

His blue-eyed gaze raked over her, taking in the long fall of her nearly dry hair, her shoulders, left bare by the thin straps of her pajama top, and the fullness of her breasts just above the brown-and-white basset hound in the center of her chest.

"Judging by your screen name, a guy might hope for some leather and lace, maybe a few fun restraints."

The image of Dylan tied spread-eagle to her bed, naked and at her mercy, sent a streak of white-hot electricity racing through her bones. Picturing herself done up in a black bustier, black fishnet stockings, and garter belt, with a long, wicked-looking whip in one hand, had her breasts swelling and her nipples turning hard beneath her top.

Did he notice? He had to notice. How could he not when it felt as though they could chip through ice?

She fought the urge to cover herself, afraid that would only draw attention to her aroused state. And the last thing she needed was for Dylan Stone to know he turned her on.

"I think you should leave," she told him in a flat voice, hoping her face was equally impassive.

Instead of looking offended or taken aback by her sudden suggestion, he merely raised a brow and quirked one corner of his full, sensual mouth.

"What's the matter, Veronica? Did I hit a nerve? Get a little too close to unveiling the red-hot mama that lurks beneath your cool, uptight exterior?"

Uptight? Where did he get off always calling her uptight? Just because she dressed professionally and refused to lower herself to his level of lazy, laid-back, so-called charm . . .

She tried to make a scoffing sound, but it came out as more of a cross between a whimper and a wheeze. "You wish, Stone."

"Actually, I do." He shifted slightly away from her on the sofa and tilted his head to one side, taking her in from head to toe. "I'm picturing you in tight black leather with lots of silver studs. High, high-heeled boots that go all the way to your . . ."

He trailed off just long enough to slant a glance at her lap, and damned if a bolt of wanton longing didn't strike her right where he was looking, right between the legs.

"Thighs," he finished, as though that had been his intention all along. "And I'm thinking handcuffs, or maybe a few silk scarves that would be soft and gentle, but keep a man exactly where you wanted him."

She wouldn't have thought it possible, but the timbre of his voice went even lower, heightening the sexual consciousness that was already coursing through her veins.

It took her a moment to regain her equilibrium, catch

her breath, and get her heart rate to return to normal. Everything within her vibrated with sensual awareness, not just of the tension in the room, but of the man across from her. And that way lay disaster with a capital D.

"You," she said, hopping to her feet, "have got a fertile imagination. No doubt brought about by the lack of interesting topics you're given to write about at work. If I were forced to cover bingo night at the VFW and Slappy the Wonder Dog walking backward on two legs in a tutu, I'd create alternate realities in my head, too."

Pushing to his feet to meet her eye-to-eye, he gave her a narrow stare and cocked one hip. "You know full well that columnists aren't given assignments. We come up with our own topics to write about."

One brow shot up, though she didn't say anything. She didn't need to; her look was enough. Yeah, as columnists, they both had free rein over what they wrote about, and as long as they kept their columns interesting enough, their editors wouldn't call them on the carpet and send them back to covering the boring and inane.

But that didn't explain why some of Dylan's columns did, indeed, feel as though they'd been low-level assignments. At least at the beginning of his employment with the *Cleveland Herald*. A fact that she'd been only too tickled to see, considering he'd stolen the job at that particular paper right out from under her.

One thing was for certain. If the *Herald* had hired her instead of Dylan, she'd have wowed them right from the start, not filled space with stories any average third-grader could have written.

Then again, maybe Dylan had been a naughty boy his first few weeks on the job and covering the ridiculous had been his punishment.

Oh, shoot! Now her brain was back on the hot-domination-sex image again.

"And for your information," Dylan added almost petulantly, "Slappy was a very cute and gifted canine."

His comment caught her off guard, and she had to bite back a grin. "I'm sure he was."

Her lips were still edging upward as she turned and made her way to the front door. "I really do think you should leave. It's late and I've got a busy day tomorrow."

"Closing down one of Cleveland's most popular delis, right?" he asked from only a few steps behind her.

Reaching the door, she slipped the chain loose and twisted the knob. "I can let that one go, if you don't mind a fair amount of rat droppings in your hoagies and potato salad."

Dylan made a face, stopping just short of the hallway. "I guess it wouldn't hurt for the health inspectors to pay them a visit. Just to be safe."

Ronnie nodded. "I agree."

"So what about this knitting thing?" he asked, holding up his yarn and needles. "Are you still going to help me out?"

Either the wine or the late hour must have had a dulling effect on her senses because she didn't even think it over, didn't weigh the pros and cons or try to figure a way out of it, she simply nodded.

"Next time, bring some Chinese or something, though. And your own beer, if you want it."

He smiled, flashing straight white teeth and the hint of a dimple in each slightly tanned, slightly stubbled cheek. "Deal."

"Good. Good night." She opened the door an inch

more, though there was already plenty of room for him to pass.

"One more thing," he said, not making the least effort to exit her apartment.

With a sigh and just managing to avoid an exasperated eye roll, she asked, "What's that?"

"My first name is Dylan. I'd like to hear you say it."

She blinked, startled that *that's* what he was still hanging around for. He was Stone; he'd always been Stone, and that's what he would always be. She didn't want to call him Dylan, or even think of him that way; it was too close to taking down the wall of enmity between them.

"You'd probably also like to hear me say men are braver, stronger, and more capable than women, but it's not going to happen."

"Come on, Chasen, I know you can do it. It's just two short syllables. D-y-l-a-n. *Dy-lan*. Dylan."

Arching a hip, she dropped her hand from the doorknob and pinned it to her waist. Her eyes narrowed, and this time when her temperature rose, she knew it had nothing to do with the wine or the sexual drought she'd been suffering for longer than she cared to admit.

"Bite. Me," she told him, enunciating each word the same as he had his name.

Instead of looking properly reprimanded, his grin widened. "I thought you'd never ask."

And before she had a clue what he was about to do, before she could formulate a reaction, he leaned in, wrapped one firm, vise-like arm around her waist, and dragged her against his chest. His hard solid wall of chest.

She had the fleeting thought that he must work out—*a lot*—in order for her to clearly feel the ridges of his abdomen through his shirt and her pajama top.

Yowza.

His mouth settled over hers, warm and soft and intoxicating. Every nerve ending in her body went numb. She stood in his grasp, thunderstruck, the arm that had been at her hip falling loose and forgotten at her side.

Several things went through her mind at once.

First, that Dylan Stone was kissing her.

Next, that *oh, my God,* Dylan Stone was kissing her!

And then, that he was a really, *really* good kisser.

Maybe if they'd done this a bit sooner, their relationship could have started out on a better foot. They might have challenged each other in the bedroom rather than through their newspaper columns.

Oh, bad Ronnie, bad. Don't think that way. He's your enemy, no matter how skilled he might be with his mouth.

She thought about pushing him away. Somewhere deep in the recesses of her brain, a voice whispered that the Ronnie whom Dylan had come to know would slap him.

But it was so very hard to work up the energy to slap him when his lips were dancing magic across her own. They pressed and then retreated. Slid slowly in one direction and then the other.

All of that she might have been able to resist . . . it wouldn't have been easy, not with her knees turned to pudding, but she thought she could have managed it . . . but then the tip of his tongue darted out, licking the seam of her mouth, and any shot she'd had at resistance dried up and disappeared like a peach left too long in the sun.

"Say my name," he ordered, the whispered words quivering against her skin, his warm breath dancing across her face.

She didn't think, didn't resist, simply opened to him, feeling flames of longing licking at her insides.

"Dylan," she breathed. And the minute she did, his mouth captured hers, sweeping inside, more forcefully and demanding than before.

Her brain turned fuzzy, her heart pounded like a jungle drum, and an almost unbearable heat pulsed between her thighs. She wound her arms behind his neck and lifted one knee to wrap her calf around his leg, her limbs moving of their own volition.

She pressed her breasts against his chest, rubbing her painfully puckered nipples along that solid wall and wishing they were both stark naked. Lower, where their pelvises were stuck together like two supercharged magnets, she felt the hard crest of his erection and knew his arousal mirrored her own.

Oh, yeah, naked would be good. Naked would be *so good . . .*

But before she could start yanking at his clothes or stripping out of her own, he broke the kiss, set her on her feet, and held tight to her elbows until she was steady, then took a single step back.

She blinked, stunned by his sudden desertion, the jarring switch from swapping spit to having twelve inches of empty space between them. Her head was spinning, making her feel slightly woozy and disoriented, and the rest of her body prickled as though it had been touched by a live wire. Even her skin felt jumpy.

It was only moderately satisfying to see that Dylan's own chest was rising and falling with a labor of breathing that matched her own.

But with distance came the return of her senses, and with those came irritation and awkwardness.

"What was that?" she demanded, crossing her arms beneath her still full and tingling breasts.

"What? You mean the kiss? Come on, Ronnie, you can't tell me it's been so long since a guy has kissed you that you don't even recognize one anymore."

"Very funny," she said, her gaze narrowing. "*Why* did you kiss me? You don't even like me. And I sure as hell don't like you."

"Could have fooled me. Unless it was some other woman trying to climb me like a monkey up a banana tree."

Her foot, which had been tapping out an angry staccato beat on the carpeted floor, froze at his words. A flush of heat bloomed in her face and down her neck, though she prayed to God it wasn't accompanied by a telltale blush. She would rather die than have Dylan know she was embarrassed by her behavior.

With any other man, she wouldn't have been. She'd have probably jumped him again and walked him straight back to her bedroom . . . if they got that far.

But with Dylan . . . well, he was right that it had been a while for her, but even if it had been ten lifetimes, that still shouldn't have made her needy enough, horny enough, or *crazy* enough to have let things go as far as they had.

"Don't get a big head, Stone. I forgot for a moment

that you're a loathsome, despicable jerk, that's all. But I'm all better now, believe me."

Before she finished her last sentence, he was already shaking his head. "Ronnie, Ronnie, Ronnie. Throwing up that armor again so soon? What happened to calling me Dylan instead of Stone?" His voice went scratchy on the last, and his brows knit in a faux frown.

"I've never called you Dylan."

"Au contraire," he said. "I seem to recall a rather breathy, passionate *Dylan* right around the halfway mark of that game of tonsil hockey. Feel free to call me that, in just that tone, anytime you want."

The corner of Ronnie's left eye started to twitch, and she had to curl her fingers into a fist to keep from reaching up to cover it. "The next time you hear me say your name with anything but derision will be at your funeral. And then, I'll utter it with such joy and elation, everyone in attendance will think I've just won the lottery."

"Ouch." His mouth turned up in a half grin. "Guess that's my cue to leave. I'll have to be extra careful crossing the street so I don't give you anything to celebrate too soon."

"Try walking close to the building along that side," she told him, pointing toward the windows at the far end of her apartment. "It will be so much easier to hit you with the anvil that way."

That brought a sharp bark of laughter, and he stepped into the hallway, head shaking. "Careful with that temper, Wile E. You know how most of those little tricks turn out—with the coyote flat as a pancake and the road-runner getting away without a scratch."

"I've got better aim," she replied as she pushed the door closed behind him. It clicked soundly, and slipping

the chain then turning the dead bolt had a cathartic effect on her blood pressure. The minute she did it, she began to relax, tension pouring from her body in waves.

Then his voice came, like a spike to the center of her
brain. "See you for our next knitting lesson!"

And in addition to his footsteps padding down the
hallway, she could have sworn she heard whistling.

Row 7

"Whoa! You actually locked lips with the Ice Queen? Weren't you afraid your tongue would freeze up and fall off?"

"I wasn't exactly thinking with my tongue," Dylan said in response to his friend's surprised question.

"Dude." Zack grunted as he twisted one rod after another on the foosball table in an attempt to stop one of Dylan's passes. The six-foot-six-inch goalie was wearing a black T-shirt with a squirrel that stretched across his wide chest. The squirrel was in a tiny suit of armor, holding up a metal shield, and beneath that were the words PROTECT YOUR NUTS.

Zack's tastes ran a little toward the never-grew-up, Peter Pan side of things. Even his apartment, where they'd gathered to eat, drink, and be merry, looked more like a theme park than an adult dwelling.

With its tall windows that overlooked the city, a massive amount of square footage, and glossy hardwood floors, most people would kill for this apartment, and do a lot more with it than the hockey player had. But because it was Zack's, it more closely resembled the loft from the Tom Hanks movie *Big*. In many respects, the

Rockets goalie was just a kid in a man's body, as his surroundings could attest.

Grace was beginning to clean the place up, adding a few mature, feminine touches, but miracles of that magnitude didn't occur overnight. Zack still had his foosball table, pinball machines, the giant plasma television on the far wall. The floor was still scuffed in places from impromptu soccer or basketball games—when it came to sports, he might play hockey for a living, but he was an equal-opportunity fan—for which a net was stuck in one corner and a hoop was attached over the bedroom door.

He also owned all the latest video game equipment, be it PlayStation, Xbox, or Wii, with every game imaginable for all three. And his idea of art was assorted street signs or posters of sports figures, anchored to the wall with whatever was handy at the time and did the trick.

He was *so* not getting his security deposit back when he moved.

Not for the first time, Dylan contemplated the fact that professional athletes got paid way too much. And he didn't get paid nearly enough.

Which was why he had no qualms about hanging out at Zack's place every chance he got to take advantage of the arcade-like atmosphere. He also had no problem letting Zack supply mass quantities of beer and pizza.

"You gonna kiss her again?" This from Gage in a low, dispassionate voice. Having lost the last round, he was kicking back on the black leather sofa, waiting to see who won the right to pick the night's pizza toppings.

Zack's horse of a dog, Bruiser, was stretched out across the remaining two seat cushions, his legs hanging over the edge, his head resting on Gage's leg, where a giant wet spot was beginning to develop from the animal's open, drooling mouth.

If Gage minded being covered in St. Bernard slobber, he didn't show it. None of them did anymore, they were so used to Bruiser's presence.

Zack had adopted the ungainly mammoth three years before from the local SPCA, when he'd been no more than a puppy. Already a gangly, massive creature at only six months of age, with a huge head and giant paws that were too big for the rest of his body, but a puppy all the same.

And though Zack wouldn't admit it under threat of death or castration, the canine was his baby. He doted on the boy, giving him free run of the apartment and feeding him whatever he was eating.

He swore the dog was a babe magnet, too. Before he'd met and fallen blades-over-brains for the fair-haired Grace, he'd had puck bunnies hanging on him like barnacles on a boat bottom, and insisted it was at least in part due to Bruiser's irresistibility.

Or maybe it was just the guy-with-a-dog thing that women found irresistible. Because Dylan was pretty sure that if the ugly brown-and-white mutt had been sitting alone on a street corner, with those droopy eyes, sagging jowls, and lines of spittle hanging from his jaw, most people—men and women alike—would run screaming.

But he wasn't here to lament his friend's strange taste in pets. He was here to gain control of pizza toppings and maybe get a little friendly advice about the situation with Ronnie.

"Doubtful," he replied in answer to Zack's question.

Negotiating a nice bank shot to spin the ball past Zack's defensive line, he brought them another point closer to pepperoni and Canadian bacon. "She threatened to drop an anvil on my head."

"An anvil? Who is she, Snidely Whiplash?" Zack wanted to know.

"More like Dita Von Teese," Dylan mumbled.

"What?"

"Nothing."

It was one thing for him to harass Ronnie about her screen name and get worked up over the erotic images it created in his brain; it was a whole other to share that sort of thing with his friends. Maybe someday, but not now.

While he was distracted by fantasies of being tied to the bed while Ronnie loomed over him in hot, skintight S&M gear, Zack shot the ball past him twice in a row to score five points and win the game.

"Yes!" his friend cheered, pumping his hand in the air. "Anchovies it is."

Dylan and Gage both groaned. Dylan grabbed a beer and joined Gage on the sofa while Zack went to phone in the order.

"We've really got to come up with a better way to decide on pizza toppings," Gage said, propping his feet on the low, glass-topped table.

"Yeah. He kicks our butts at anything sports-related every single time."

"How good do you think he'd be at Rock, Paper, Scissors?"

"My guess is, he'd go for rock."

"We could always challenge him to a game of Scrabble," Gage added. "That ought to trip him up."

"Well, I don't know about you, but I think the two guys who aren't getting laid on a regular basis should be the ones to choose what kind of pizza they get. I mean, we deserve some kind of consolation prize, don't we?"

"Speak for yourself," Gage intoned.

"Oh, yeah?" Dylan turned to the somber, stone-faced cop. "You telling me you've been getting some since you split with Jenna? Because your mood lately would indicate otherwise."

Gage's expression turned even darker, which was really saying something. He flipped Dylan the bird at the same time he muttered, "Fuck you."

Dylan didn't take offense at the remark. It wasn't the first time one of his friends had told him where to go or what he could do with himself, and it wouldn't be the last.

And with Gage, they were all willing to cut him a little more slack than usual. He probably shouldn't have brought the man's ex-wife into the conversation to begin with. That was still a sore subject and, Dylan suspected, the direct cause of Gage's continued sullenness. The man had never been much of a talker to begin with, but for the past year or so he'd been practically catatonic compared with his old self.

"What are we talking about?" Zack wanted to know when he reentered the living room.

"Dumb jocks," Gage supplied.

"And jerks who are getting a regular supply of sex making their friends suffer through anchovies on their pizza."

Zack moved to the low, black leather chair that matched the couch and was cocked at an angle in front of the coffee table. The air blew out with a whoosh as he dropped his two-hundred-plus pounds onto its over-stuffed seat cushion.

"Jealousy is an ugly trait, gentlemen. Crack all the jokes you want about my intelligence, I'm still the one who gets to shag a beautiful woman every night *and* kicked both your asses at foosball. Foosball," he said again, shaking his head with exaggerated disappointment. "What a couple of wusses. I'd be afraid to get on the ice with you two. I might be brought up on manslaughter charges just for looking at you funny."

Dylan and Gage exchanged a glance.

"When the pizza gets here," Dylan said, "you distract him. I'll pay the delivery guy and spit on his slices."

"Deal," Gage agreed.

Zack made a rude gesture with his right hand. "Yeah, yeah, I'm real scared. Stop whining and tell me more about feeling up the Ice Queen."

"I didn't feel her up. We didn't get that far."

"Still. I know she's Grace's friend and all, but I didn't think she was capable of thawing enough to get her legs apart, let alone wrap one around your ass."

Dylan frowned. "Don't talk about her like that. She's not that bad."

A couple of seconds of dead silence passed, and he knew his friends must be questioning his sanity. From the time Ronnie had first started getting under his skin with her emasculating challenges and razor-sharp tongue, he'd said stuff like that and worse, and Zack and Gage had been there to hear most of it.

But ever since he'd been in her apartment and she'd actually been civil to him for a short window of time, his opinion of her had begun to shift.

Not swing a full 180 or anything bizarro like that, but alter. Subtly.

"It was kind of odd," he said.

"Why? Did she have a forked tongue?"

Dylan frowned. "Not the kiss, just . . . it. The whole visit."

The doorbell buzzed and Zack jumped up to retrieve the pizza. He returned in record time, and no sooner had he set the box on the low table than Bruiser's ears perked up, his head lifted, and he hefted his bulky, two-hundred-pound weight off the couch and over to Zack.

Zack peeled a slice of pizza away from the rest of the pie, folded it in half, and held it up for the dog, who devoured it practically in one gulp. Only then did Zack pull out a slice for himself and pass the box around to the others.

Used to Bruiser getting first dibs, they dug into the hot, crusty pie, anchovies and all. And Bruiser, knowing he wasn't going to get another whole piece of pizza, settled at a spot an equal distance among the three men in the hope of being the recipient of a few crumbs or left-over crust.

"So go ahead," Gage put in after they'd each consumed a full slice and downed half a beer. "Tell us what was so odd about your trip to Ronnie's place."

"She was nice to me, for one. Half the time, anyway. And she was wearing these cute little pajamas with basset hounds all over the bottoms and one right in the center of the top. It was disturbing to say the least. I've never seen her in anything other than prissy, top-of-the-line business attire."

He stopped short of telling them about her screen

name. He hadn't quite come to terms with that one himself.

Not that he had any particular qualms about spilling her secrets to the world. Thinking back on his Pink Panty–seeking mission into the biker bar on the outskirts of town, he was tempted to rent a billboard and stick the user name up there, right along with a Photoshopped picture of Ronnie in coordinated dominatrix gear.

But it never hurt to keep some ammunition in the arsenal. He'd save that little piece of information for later, when he was really pissed and needed to vent.

"She does have a nice set of sweater puppies," Zack remarked around a mouthful of pizza, "so I get the choice in sleepwear."

While his friend was right about Ronnie's ample assets, the comment still caused Dylan's jaw to tense.

"That's not what I'm talking about. I'm talking about . . ." He shrugged, searching for the words to describe his feelings about his time spent at Ronnie's apartment.

"I don't know. You know Ronnie. You've seen her at The Penalty Box. She's always so well put together. Looks like she just stepped off the cover of some fashion magazine, with her designer clothes and shoes, never a hair out of place."

"What? Was she a scraggly mess in rags from the Goodwill store when you dropped by?"

Dylan's brows knit as he picked pieces of anchovy off his second slice of pizza and fed it to the dog, who had proven long ago that he would eat anything.

"Nah. Her hair was still damp from the shower, but she looked good enough." Good enough to eat, if truth be known, but he didn't say that.

"It was more the apartment that threw me. It was kind of . . . Spartan. I would have expected something that looked like Martha Stewart had decorated, but instead it was more thrift store mix-and-match. The couch, the TV, the coffee table . . . they had to be at least ten years old—and they looked every minute of it. She had a radio, not a stereo. Not even a CD player that I could see. And a VHS machine, but no DVD player, and hardly any tapes. None of her dishes matched, at least the ones I saw. The artwork on the walls was kind of old-fashioned and almost creepy, like the stuff you see at the dentist's office. And she had recycle bins next to the kitchen."

"Recycling is good," Zack said. "I recycle. Everybody should."

"Don't you mean Magda recycles for you?" Gage asked, monotone.

"She's my housekeeper, it's her job. But I pay her to do it and make sure no one throws anything recyclable into the trash so she doesn't have to dig it out."

"You Prince Charming, you."

This time, Gage was on the receiving end of a single-finger salute.

"I'm with you on that, and you're more than welcome to my beer bottle when I'm finished with it, but in a million years would you ever have pictured Veronica Chasen living in anything other than fashion-forward comfort, maybe even near-luxury?"

"Maybe it's all hand-me-downs from a dead grandmother with lousy taste or something," Gage offered.

"Maybe."

"Or maybe she's trying to save a buck and doesn't get much company, so it doesn't matter," Zack suggested.

"That's just it. Who spends *beaucoup* bucks on their wardrobe but skimps at home?"

Zack shrugged. "A woman? Women do all kinds of crazy things for all kinds of crazy-ass reasons. Grace has this weekly face thing she does, and she won't let me be anywhere near her when she does it. So once a week, she refuses to come over here and won't let me go over there." He spun a finger next to his ear to indicate his fiancée was Looney Tunes.

From his spot on the sofa, Gage cocked his head. "So what are you going to do once you're married?"

"Beats me." He took another big bite of pizza, chewing while he talked. "Hopefully she'll wait until I'm on the road to go all *Night of the Living Dead* on me."

Bringing the conversation back to Ronnie, Dylan said, "But wouldn't you think that someone who wanted to pinch pennies or watch their budget would try to save money with *everything* she buys? How much sense does it make to buy a cheap television set, then spend six hundred dollars on a pair of designer shoes?"

"Not much," Zack agreed. "Then again, how much sense does it make to kick your hot and horny boyfriend out of bed because you need to moisturize? Women are nuts half the time. But if you tell them that, they go even nuttier."

"It's better to just mind your own business and let them be," Gage volunteered. "That's why God created *Monday Night Football* and Saturday-night hockey games . . . to give us guys a break and a few hours of much-needed sanity."

Dylan eyed his two friends, tapping a thumb against the side of his rapidly warming bottle of Michelob.

"You two ever fly this little theory past your significant others?"

They exchanged a glance, then broke out in wide, matching grins. "Hell, no," they both replied at exactly the same time.

"Well, I can't figure her out, that's for sure. All this time, I've thought she was this steel-heeled bitch who could burn a man to ashes at fifty paces. Now I'm not so sure. Something about the way she lives doesn't jibe with the woman you see in public."

Zack raised a brow and washed down his last bite of pizza with his last swig of beer. "You're the reporter," he said, wiping his palms on his gray Champion shorts. "Why don't you investigate her and see what's up?"

Dylan hadn't thought of himself as much of an investigative reporter lately. Not since he'd gotten stuck writing lackluster columns that mostly revolved around trying not to let a woman with a chip on her shoulder from a rival paper kick his ass.

But his friend had a point. There were bells going off in his head, telling him that all was not as it seemed with prissy Miss Veronica Chasen. And suddenly, he very much wanted to find out what made her tick.

He just hoped he didn't discover that she was a time bomb, about to blow up in his face.

Ronnie bustled into The Penalty Box behind Jenna and Grace. It was just the three of them tonight; everyone else from their knitting group had opted to skip the trip for after-meeting drinks.

As soon as Ronnie saw Dylan sitting with Zack and Gage at a table in the center of the bar, she began to wish she'd done the same. She just had no stomach for dealing with him tonight.

Not *anymore,* anyway. She'd already had to bite her tongue, curl her fingers, and count to a thousand when he'd shown up at The Yarn Barn for her previously Jackass-Free weekly knitting meeting.

Everywhere she turned lately, he seemed to be there. Her apartment for one-on-one tutoring . . . he'd dropped by again two days after The Kiss, and just as she'd flippantly demanded that night, he'd brought Chinese.

She hated him for that. Not only for showing up *again*—at her home and sanctuary—when she would have much preferred he disappear from her life altogether. But also because it appeared she'd finally met a man who actually listened and followed through, and wouldn't you know it had to be him.

But it wasn't just the visits to her apartment or the usurping of her personal girls-only . . . *it really should be girls-only!* . . . knitting group. He'd also begun e-mailing her at work. And to add insult to injury, each and every one began with some horrifying BDSM salutation.

Dear Domiknitrix . . .

Mistress Ronnie . . .

Dear Ronnie, O, exalted mistress of yarn and pain . . .

She really wanted to smack him.

It wasn't just his knowledge and abuse of her personal screen name that made her blood pressure rise, though. Oh, no. It was the fact that he was practically cyberstalking her.

He e-mailed to ask if she was going to be home on a certain day, at a certain time. To which she'd responded with an emphatic *No,* but was then proven a liar when he showed up, anyway.

He e-mailed to ask about this stitch or that stitch, even going so far as to attach a digital picture of where he'd gone horribly wrong trying to knit a few rows on his own. That, she had to admit, had given her a few moments of sadistic glee. Yes, she was supposed to be helping him learn to knit and knit well, but she wanted to win their bet more, and that required him *not* to do a good job.

Today he'd e-mailed her about coming over after knitting group, but Ronnie hadn't responded. She didn't want him coming over, and she *thought* she'd be able to avoid him simply by keeping the lights off and refusing to answer the door once she got home. She'd never expected him to show up at The Yarn Barn, and hadn't thought far enough ahead to realize that he might be at The Penalty Box when she showed up with the other girls.

It was enough to make a girl want to move . . . or at least drive her to drink.

Which was exactly what Ronnie intended to do tonight.

Following Grace and Jenna to a nearby booth, she slipped onto the bench across from them and plopped her carryall down beside her. She'd gotten hardly any decent knitting done tonight at group, too distracted and annoyed by Dylan's presence to concentrate. And that only pissed her off all the more. At the rate she was going, she'd never finish this damn sweater, and with all the good-natured help Dylan was getting from Charlotte, he probably *would* finish his project.

She thought it might be the beginnings of a scarf,

but wasn't sure. It hadn't quite taken shape yet. Unless you considered *scary-ass blob* a shape.

The truth was, whatever he was working on really should have been unraveled and started over, but he'd done that so many times already, she suspected he just wanted to move forward and learn something beyond casting on before any more time passed.

The next time he showed up at her apartment uninvited, though, she might very well make him rip it all out. It would serve him right, and it would also get her that much closer to winning the challenge.

A waitress in navy-blue hot pants and a Playboy Bunny's version of a hockey jersey—The Penalty Box's idea of a uniform—appeared at the table to take their orders.

"I don't know about you," Grace said, "but I'm in the mood for something really sweet and different. How about a pitcher of Mudslides?"

Jenna nodded as Ronnie imagined the bartender's reaction to that request. Before Grace had started hanging out here and dragging her female friends along with her, she suspected Turk had never even heard of half the fruity, girlie drinks they ordered on a regular basis. To him, a mudslide had likely been something he only heard about on the news, followed by the words "still searching for survivors."

Up until a few months ago, she doubted the Box had even owned a blender. Now—on Wednesday nights, at least—it could be heard whirring away in the background on a regular basis.

"That'll do for starters, but I'm telling you right now, I'm going to need something stronger before the night is over."

"Oooh, bad day?" Grace asked as the waitress wandered off toward the bar, scribbling on her notepad.

Grace didn't know the half of it. Normally, Ronnie would have shared her frustrations with her friends while they were at their knitting group. Frustrations, successes, a few dirty jokes . . .

But thanks to Dylan's intrusion, she hadn't been able to talk to them about anything tonight. She felt like an overblown balloon about to explode.

She hadn't realized until very recently just how much she relied on the Knit Wits to keep herself sane. They were more than just casual acquaintances brought together by a love of yarn and needles. They were friends and confidantes, and maybe even amateur therapists.

Thank goodness. Otherwise, Ronnie was afraid she'd have to go into debt just trying to keep her mental health in order.

"Bad lifetime," Ronnie muttered in response to Grace's question.

"Awww." Jenna reached across the table to pat the back of Ronnie's hand. "You look positively miserable. What's wrong?"

Pressing her fingers into her eye sockets until she saw stars, Ronnie said, "He's driving me insane."

There was no need to specify who. There was only one man in her life—*in the known universe*—who could induce a migraine of this size and magnitude, and her friends knew exactly who it was.

"He's calling me now, at home and at work. And e-mailing me almost daily. If I had known this knitting challenge was going to become such a nightmare, I'd have made him turn tricks on Lorain Avenue or something instead. Dear God!"

The waitress arrived then with their order, and they took a moment to pour three tall glasses of frothy brown Kahlúa-laced drinks.

"This is amazing," Jenna said after a few strong sucks on her straw.

"Turk deserves an award for his skills behind that bar," Grace added. Then she turned a pointed glance in Ronnie's direction. "Maybe you should hang around until after closing and thank him with a little naked slap and tickle."

Mudslide went down the wrong way and Ronnie choked. "Dear God," she coughed, covering her mouth with a napkin as she struggled for breath. "That's disgusting. What is wrong with you?"

"I think she's been spending too much time with Zack. He's starting to warp her brain," Jenna said with a giggle.

Grace rolled her eyes. "Oh, come on. You can't tell me you haven't thought about it. Turk is one fine male specimen." She wiggled her left ring finger in front of her. "If I weren't spoken for, I might take a bite out of that luscious ass myself."

At that, it was Jenna's turn to go red in the face and nearly choke on her drink.

"Are you sure this is your first drink of the evening?" Ronnie said with a smile.

Grace made a noise that sounded an awful lot like *pshaw*. "You can't tell me you haven't thought about it. He's a gorgeous hunk of man."

Ronnie's gaze slid across the room and over the unwitting subject of their bawdy conversation. And the alcohol in her Mudslide must have started to kick in, because her mind was suddenly right down there in the gutter with Grace's.

"He is attractive. But he's roughly the size of an eighteen-wheeler, for God's sake. I'm not sure I could handle that much man; he's likely to split me in half."

"Ronnie!" Jenna gasped.

"Well, one of you should do something with *someone*," Grace told them. "I hate to break it to you, but you both need it. *Bad*."

Jenna might have been horrified by Grace's suggestion, but Ronnie certainly wasn't. She'd be the first to admit it had been too darn long since anyone besides BOB (her battery-operated boyfriend) had made her scream, shudder, or anything else.

Well, except for Dylan. She may not have screamed aloud, but he'd certainly made her shudder.

And the memory of him kissing her made her shudder all over again. Her stomach clenched and she had to shift in her seat to stifle the itch building between her legs.

Shit, shit, shit. She really was in trouble if the thought of having sex with Dylan turned her on more than the thought of having sex with the incredibly hot and masculine bartender.

She glanced at Turk again. Then another decent-looking guy at the bar. One standing with a group of friends at the back of the bar. Zack. Gage.

Dylan.

Shit. Her Orgasm-o-Meter didn't even flicker while contemplating any of those other men. But aim it at Dylan Stone and she nearly came in her seat.

Slouching down in the booth, she crossed her arms

over her chest and grumbled, "Says the woman who's been getting the long, slow one slipped to her every damn night. Lucky bitch."

"That's right. Although it isn't always slow," Grace agreed with a wink, while Ronnie wondered if she could drown herself by sticking her head in what was left of the Mudslide mixture in the pitcher on their table-top. "Which means I know of what I speak, and you two should listen to me. Ronnie is so tense, she's likely to shatter if a stiff wind blows by. And you, Jenna . . . It's been a year already. You've got to get over Gage and the divorce and move on with your life. Find someone, *anyone* to rip your clothes off and remind you that you're an attractive, vibrant, multiorgasmic woman."

Ronnie blinked, meeting her friend's gaze.

"What?" Grace wanted to know. Then she threw up her hands and leaned against the back of the booth. "You two can't be mad at me. It's nothing you didn't need to hear, and we've said way worse to each other. You guys are the ones who told me I was an idiot to date, let alone marry, a professional hockey player because he'd be a jerk and a cheat and break my heart."

Her voice rose with every word, as though she was truly worried she'd upset her best friends.

But Ronnie was much too preoccupied to be offended. Pushing her glass away, she swallowed hard and lowered her voice. "I'm not going to sleep with Turk or anyone else. But there is something I need to tell you."

Row 8

For the first time in as long as Dylan could remember, high-pitched, trilling laughter was not floating over from the girls' booth. He'd seen Ronnie come in, along with Grace and Jenna, and had been watching her from the corner of his eye ever since.

He couldn't stop thinking about her mouth. The taste of her. The feel of her. That brief, powerful kiss that had knocked him for much more of a loop than he ever would have expected.

Sometimes he thought he could still feel her lips moving beneath his, her body pressed against him like a second skin.

Zack and Gage were in the middle of a heated debate over last week's game where the Cougars beat the Rockets four to two. Dylan listened with only half an ear, the rest of his attention on the women across the room.

Rather than tossing their hair and laughing raucously over brightly colored drinks as he was used to seeing, they seemed strangely subdued. Heads bent together, small glasses of amber-colored liquid and a few empty bottles among them, their expressions serious. He was curious about what they were discussing, and even attempted to read the women's lips until he was forced to admit that wasn't one of his strong suits.

Several minutes later, a waitress came to clear their table, and the ladies began digging in their respective purses for money to pay the tab.

When Ronnie slipped out of the booth to stand, she faltered a little, reaching out for the edge of the table to steady herself. Grace moved to her side to take her elbow and whisper something in her ear. Ronnie shook her head and turned, taking a few careful, measured steps toward the bar entrance.

Before he'd even thought through what he was going to do, Dylan pushed to his feet and started forward. Grace was saying something else, and Ronnie nodded, but he broke in, not wanting them to finish what he was pretty sure they were talking about.

"Hey," he said, sounding too chipper even to his own ears.

All three women lifted their heads and turned in his direction.

"Dylan," Grace and Jenna both greeted him . . . less than friendly because of their loyalty to Ronnie, but still polite because of his relationship with their significant or formerly significant others.

Ronnie merely glared.

Even from where he stood with a foot or two of empty space separating them, he could tell she was drunk. Not hold-on-to-the-grass-to-keep-from-falling-off-the-earth drunk, but definitely too inebriated to drive herself home.

Getting right to the point, he said, "Looks like somebody had too much to drink. Can I offer you a ride home? Your place is right on my way."

Well, if he took the long route.

For a moment, no one responded. Ronnie's mouth turned down in a frown, then Grace piped up.

"That would be great, thank you so much. I really wanted to go home with Zack, but I wouldn't feel right about not seeing Ronnie home safely first." She actually reached out to grab both Dylan's and Ronnie's arms and link them together, presumably to keep her tipsy friend from toppling over.

He expected Ronnie to pull away, to immediately yank her arm back and maybe even shake it to dispel the cooties she might have picked up by touching him. Honest to God, she was the prickliest, most tightly wrapped person he'd ever met. But instead, she left her hand where it was and only her fingers moved, curling into talons that dug into his forearm.

"You're leaving me?" Ronnie nearly shrieked at Grace in what he was sure she thought was a stage whisper. "After everything I told you tonight? What kind of friend are you?"

Far from chastised or offended, Grace merely smiled and leaned in to kiss her friend's cheek. "I know you don't think so right this minute, but I'm doing you a favor."

Then she moved even closer and whispered something directly into Ronnie's ear.

Ronnie reared back, horror etched into every line of her face. "I'd rather take my chances with Turk!" she bellowed, her voice carrying over the music and other high-volume noises from the crowded bar.

Several Box patrons—including the towering, muscle-bound bartender—turned their attention to her. She lowered her voice and growled, "Traitor."

"You'll thank me later," Grace said, patting Ronnie's hand before looping an arm through Jenna's.

Then she turned to Dylan. "She'll feel better after a good night's sleep. I hope you can see that she gets one."

Was that a sparkle in the blonde's eye? A subtle wink or maybe a thinly veiled suggestion? He blinked, studying her again more closely, but whatever had been there was gone.

He must be imagining things. Maybe he'd had too much to drink himself—though it usually took more than two beers for him to start hallucinating.

But just the hint of insinuation from Zack's fiancée had his blood firing up and catching the first train south. Helping Ronnie get a good night's sleep sounded like a good idea to him, and he could think of any number of ways to get her there. Sixty-nine. Around the world. Ride the pony. Even plain old missionary would be fine with him, as long as she was naked and burning beneath him.

"Okay, time to go," he said, more to himself than to her. He needed to get out of there, out into the chilly night air to cool off before he overheated.

Although she moved with him as he crossed the room toward the door, that didn't keep her from arguing. "I don't need you to give me a ride," she told him. "I haven't had that much to drink. I can drive myself. Or I can go home with Jenna. Or I'll wait until Grace and Zack are ready to leave and go with them."

Dylan cast a look back over his shoulder at the table where the four of them—Zack, Grace, Gage, and Jenna—were now gathered. Grace was perched happily on Zack's wide knee while Gage and Jenna sat about as far apart as humanly possible while still being seated at the same table.

"I don't think they want to be bothered with you to-night."

"Bite me, Stone."

Reaching for the door handle, he ushered her outside ahead of him, still holding on to her arm in case she lost her footing. He sighed as they made their way down the sidewalk toward The Penalty Box parking lot at the side of the building.

"We've been through this. Under the right circumstances, I'd be happy to, as long as you promise not to be too rough with me in return. I wouldn't want to get the spiked heel of one of your domiknitrix boots jabbed in the middle of my spine."

When they reached his jeep, he unlocked the passenger door and let her in, making sure she was properly seated, all limbs and clothing inside, before slamming the door. She remained silent that long, but as soon as he slid behind the wheel, she was ready with a sharp retort.

"If you're ever lucky enough to even *see* my boots, I won't be putting the heel in the middle of your back, Stone."

"I don't know," he said with a chuckle, his fingers tapping out a meaningless staccato beat on the steering wheel as he pulled onto the street. "I happen to think I could give you a run for your money in the sack. You may have the whips and leather chaps, but I've been known to bring a woman to orgasm a dozen times in one night."

She gave an unladylike snort. "And who might that have been? Bambi, your blow-up doll?"

"No. I assure you, all the women I've been with have been very real."

"Uh-huh. Well, then, I've got news for you, Stone.

Whichever *real live woman* you claim to have done that with was faking it. Twelve times over . . . she must have been quite the accomplished actress. Either that or a consummate professional—the kind who charges by the hour."

He slanted a glance at her, and even in the dark confines of the jeep, Ronnie could see the amused arc at the corner of his mouth.

"You're just jealous. When was the last time a man made you come more than once in a night? I'm betting . . . what? . . . senior year of high school, junior year of college?"

That was something she definitely did not want to discuss.

And how was it that this man—man, jerk, asshole—knew just what to say to make her head pound and her stomach churn?

Hadn't she just been brooding over how very long it *had* been since anyone other than she herself had rocked her world, curled her toes, or made her see the face of God?

Two hundred sixty-one days and counting, she thought with derision.

In response to his question, she mumbled a less-than-impressive, "None of your business."

At this point, Ronnie didn't even care that she was making a fool of herself in front of her sworn enemy. Kahlúa and vodka and beer, and possibly a couple of shots of whiskey, all mixed together to fog her brain and slow her synapses.

She needed some food or coffee, or at the very least a nap . . . and to be as far away from Dylan Stone as possible.

"Care to take me for a test run? I'd be willing to give you two or three big Os on the house. If you like them, you can come back for the whole shebang."

"And if I don't?" she retorted. "How exactly would I go about requesting a refund?"

He flipped his signal for a right turn, then in true macho-man fashion straightened his spine and clipped out, "I've never had any complaints."

"Maybe you just weren't listening. Or maybe you were asleep. That's what most men do, right? Get off, roll over, fall asleep."

Pulling up to the curb beside her apartment building, he cut the engine, palmed his keys, and released his seat belt. He turned slightly to face her, and she could clearly read the confidence in his expression in the glow of an overhead streetlight.

"I'm not most men."

She stared at him for a long minute, then she raised a brow and asked innocently, "Really? Does that mean you don't even bother getting off before you fall asleep? You just go unconscious right in the middle? Now I feel even more sorry for your dates. This also explains that whole *twelve orgasms in a night* assertion . . . you must have dreamed them."

With a scowl, he climbed out of the jeep and came around to assist her. She wiped the wide grin off her face just as he yanked her door open and reached for her arm.

Gathering her purse and tote and straightening her skirt, she lowered herself to the sidewalk, pleased when she teetered for only a second. And that was due entirely to the height of her heels, she was sure.

"Why do you drive a jeep?" she asked as they headed for the front of her building.

"Because it's too heavy to carry."

Caught off guard by his reply, Ronnie laughed. Not just a light, amused chuckle, but a full belly laugh that ended with an unladylike snort.

Embarrassed, she covered her mouth, then lost her balance and leaned heavily into Dylan's side. He caught her, helped her right herself, then slid an arm around her waist to keep her that way.

"You okay?"

She nodded. "Sorry."

He led her to the elevator and pushed the button. A second later, the doors opened and they stepped inside.

As the elevator moved upward, she said, "I meant that I didn't picture you as a jeep type of guy."

"Really? What type of guy am I?"

She shrugged, and was pleased when the action didn't cause her to waver a bit. "I don't know. I guess I expected you to drive some flashy red sports car. Eye candy to draw in all those hot, vapid females."

He met her gaze, lifting a brow. Had she noticed before what a lovely shade of blue his eyes were? Sort of a cross between a robin's egg and a clear summer sky.

She licked her lips, swallowing hard in sudden awareness—of his handsome, masculine features . . . their close proximity . . . the growing throb deep within her sex.

"I don't need a fancy car to attract women," he said softly, his mouth only inches from her own. "And I'm not particularly interested in the kind of women who would be attracted to a fancy car."

"Oh."

The elevator came to a stop, whispering open, and

Dylan started forward. She moved with him, perfectly in sync, perfectly steady.

When they reached her door, she held out the arm that balanced her purse and tote, and Dylan took the initiative to dig inside, find her keys, and let them in. The apartment was silent and dark, but not pitch black. Across the room, the blinds had been left open, making the room partially visible in the glow of the moon and lights of the city.

Ronnie stood with her back pressed flat to the closed door, her mind racing in tandem with her heart. She was about to do something certifiable. Completely out of the norm for her.

And yet it was exactly what she wanted to do most in the world at that precise moment.

"Where's the light switch?" Dylan asked, feeling along the wall beside the doorjamb.

"Leave them off."

He paused, dragging his attention back to her. "Ronnie . . . as much as I like where this is going, I'm not the kind of guy who takes advantage of women under the influence."

Her vision had adjusted from the brighter light of the hallway, and she could easily make out his broad silhouette, so she knew he could see her, as well.

"I know exactly what I'm doing, Stone," she said, her head surprisingly clear from the adrenaline coursing through her system. "I want a baker's dozen."

She licked her lips nervously, dropping her bags to the floor and then fisting and unfisting her hands at her sides. *When in doubt,* she thought, *fall back on what you know,* and what she knew when it came to Dylan Stone was competition.

"But if you fail to live up to your end of the bargain," she added boldly, "I get your jeep."

The seconds ticked by like hours while she held her breath, waiting for his response. A part of her was terrified he'd turn her down, while another part couldn't believe she'd actually propositioned him.

But before she could change her mind, maybe fake passing out in a drunken stupor, he closed in on her. His hands came up to flatten against the door on either side of her head, his arms boxing her in.

The heat of his body surrounded her. The scent of his spicy, woodsy aftershave—or maybe it was cologne—filled her nostrils, reminding her of everything a man could be. Everything a man and woman could do together in the dark, with their clothes off.

She shivered, overwhelmed by the sensations engulfing her, and tried to close her eyes, but his gaze locked with hers and she was trapped. Mesmerized. Caught in his seductive spell. A ball of caterpillars wiggled and writhed at the base of her stomach, making her suddenly weak in the knees.

He leaned forward, his hot breath dancing across her face and raising gooseflesh everywhere else. Then he whispered one word. One single word that sealed her fate.

"Deal."

Row 9

His mouth, when it covered hers, was soft and warm, and sent shocks of electricity past her lips, through the cords of her neck, into her shoulders, down her arms, through her torso, into her throbbing center, and down her legs to the tips of her toes.

She felt singed. Dizzy. As though she'd been out in the cold too long and her extremities were beginning to get frostbitten.

But only for a moment. A moment of stunned silence, and then her body responded, her system jumping into stark, needy overdrive. Grabbing the sides of his head, she threaded her fingers into his silky blond hair and held him steady while she deepened the kiss.

Their tongues tangled. Their bodies rubbed. She moaned deep in her throat and started moving him backward, farther into the apartment.

She felt out of control, but didn't care. Her hands fumbled at the collar of his shirt, pulling at the buttons, sending a few flying as she yanked the material from the waistband of his jeans.

She shoved the light blue, long-sleeved shirt off over his shoulders, along with his jacket, uncaring that they caught at his elbows because his hands were equally busy lowering the zipper at the back of her skirt and driving his fingers up beneath the material of her blouse.

When the backs of his legs hit the edge of her coffee table, they stopped moving, but continued to strip each other. He shrugged out of the shirt, then let her draw the white cotton undershirt beneath up and over his head. Both got tossed somewhere off to the side, out of the way.

My God, his chest was amazing. Broad and muscular, smooth in places, covered with a dusting of coarse blond hair in others. She especially liked the line of curls that led from between his well-defined pectoral muscles all the way down to disappear into the waistband of his denim jeans.

The rough pads of his fingers skimmed her waist and hips as he lowered her skirt, letting it pool around her feet on the floor. Then he stroked upward, beneath the hem of her blouse, to the undersides of her breasts. His lips caressed the pulse at her throat while he reached around and unfastened the hook of her bra.

Letting her head fall back, Ronnie reveled in the pleasure of having his mouth and hands on her body. Oh, yes, this was what she wanted, what she'd missed and been clamoring for.

He spilled the blouse down her back, then followed by sliding the straps of her bra off her shoulders and arms, leaving her bare from the waist up. She should have felt awkward or self-conscious standing in her living room half naked in front of this man, but instead her nerve endings tingled with awareness and sweet anticipation.

Dylan cupped her breasts, running the sides of his thumbs back and forth across the rigid peaks. Desire streaked from where he touched her with those big, slightly callused hands all the way to her core, making her bite her bottom lip to keep from crying out.

She grappled at his fly, desperate to free him. To feel him, taste him, have him inside her.

At the same time, they stumbled around the coffee table until he tripped and fell flat on his back on the couch, with her falling right on top of him. He grinned, and she caught herself grinning back, her hand still stuffed down his pants, cupping the impressive swell of his erection.

When was the last time she'd been amused during sex? Considering she could barely remember the last time she'd *had* sex, not remembering the last time she'd laughed during didn't come as much of a surprise.

Dylan widened his legs, letting her settle more comfortably between. His hands were still on her breasts, squeezing and tweaking.

"Damn, you feel good," he muttered, lifting up enough to lick the jut of her collarbone.

She wiggled her fingers, trying to get a better grip on his arousal through the thin barrier of his underwear. The metal prongs of his zipper dug into the back of her hand, but she didn't care.

"I want your cock in my mouth."

"Jesus." He jerked, and the body part in question grew even larger against her fingers. "If you're looking for ways to make a guy come in his pants, that's a good one."

His voice was harsh, nearly hoarse, and she could feel the tension thrumming through his body.

"I'll make a note," she said. "But I'd rather you saved it until you're inside me."

Another shudder racked him from head to toe. "All right, that's enough. Time for a little payback."

He jackknifed into a sitting position, then pushed her back until she was the one lying flat on the sofa. She watched him hovering above her and couldn't resist reaching up to feather her fingers through his hair.

Leaning in, he kissed her—not hot and desperate this time, but long, soft, and slow.

Something inside of her melted with that kiss, turned pliant right along with his lips on hers, pummeling at the barriers she'd built up around her and kept strong for so many years.

"I've waited too long for this," he murmured against her mouth. "I'm not going to let you rush me or speed me through to the finish line before I've thoroughly enjoyed myself."

She met his gaze, licking her lips as his words sank in. "You've thought about the two of us, together like this?"

He stared down at her, one side of his mouth twisted up in a cocky grin. "Oh, yeah."

"But we hate each other."

With a shake of his head, he said, "You know that *When Harry Met Sally* . . . thing, where they say men and women can't be friends for long without sex being thrown into the mix? Well, I don't think they can be enemies, either. I've been fantasizing about fucking you since the moment we met. Your ass drives me crazy."

"My ass?"

The other side of his mouth quirked upward as he lowered his head to the curve of her neck, licking, nibbling. "You've got a great ass. Kind of like an apple, all juicy and begging for a big bite." His mouth trailed down to the upper swell of her breast. "Every time I see you at The Penalty Box in one of your tight, sexy skirts, I get a hard-on and can't move for half an hour."

"I didn't know that," she said softly.

"I should hope not." His tongue darted out to lick one puckered nipple. "I've gone to great efforts to make sure *no one* knew how horny you make me. It hasn't been easy, either. Do you know how hard it is to come up with excuses not to get up for another round of beers or play a game of pool with your friends?"

"No." She slipped her hand down his bare chest, into the open fly of his jeans to cradle his impressive package. "How hard was it?"

He groaned, arching his pelvis to press himself even more fully against her hand. "You tell me."

"It feels pretty hard. Can I give you a suggestion of where to stick it?"

His groan deepened and he thrust into her hand once more before pulling away and physically moving her arm up over her head.

"You," he said, "are a dangerous woman. But stop trying to distract me. It won't work, and you're only delaying your own pleasure."

Ronnie spread her legs even wider, tilting her hips to rub suggestively along the flat plane of his abdomen.

"Then get busy, Stone. You promised me a dozen orgasms, and so far I'm still sadly orgasm-less."

A chuckle rasped up from his diaphragm. "Is that even a word?"

"Maybe not, but it's certainly a sad state of affairs."

"Well, then, let's see what we can do about that."

He finished teasing her breasts, licking the tip of one, massaging the other. Then his mouth moved farther south. When he reached her waist, he began tugging at her panty hose and the high-cut, barely there black lace panties beneath.

As he revealed more and more intimate flesh, his mouth followed, placing hot, openmouthed kisses along her midriff, around her belly button, over the slight rise of her lower abdomen. While his lips lingered there, just above the dark curls of her mound, his fingers continued to skim the panties and panty hose down her legs and off over her feet. Her shoes fell to the floor, one at a time, with a heavy clunk, then he lifted her right leg high onto the back of the couch and pushed her left to dangle over onto the floor.

She was spread wider than she would have thought possible, open to his heavy-lidded, passion-laden gaze and erotic ministrations. And she liked it. Shivered with longing for more.

Dylan hooked his arms around her upper thighs and inched down toward the end of the sofa, just above the pink, pulsing tissue of her exposed vulva. His warm breath danced across her most intimate flesh, causing her lungs to hitch and her nails to dig into the overstuffed sofa cushions.

Mouth lowering, he licked a long, slow line along the full length of her aching sex.

"You taste like honey," he murmured, so softly she almost didn't hear. "All thick and sweet."

She didn't think his comment required a reply. And thank goodness, because she was having enough trouble just keeping her eyes from rolling back in her head.

And what he'd done so far was only the beginning.

Soon he was feasting on her like a starving man. His thumbs parted her farther and he slowly pressed a single finger inside her while his tongue swirled and fluttered.

She was panting now, her hips rising and falling gently as the pressure of oncoming release began to build. Filling her even more fully with a second finger, he focused his attention on her swollen, oversensitized clitoris.

The minute he touched her there, pleasure unlike any she'd felt before gathered at her very core. She grabbed for his head, but rather than push him away, she held him closer, desperate for more.

"Say my name," he ordered, the words vibrating against her skin, adding to the sharp pressure of building release.

"Shut up and keep going, Stone," she answered thickly, and could have sworn she felt him smile.

"My first name. Say it, or I'll stop."

Her inner muscles clutched at his fingers, which dug deep and hit her in just the right spot. Her throat was so tight, she could barely speak, but she managed a stuttering, "You're a sadistic bastard."

He continued to lick and suckle and fill her with his hand, but his movements had slowed, and she was almost desperately afraid he really would stop what he was doing when she was so close, so very close to shattering into a million pieces.

"I know," he said. "So do it before I get really mean."

With a groan of frustration, she surrendered. "Dylan," she ground out. "Dylan, Dylan, Dylan."

He caught her clit with his teeth, at the same time giving it one final stroke of his amazing, masterful, talented tongue, and she fell apart.

A million had been a gross understatement. If she counted to a billion, a trillion, a gazillion, it still wouldn't come close.

Her fingers tangled in his hair so tightly, she wouldn't have been surprised if she'd drawn blood. But at that point, she really didn't care. She continued to ride his face in one long, drawn-out, explosive orgasm until every drop of blood seemed to leave her veins, every particle of air seemed to vacate her lungs, and every thought seemed to seep out of her brain.

She didn't bother opening her eyes. Couldn't have, even if her life had depended on it. She was, quite simply, wrung out. As limp as a rag doll left out in the rain.

She felt Dylan shifting above her, drawing himself back up the length of her body. The rough denim of his jeans brushed along her inner thighs, and it surprised her to realize that he was still partially dressed. She'd been too lost in her own pleasure—and what a paltry word that was for what he'd done to her, she thought—to even notice.

"Now I'm happy," he whispered, pressing a soft kiss to the corner of her mouth at the same time he brushed damp tendrils of hair behind her ear. "And that's one."

If that was one, Ronnie wasn't sure she'd survive orgasms two through twelve. And, dear God, she'd insisted on a baker's dozen!

No, she definitely wouldn't survive thirteen. She hardly had enough energy now to breathe, let alone work up to another climax.

Nope, she was done for. Dylan was on his own for the rest.

She was pretty sure she told him all that. It sounded

good in her head, anyway, and she thought her lips
were moving.

But then he began kissing her, and she figured that
either she hadn't said it out loud, or he was choosing to
ignore her.

It would be just like him to disregard her wishes and
go straight to pleasing himself.

Except she had to admit that what he'd just done for
her—*to her*—hadn't been selfish at all. Far from it.

Then he deepened the kiss, and she tasted herself on
his tongue, felt the press of his steel-hard erection between her legs.

Oh, boy. She'd been wrong. Very, very wrong. Already, her juices were flowing once again, her body
turning warm and loose in preparation of another earth-
shattering race to completion.

"Ready for number two?" he pulled back far enough
to ask.

She slid a hand between their bodies to cup his stiff
cock. It gave a little twitch, and she grinned. "What do
you think?"

He thought he'd been damn lucky to have lasted this
long. He couldn't remember ever being this hard, this
swollen and aching for release.

Being with Ronnie was like fulfilling every erotic
fantasy he'd ever imagined. She was lush and gorgeous,
filling his hands and stretching out along his body like
she'd been made for him.

From the top of her head to the curl of her toes, she
tasted both hot and cool, sweet and spicy. He could
have remained between her thighs, lapping at her sweet
folds forever. Kissing both her mouth and sex reminded him of relishing a particularly delectable

dessert . . . something rich and exotic that you wish would never end.

She was also amazingly responsive. He touched her, and she went off like a box of Chinese firecrackers. She pressed herself close, writhed in pleasure, took everything he gave and begged for more.

It had been a long time since he'd enjoyed eating a woman out quite that much. Usually it was something he did just to prime the pump . . . a little obligatory foreplay so the gal would be more than ready when it was his turn to race to the finish line.

But with Ronnie, he wasn't thinking about the shortest route between Point A and Point B, the quickest way to get what he wanted so he could get dressed and go home. If anything, he was busy pondering methods of giving her what he'd promised while drawing out the pleasure for himself.

A dozen orgasms in one night. Yeah, he'd been blowing smoke when he threw that one out there, just trying to get a rise out of her. But she'd called him on it, and now he had no choice but to go through with it or be proven a liar.

And he wasn't going to let that happen. This was Ronnie he was talking about; she'd never let him live it down. He'd spend the rest of his life listening to her up on her soapbox, crowing to her friends and chapping his ass about how he'd claimed he could bring a woman to orgasm twelve times in one night, no problem. And that he'd failed.

No way was he going to give her that satisfaction.

So he'd give her the other kind—a dozen times in a row—if it killed him.

Shouldn't be too difficult, provided he could keep from coming in his pants before she hit her second one.

And at the moment, that was a real possibility.

Her legs were wrapped around him like a vise, bringing his cock flush with her crotch. It didn't matter that he was still fully encased in jeans and cotton briefs, he could still feel her moist heat as though they were skin-to-skin. Which was exactly how he wanted it.

Without taking his mouth from hers, he lifted his hips, shrugging out of his pants and shorts and kicking them aside.

Everything in him screamed to connect with her. To just slip inside, *now,* and give them both what they were panting for.

Thankfully, he still had enough cylinders firing to know better than to get any closer until he'd donned a raincoat. Of course, the only rubber he had with him was in his wallet, in his jeans, which were now somewhere on the floor.

"Shit," he swore, tearing his mouth away from her ever-ravenous kiss.

She opened her eyes to study him, her chest, with those firm, round, marvelous breasts, rising and falling with great, gulping breaths. "What?"

"Condom."

Confusion clouded her eyes for a second, and then understanding dawned. Her lips rounded in a small O of dismay. "Do you have one?"

"Yeah, I've just got to . . ."

Moving was about the last thing he wanted to do, and damned if it wasn't painful, to boot. But he shifted away from her, going up on one knee on the sofa and reaching for his pants, which had landed farther away than he'd thought.

With a grunt, he pulled them back and dug in the rear pocket, extracting his wallet and then the lone condom packet that resided there. Tossing the jeans aside once more, he tore the little plastic square open with his teeth and removed the circle of latex.

"After this, we're in trouble," he warned her, rolling the rubber down the full length of his straining erection. "This is the only condom I've got with me."

Sitting up, Ronnie got to her own knees in the center of the couch and ran a hand over his shoulder just as he finished covering himself. "That's all right. I think I've got some more in the bathroom."

The relief that washed over him made him want to weep. He hadn't made love to her a first time yet, and already he was anticipating rounds two, three, four . . .

"Thank God."

His arms snaked around her waist, pulling her tight. Her breasts flattened against his chest. Her soft curls and the slight convex curve of her abdomen trapped his penis, sending it even higher than it already was.

He kissed her lightly, letting his palms glide over the expanse of her slim back, feeling the smooth skin, the long lines of sleek feminine muscle. He cupped her delectable rear end triumphantly, finally having his hands on the world-class ass he'd been all but slavering over for months.

One after another, a Kama Sutra of positions ran through his head. Did he want her on her back? On her knees? Straddling him?

He wasn't sure; all he knew was that he wanted inside her. Badly. Now.

To that end, he leaned back, lifting her a few inches off the sofa. With a hand on the back of her thigh, he raised one leg up and over his hipbone.

She caught on quickly, raising her other leg so that he was supporting her entire weight. The tip of his penis was poised at her opening and he had to breathe carefully through his teeth to keep himself under control. To keep from plunging forward and slaking his lust, to keep from going off too soon and ruining it for both of them.

Sitting back on his heels, he braced himself in the center of the sofa, one arm wrapped firmly around Ronnie's back. Then slowly, heart pounding in his chest to the same beat as the throbbing in his cock and balls, he brought her down.

She felt like heaven, like a hundred thousand feather strokes to the most sensitive part of his anatomy. Air hissed through his teeth and his eyes screwed shut before he was halfway inside. At this rate, he might not make it all the way in.

"Christ, you're tight," he bit out.

He could feel her breath in his ear as she clutched his shoulders, raked her mouth across his ear, the column of his neck where his muscles stood out in stark relief.

"Yeah, sorry about that," she said brokenly. "It's been a while."

A streak of possessiveness gripped his gut at her admission, making him grasp her even tighter and bring her down another inch. They both groaned at the frisson of sensation the action created.

Call him a Neanderthal, but he liked knowing she hadn't been with another man recently. That while he'd been fantasizing about her incredible ass and having her use her mouth for something other than slicing him to ribbons, she hadn't been sharing the benefits of those gifts with some other guy.

"Wrap your arms around my neck," he told her.

They were already close, draped haphazardly over his shoulders, upper arms, upper back. But she followed his instructions, bringing them up just a bit higher to circle his neck and hug him tight. Her breasts pressed into his chest, the rigid diamond peaks cutting into his pecs and making him glad he'd been born a man so he could enjoy the many wonders of a woman's body.

"Now hang on," he warned. "This may not take long."

Either she didn't mind or she wasn't paying attention, because she simply tightened her hold on his neck and started kissing him—hot, openmouthed, voracious.

He cupped her buttocks, his fingers flexing and releasing the soft, fleshy globes. With a single yank, he drew her the rest of the way down his rigid length until he was fully engulfed, surrounded by her slick warmth.

Her muscles contracted, gripping him like a vise, and he groaned. The sound poured into her mouth and rolled through both of them.

Rather than thrust, he brought her up and then down. Slow, short strokes at first, drawing out the pleasure. Then longer. Faster. Harder.

It didn't take long for the pressure to build, for the need to become almost unbearable. No matter how fast he moved her over him, it wasn't fast enough. No matter how hard he pounded, it wasn't hard enough.

Even through the fog of lust clouding his brain, he had the presence of mind to slip a hand between their bodies and find her clit. She may not have needed it—

she was bouncing and moaning enough to come all on her own—but if she didn't, he'd be one behind.

His fingers slipped easily in her slick juices, and he scissored his fingertips over and around the swollen bud of her desire. She stiffened almost immediately, her mouth breaking away from his to cry out. Her nails dug into his back. Her internal muscles clamped down hard enough to make him dizzy while she convulsed in his arms.

That was all it took to send him over the edge. He brought her down on top of him one last time as fire shot through his veins and out his dick. His hands flexed on her buttocks and he gave a shout as the most powerful orgasm of his life rocked through him.

Seconds and then minutes ticked by. The room was silent except for the sounds of their mingled, labored breathing.

Dylan remained perfectly still, holding Ronnie slightly above him while he waited for the feeling to seep back into his bones. He was empty, wrung out. After what he'd just experienced, he wasn't sure he'd ever walk again.

Lifting her head from his shoulder, Ronnie gazed down at him through glazed, sleepy eyes. A fine sheen of perspiration covered her skin, keeping her pressed to him like plastic wrap. Her glorious mane of mahogany hair spilled down her back and framed her face in long, tousled ringlets. A few stray curls clung damply to her hairline, and he somehow found the strength to reach up and brush them aside.

"That was two," she murmured, her lips pink and swollen from his kisses. If he'd ever wondered at the term *bee-stung,* he now had his answer.

Sounding almost despondent, she added, "I don't think I can handle ten more."

"Eleven," he corrected. "You wanted a baker's dozen, remember?"

Pressing a light kiss to her mouth, Dylan ran his tongue lightly along the seam. Some dark, primitive instinct was driving him to make those lips pinker, puffier. Never mind that he was exhausted, drained, running on empty. He already wanted her again, or at the very least wanted to possess her again, mark her as his.

"Oh, God," she nearly whimpered.

"Sorry, sweetheart, even He can't help you now."

Row 10

Ronnie was conked out on the sofa, as close to uncon-
sciousness as it was possible to be without actually
drifting off. He'd sexed the temper right out of her.

Which would be a lot easier to strut about if she
hadn't pretty much done the same to him. He was lucky
he was still breathing, let alone able to walk to the john.

He made his way across the soft carpeting stark
naked, leaving Ronnie half curled up, half sprawled,
with her head resting on the arm of the couch.

After disposing of the used condom and cleaning
up, he decided to see if he could find those extra rub-
bers she'd mentioned. He wasn't quite up to round two
yet—literally—but he'd been a Boy Scout as a kid and
still liked to be prepared whenever possible.

As long as Ronnie was lying prone and acquiescent
in the other room, it seemed like a good time to snoop
a bit, too. He may have spent the last year being a low-
level, insignificant, small-town columnist instead of
doing the hard-hitting stories and interviews he'd always pictured himself writing, but that didn't mean his
reporter's instincts had dried up entirely.

There was nothing of consequence on the shelves

over the commode, just towels and washcloths in colors that matched the room's English rose garden decor, and a small bowl of potpourri.

The medicine cabinet didn't reveal much more, except that she seemed to buy a lot of generic items. A toothbrush and tube of toothpaste, some Band-Aids, a bottle of pain reliever, a few tubes of mystery ointment, and some feminine hygiene products he preferred not to investigate too closely. Not all of them were no-brand, but a lot of them were.

Next he checked the cabinet under the sink and found extra rolls of toilet paper, a bottle of mouthwash, a set of hot curlers. What caught his attention, though, was the personal manicure set and boxes of hair dye.

Ronnie was a fashion plate, no doubt about it. Gorgeous and more put together than any other woman he knew—never a hair out of place . . . well, except when she'd been fucked within an inch of her life, he amended . . . never a thread out of style, never a chip in her perfectly shaped, painted nails.

And he—as well as everyone else who'd had the pleasure of looking at her, he'd be willing to bet—had simply assumed she attained that perfection at a professional salon. He never would have guessed she colored her own hair and manicured her own nails so flawlessly.

His mouth pulled down in a frown as he considered that. What did it mean? What did it say about her?

Was she cheap or just being frugal? Or maybe she was in trouble financially.

She shouldn't be, since she probably earned only slightly less than he did with her job at the *Sentinel* and she seemed to be living well within her means. Of course, he had no idea if she'd racked up a boatload of debt or had a gambling problem.

Somehow, he couldn't see her getting carried away with online poker or putting money down at the track. Betting on next fall's most popular colors, maybe, but not the ponies.

He wasn't sure what was going on with her or why she felt the need to put on such a show when the real Ronnie was apparently more down-to-earth than she let on, but he planned to find out.

"Did you fall asleep in there?" her groggy voice called out, jerking him out of his reverie. Although he shouldn't feel guilty just for snooping through her bathroom, his conscience gave a small twinge, sending heat to his cheekbones.

Straightening from his crouched position in front of the sink, he opened the door and stalked back out into the living area. "I was just looking for those extra condoms you said you had. I expected you to fall asleep, though."

Her lashes fluttered as her eyes popped open, but she didn't raise her head from the arm of the couch. "I just need a few minutes to recharge. Did you find them?"

He shook the box in his hand, relieved when more than one packet shuffled around inside.

"I hope they're still good."

"How old are they?" he asked.

She made a face, letting her eyes slide closed again. "How long has it been since Bush Senior was in office?"

Her deadpan reply nearly made him laugh out loud. She might drive him crazy 95 percent of the time, but she did have a great sense of humor.

Reaching the sofa, he patted the right cheek of her sexy bare ass before gently lifting her legs to slip beneath them and sit down. He draped them back across his lap, leaving her on her side, and studied the box.

"Let's see if the fine folks at Trojan can tell us what we need to know."

When the back of the box didn't reveal a "use by" date, he started flipping it end to end. There, along one of the openings, was a stamp of the product ID number and a date.

Praise Jesus. "We're good for another six months."

That brought Ronnie's head up a couple of inches. "Really?"

"Yep." He pried the end with the expiration date open and dumped the contents onto the coffee table. It was a box of twelve and there were nine left.

One brow shot toward the ceiling as he considered that. He had no business wondering when she'd used the other three or with whom . . . but, dammit, *he did*. And he wanted to kick the anonymous Mr. Lucky's ass.

Which was a completely ridiculous thought for him to be having. He wasn't planning to marry Ronnie, he just wanted to shag her for a few hours. Or maybe a few days here or there, scattered throughout a few months.

Point being, he wasn't the first man she'd been with and he wasn't going to be the last, so he should stop worrying about things he couldn't change and shouldn't care about to begin with, and get back in the game.

Leaving the condoms where they were, he stretched out in the narrow space between Ronnie and the sofa back and brushed her hair aside to kiss the back of her neck.

"Ready for number three?"

She moaned, but he didn't miss the slight shift of her bottom tilting closer to his groin.

"Are *you*?"

He chuckled, his teeth nipping lightly at the lobe of her ear. "I don't need to be ready. This bet doesn't require *me* to come thirteen times in one night, only you."

She moaned again, turning her face away. "Remind me to keep my mouth shut from now on."

His lips continued to trail down the side of her neck, over her shoulder, along the line of her upper arm, while his hand sneaked around her front to toy with the firm globes of her breasts.

"That's been my recommendation on many occasions, if you recall. You never seem to take my advice."

"I will from now on, I swear."

He chuckled. "Right. The day that happens, be sure to alert the media." Pausing a moment for effect, he added, "Oh, wait, I am the media."

His joke was rewarded with an airy laugh. But it didn't last long when his fingers wandered lower. She made a mewling sound in the back of her throat and arched into him.

He was no superman, and no perpetually erect porn star, either. But even if he'd been three hours in his grave, feeling the soft curve of her buttocks pressed against his crotch would have given him a chubby.

"Roll over," he whispered, keeping a hand at her waist while she moved closer to the edge of the couch so she wouldn't accidentally topple over. At the same time, he got up on one knee and straddled her.

She was on her stomach now, head turned to the side, her cheek resting on her folded arms. Gathering the long strands of her dark hair, he twisted the mass into a makeshift ponytail to make room for his hands to gently knead the line of muscle between neck and shoulder.

"Mmmm. Is this one of those Happy Ending massages I've heard so much about?"

He smiled, continuing to work his way over her shoulder blades and along the slim expanse of her back. Her muscles were anything but tense, so she probably didn't really need a massage, but he was enjoying himself. And getting her all soft and pliant was one step closer to giving her a third orgasm.

"It could be."

"Would it be politically incorrect for me to say I'm glad you aren't a petite Asian woman?"

He laughed aloud at that one. "Probably, but I won't turn you in, since I concur. If you're not careful, though, I still might walk on your back."

"If it feels as good as this," she told him, "go right ahead."

He crawled backward, coming to rest at her knees rather than—as much as he'd liked the position—over her ass. The tattoo emblazoned high on her left butt cheek caught him off guard, sending a bolt of desire from his chest, to his gut, to his balls, which tightened at the sight.

It shouldn't have jolted him quite so much, since he'd known it was there somewhere. He'd just never seen it before. And even though she'd been naked much of the evening, she'd mostly been facing him, giving him little chance to view that portion of her posterior until now.

Major oversight on his part. He should have yanked her skirt down and turned her around first thing.

He'd speculated about this tattoo, wondering where it was and what it meant. Brushing his palm over the fancy black Chinese symbols, he slid his hand down another fraction until he could lean forward and press his lips to the design.

"I've fantasized about this tattoo, you know."

He didn't know what possessed him to make the confession, but there it was.

"As amused as I was by your determination to go through with that particular challenge, I respected you for it, too."

She shifted slightly, turning her head a fraction to look back at him. "Lots of people have tattoos," she told him. "It's no big deal."

"Yeah, but most people actually *want* a tattoo and go into it with enthusiasm, knowing what they want inked on their bodies for the rest of their lives. Somehow I can't picture you as being interested in body art or already having a design in mind."

"No, you're right. It took me a while to work up the courage . . . and to decide what to get and where to put it."

"Good choice, on both counts. But I have to admit, I'm dying to know what this symbol means." He ran his fingertips over it again, a feather-light touch that brought goose bumps to her bare flesh.

Twisting at her waist, she came half around to meet his gaze. A hint of a grin tugged at the corners of her mouth, and a glint of mischief danced in her chocolate-brown eyes. "Are you sure? I don't think you'll like it very much."

"I can handle it," he assured her, not sure whether to be worried or amused.

Shrugging one slim shoulder, she said, "Fuck you."

The sudden verbal assault made him blink. They'd been having a good time, an amicable time, even. He hadn't expected her to turn on him and tell him off quite so succinctly.

"I was about to," he replied flippantly, and though he considered climbing off her to go in search of his pants, he didn't move.

"No," she said, shaking her head. "That's what it means. It's the Chinese equivalent of 'Fuck you.'" An airy chuckle spilled past her lips. "I was none too happy with you at the time, and if I had to permanently mark my body with something I didn't really want, I figured it should be memorable and mean something. 'Fuck you' seemed to sum up my feelings pretty well. It wasn't easy to track down the symbol, though . . . Grace and Jenna helped me with that."

Dylan studied her for a minute or two, letting her explanation sink in. It wasn't every day a woman branded herself with an invective directed at one specific person, and even though he felt like a complete dope because of it, he was ridiculously pleased to be that person.

For the rest of her life, she would wear that tattoo.

For the rest of her life, every time she saw herself naked in the mirror, she would be reminded of him.

Every time she slept with some random jerk-off, he might not know it, but he'd be looking at or stroking a brand that said Dylan Stone had been there first. Long before he'd gotten her into bed, he'd been in her periphery, in her head, under her skin.

"Have I ever told you that you're a very scary woman?" he asked.

"Scary in a good way, or scary in a bad way?"

He grunted, not sure whether to be amused or intimidated. "Both."

"Thanks. I think. I just hope the damn thing really does mean what I think it means. We did the best research we could, but I may never know for sure if I got it right. For all I know, I may have 'Made in China' stamped on my ass."

She slapped a hand across her face and rolled her head back and forth on the arm of the sofa. "God," she groaned, "do you have any idea how angry I was with you over that challenge? I wanted to kill you, and now here I am having sex with you. I need serious counseling."

Biting the inside of his mouth to keep from laughing, he said, "I'll keep that in mind for a future column."

The hand fell away and her eyes went wide. "Don't you dare," she warned, her voice going low and as close to *The Exorcism of Emily Rose* as he'd ever heard it. "If you print a word of anything I've told you or of anything that happens here tonight, I swear to God you'll be sorry."

"Oh, yeah?" he taunted, this abrupt confrontation turning his blood hot and sending it rapidly to all the right places. "What will you do?"

She sat up a fraction more, flames leaping in her wide, round eyes. "I'll rip open your chest and carve the Chinese symbol for 'Fuck you' into your still-beating heart. And then . . ."

Quick as a shot, her hand darted out to grab him by the danglies. He yelped and tried to pull back, but she held him tight, her fingers flexing on the verge of painful around both his dick and his tea bags. Shit, this woman meant business, and she *was not* messing around.

When she spoke again, her tone was frighteningly soft and calm, a full-180 switch from seconds before. "And then I'll get nasty."

For a moment, they both remained perfectly still. She seemed determined to make her point, and he was afraid of being the recipient of a sex change he hadn't signed up for.

Then he swallowed and inclined his head. "Got it. Tonight is off the record, no exceptions."

When she smiled sweetly and loosened her hold on the family scepter and jewels, fresh air flooded his lungs.

"Thank you." She released him entirely and laid back down. "Now, shall we continue on our way to number three?"

How she could go from threatening his life—and worse, his manhood—to being ready for another round of mind-blowing sex in the space of a heartbeat only confirmed his belief that she was a scary, scary woman.

So how demented was it, then, that he found himself growing harder than before and even more eager to be inside her again?

Yep, she was scary, all right, but he was obviously one sick puppy.

"Turn over," he growled out, determined to reassert his masculinity and return the testosterone level in the room to an even keel.

"Why?" she asked, eyeing him suspiciously. "You aren't going to spank me for grabbing your crotch, are you?"

At that suggestion and the image it invoked, his dick trembled and headed a fraction farther north.

"Maybe," he said, careful to keep his expression

blank. "But if you don't roll over, then the answer is definitely."

Her tongue darted out to wet her dry lips before she did as he'd commanded, sliding back to rest on her stomach. Only the stiff line of her spine alluded to the fact that she wasn't entirely at ease.

For several long minutes, he stayed where he was, simply staring at her. Taking in every curl, every curve, every dip and plane.

Then he reached out for a condom packet, deciding he might need one soon, after all.

Ronnie awakened slowly to sun streaming through her bedroom window and every muscle in her body aching from overuse. Squinting against the bright light, she turned her head to find Dylan stretched out beside her.

He was flat on his back, spread-eagle, looking about as dead to the world as a person could get. And no small wonder, after the energy he'd exerted last night. He'd brought her off time and time again—with his mouth, his fingers, his cock. He'd taken her in ways she hadn't known were possible. On her back, on her side, straddling him, sitting on his lap . . .

Her favorite, she thought—if she could even pick a favorite out of the myriad pleasures she'd experienced all through the wee hours—had been when he'd bent her forward over the back of the sofa and fucked her silly while she stared through the open curtains at the shining city lights against a blanket of black.

She remembered wondering at one point if anyone could see them; if some voyeur might be out there with a pair of binoculars, watching as Dylan made her scream. The possibility had only heightened her pleasure and the ensuing orgasm.

She'd never thought of herself as the kind of person who would get off on being spied upon during the throes of passion.

But then, she'd never thought she could come so many times in one night, either. Or that she'd ever find herself waking up after a night of hot monkey sex with Dylan Stone in her bed.

Heaven help her, but she seemed to be having one revelation after another lately.

The mattress dipped beneath Dylan's considerable weight . . . her poor bed wasn't used to having a big, muscular man in it any more than she was . . . and threatened to pull her into the center, right up against him. It would have been so nice to let gravity do its thing so she could curl up beside him and snuggle into all that solid male warmth.

God, he looked good. Sexy and slumberous and good enough to eat.

She licked her lips at the prospect, then turned resolutely and regretfully away. As tempting as it might be to wake him with a few kisses and light strokes to the proper areas, she couldn't justify dragging this on any longer.

Last night, she'd been tipsy and horny and willing to shove her better judgment aside to discover if all Dylan's bragging about being able to bring a woman to orgasm a dozen times was valid or just so much boasting swagger. And—much to her delighted dismay— she'd learned he was as good as his word.

She couldn't be sure if he'd given her the promised thirteen or only the bragged-about twelve . . . she'd pretty much lost count after number five or six. But since the night had gone on and on after that, and he'd continued to make her come and come, she had no doubt he'd reached his goal and possibly surpassed it.

She'd never before been this sore just from sex alone. It was a good sore, if there was such a thing, but muscles she hadn't known existed screamed in protest as she climbed from the bed and quietly made her way to her closet for a robe.

Thank God he hadn't felt the need to stimulate her clitoris every time he brought her off, otherwise she was afraid that tiny, most valuable part of her anatomy would have shriveled up and fallen off halfway through the evening.

She winced as she shrugged into her long lime-green-and-turquoise robe, glancing back over her shoulder at Dylan to make sure he hadn't stirred.

It was after nine o'clock, which meant she was late for work. She should have felt guilty, but didn't. The number of times she'd been late or called in sick could be counted on one hand, so they certainly weren't going to fire her. She would simply call in and let them know she'd be there in an hour or so, then make up for the lost time at the end of the day.

Making her way out of the bedroom, she went to the kitchen to place the call, then backtracked to the bathroom for a quick shower. By the time she returned, she felt better. Steadier, stronger, more resolute about what needed to be done.

She was digging in the drawers of her bedroom dresser when she heard a deep groan and the squeak of the mattress behind her. Slanting a glance over her shoulder, she saw Dylan stretching, rubbing a hand over his face and through his hair, then sitting up in the middle of the wide bed, only a corner of the white sheets draped across his torso keeping him from being completely nude to her view.

"Morning," he said in a low, gravelly voice. His eyes were drowsy with sleep, and his lips were twisted into an endearing half smile.

"Good morning," she replied, keeping her tone even and free of emotion as she went back to what she'd been doing.

He slid to the end of the bed and climbed to his feet. Leaving the sheet behind, he padded bare-ass across the room and down the hall to the bathroom.

She let out a breath she hadn't realized she'd been holding as she pulled a pair of panties from her underwear drawer and stepped into them. He returned to the bedroom just as she was fastening the hook of a matching fire-engine-red bra.

Moving to the closet, she pulled out a pair of charcoal slacks and a white blouse, mindful of his gaze remaining hotly on her the entire time from where he leaned casually against the open doorjamb.

"Are you sure you want to do that?" he asked. "If you stay naked, we can have some more fun."

She would have been lying if she'd said his suggestion didn't make her legs quiver just a bit and a streak of heat roll through her belly.

Get a grip, Ronnie, she told herself sternly.

"Don't you need to get to work?" was her evasive reply.

He shrugged negligently and gifted her with another one of his cocky but seductive grins. "I'll call in sick."

"Don't bother," she told him, buttoning the blouse and

tugging the hem into an even line on the outside of her slacks. "I'm late, but I'm still going in. You should, too."

She should have borrowed a page from his work ethic, though, and taken the day off herself. She was stiff, and tired, and in no mood to put in a full eight hours.

But as much as she would have liked to stay home and recoup, she needed equally to get away from Dylan for a while and shake him from her system.

Seconds ticked by in silence while Ronnie examined her reflection in the mirror above the dresser. Her hair was a wet, tangled mess, making her look like something the cat had dragged in, and her face was devoid of makeup, leaving her somewhat glossy and pale. But she could fix that with a few minutes under the hair dryer and a quick application of foundation, blush, eye shadow, and lipstick. It would take her all of ten minutes, and then she would be out the door.

From the corner of her eye, she noticed Dylan turning and disappearing down the hall while she affixed a thin silver chain and pendant around her neck and stuck silver earrings into her ears. The tension in her limbs seemed to lessen without him standing there, in the buff, watching her like a big cat stalking its prey.

Her relief didn't last long, however. No sooner had she put on her jewelry and turned, intending to walk to the bathroom and finish getting ready, than he reappeared, a glint of determination in his blue eyes.

He was wearing his jeans, pulled up and half zipped, but still left unbuttoned, making her realize he'd gone back into the living room to collect them. He hadn't bothered with a shirt, though, leaving his muscular chest spectacularly bare.

It had been so dark last night that she hadn't had a chance to really study him, to note what a fine male specimen he truly was. He had the figure of a Calvin Klein model. Smooth planes meeting firm delineations, with two perfectly round, bronze nipples in the center of his pectorals that begged to be stroked, teased, licked . . .

Oh, crap, she was getting wet again. She didn't have time to be turned on, didn't want to be turned on. Not again. Not by him.

He stood in the doorway with his legs slightly spread in a near-military stance, his hands at his hips, blocking her exit. And the expression on his face told her he was no longer interested in luring her back into the sack. He had something on his mind, and he meant to get to the bottom of it.

"You wanna tell me what's going on?" he finally asked.

It took her a moment to swallow down her growing arousal and remind herself of her plans for the day: get rid of Dylan; make it clear they were done, over, finished, *finito;* and get her butt to work.

"Nothing is going on," she said, stealthily evading his penetrating gaze by tugging at the cuffs of her blouse, checking that the front buttons were straight, scrunching the damp roots of her hair. "I'm getting ready for work."

She moved to get around him, but he shifted to keep her where she was.

"Uh-uh. You're avoiding me, and I want to know why."

"I'm not avoiding you," she all but snapped. "I'm looking right at you."

Of course, she wasn't. She was looking at a spot just past his left shoulder. But close enough.

"You're buzzing around as fast as you can so you can get dressed, get ready, and get away from me. So what's the deal? Morning-after regrets?"

This time, she did meet his eyes. Mouth flat, fingers curled tight at her sides, she said, "All right, yes. Yes, are you happy now? Last night was a mistake. I had too much to drink and my defenses were down, otherwise you know you wouldn't have gotten two steps inside my door."

One dark blond brow rose. "You can't claim you didn't want it."

He had her there. She'd not only wanted it, she'd begged him for it—numerous times.

"No, I can't say that," she admitted, her voice soft with reluctance. "I just shouldn't have wanted it with you."

Row 11

Well, there you had it. He'd asked, and Ronnie being Ronnie—blunt and sharp-tongued to a fault—she'd answered.

She'd wanted to get laid, just not by him.

Nothing like a good, swift kick to the peaches to wake a guy up in the morning.

"I guess that's honest enough," he muttered.

"I'm sorry, Dylan," she apologized, more sincerity than he would have expected brimming in her eyes. "But you can't think that it was anything more than sex for sex's sake."

"Freaking fantastic sex," he grumbled.

"Yes. Fantastic sex," she agreed, "but still just sex."

She made another move to bypass him, and he shifted to the side, arms falling from his hips to let her.

Following her down the short hall to the bathroom, he said, "I wasn't planning to ask for your hand in marriage, but after last night, I thought we could maybe start hanging out a little more. Is it such a crime to be friends with benefits, no strings attached?"

She turned to face him when she reached the bathroom. "But we're not friends."

At that, she closed the door behind her, shutting him out. A second later, he heard a hair dryer click on, and realized he'd been summarily dismissed.

In her dreams, he thought, and spun on his heel to return to the living room and collect the rest of his clothes. He finished zipping his pants and yanked his undershirt over his head, then sat on the sofa to pull on socks and shoes.

When the hair dryer shut off, he got up, shrugged into his shirt without bothering to button it, and stalked back to the bathroom, positioning himself outside like a sentinel. He didn't know what she was doing in there, but it took several minutes more for the door to creak open and her to reappear.

She stopped in her tracks, startled to find him only inches in front of her. Her hair was now dry and styled, hanging all around her face and shoulders in dark brown waves, and her face was tastefully covered in a light layer of makeup.

Her appearance shouldn't have hit him in the solar plexus with quite as much force as it did. She looked different dressed and made up than she did naked and sprawled beneath him in wild abandon, but damned if he could decide which was his favorite. Either way, she turned up the heat and made his cock throb with wanting.

"I thought you would have gone," she said quietly, unaware of the press of a particular stretch of flesh growing behind his fly.

"We aren't done talking."

When she slipped past him and headed for the kitchen, he let her go, but followed right along.

"What's left to say?"

"We may not be friends, but we make pretty good lovers," he pointed out. "What's wrong with that?"

Ronnie stood at the kitchen counter, digging through her purse. Then she grabbed a banana from a nearby fruit bowl and tossed it inside, on top of the handbag's other contents.

"I don't make a habit of sleeping with men I don't care about, let alone ones I publicly despise. You may be used to having indiscriminate sex with all manner of friend and foe, but I'm not."

Shrugging into her coat and throwing the strap of the purse over her shoulder, she brushed by him again, making a beeline for the front door.

She was back to being snooty and stuck-up, but instead of raising his hackles the way her attitude usually did, he found himself fighting a grin. Ronnie Chasen might be ornery and prickly for most of her waking hours, but now he knew the fire and passion that hid behind her Little Miss Priss exterior.

Since he'd entered her apartment with nothing but the clothes on his back, he had nothing to collect except his jacket before following her out. Waiting for her to lock up, he slipped his hands in the front pockets of his jeans, then walked with her down the hall.

"All right, no sex, then," he agreed amicably. Maybe too amicably, judging by the suspicious glance she slanted in his direction.

But he was confident in his abilities. The sex hadn't been just run-of-the-mill, okay whoopee, and he was betting that the next time Ronnie got horny, she'd forget her bright-light-of-day resolve and decide that maybe another ride on the Stone Pony wouldn't be such a bad prospect, after all.

But if she could hold out for a while, so could he.

"That's it?" she asked. "Okay, fine, no argument now, even though you've been arguing with me since you woke up?"

"Yep," he said as they stepped into the elevator and turned in the age-old habit of facing forward. "I just wanted to make it clear that I didn't coerce you into anything last night. You might have had too much to drink at the Box, but you were right there with me. I didn't take advantage of you, and if you'd told me to stop—which I gave you ample opportunity to do—I would have."

"No, you didn't take advantage of me," she acquiesced. "Any stupidity was entirely my own."

"Careful, sweetheart. If you keep flattering me like that, my head might get too big to fit through the door when we try to step off this elevator."

Her brows met in a scowl and he got the distinct feeling she was resisting the urge to stick her tongue out at him, which almost made him laugh.

"So we'll go back to our original setup," he continued. "Sex-free knitting lessons. It won't be nearly as interesting, but I can deal with it if you can."

The elevator doors slid open and he stepped out of the car, taking a few strides toward the front entrance of the apartment building before he realized Ronnie wasn't with him. Glancing back, he found her still standing inside the elevator, staring at him with a rather pale, blank look.

Retracing his steps, he asked, "What's wrong?"

Shaking her head, she seemed to snap out of whatever daze had held her frozen. She marched past him and out the double glass doors, and he was forced to hustle to catch up to her.

Honest to God, this woman could teach classes on keeping a man on his toes. He couldn't remember ever trailing after, sniffing after, or lolling after another woman the way he had Ronnie just this morning. And if anyone had told him he'd be acting this way without receiving a full frontal lobotomy first, he'd have laughed them off the planet.

"I think it would be better if we stopped the knitting lessons, too."

"Why?"

They were making their way rapidly along the sidewalk to one of the apartment building's two small parking areas. He didn't have the heart to tell her they were heading in the wrong direction. Or maybe he was simply enjoying her snit too much, and was willing to walk a few extra yards if it meant observing the stick-up-her-butt mood awhile longer.

"Because it doesn't make sense. It didn't make sense before, but now that we . . ."

"Took the last train to Fucksville?" he supplied.

Her brow rose at his choice of words, even though she'd been the one yelling "All aboard!" last night.

"I think it would be better if we went back to avoiding each other as much as possible. You're certainly capable of losing your latest challenge all on your own."

"Oh-ho!" he chuckled. "Nice one. But with or without you, I'm not going to fail."

They'd reached the parking lot and stopped walking. Not beside any vehicle in particular, just stopped and were standing there. Dylan suspected Ronnie was trying to be inconspicuous while she scanned the lot for her car.

"Know what I think? I think you want to stop with the knitting lessons because you're afraid you won't be able to control yourself around me anymore. You'll be sitting there, watching me wrap my yarn around that long metal needle, and you'll get so hot, you'll jump my sexy bones."

Her head whipped around, and if eyes could be fitted with laser beams, he'd have been a crispy critter smoldering on the blacktop.

"You really are mentally unstable, do you know that?"

"Chicken."

"I'm not a chicken. I just don't think it's a good idea," she said, her tone growing sharper. Then she cast a disparaging glance up and down his tall frame. "And I would not be even remotely tempted to jump your bones, believe me."

This was what he loved about Ronnie. *This* was the relationship he was used to, what made his blood pump harder and brought all of his competitive instincts to the fore.

"Wanna bet?" His two favorite words, and the question he knew Ronnie wouldn't be able to resist.

"Are you saying I can't get through an evening in your presence without introducing sex to the mix?" Her eyes had narrowed, her mouth thinned into a stiff line.

It took all of his strength not to grin at her response. "That's what I'm saying. And the only way to prove me wrong is to continue with the private knitting lessons."

He lowered his voice to a near whisper and leaned close enough for his breath to stir her glossy brown hair. "The two of us, all alone in your apartment. My

irresistible sex appeal. It will be too much for you to
handle. You'll fold like an origami swan."

She pulled back, glaring at him, a dusting of pink
tingeing her high cheekbones. "You're a jackass, Stone,"
she told him tartly. "And I hate to bruise your ego, but
you're not the least bit irresistible. You're undoubtedly
*re*sistible. So come on over. I'll teach you to knit and
manage to keep my clothes on the whole time."

Now he did grin like an idiot. "We'll see. In the
meantime, I have some bad news for you."

"What now?" she asked, sounding exhausted already
at only ten in the morning.

"Your car isn't here. It's still at The Penalty Box. If
you want to get to work anytime soon, I'll have to
drive you—either to the *Sentinel* offices or the Box,
it's up to you."

"You're both traitors," Ronnie told her friends, her needles clacking together angrily. The madder she was, the
faster she knit, and right now she was about twenty degrees past thoroughly pissed off.

The three of them were seated in the living room of
Charlotte's hundred-year-old farmhouse. Grace and
Jenna were perched on an ancient red brocade and mahogany settee, faded and frayed with wear. Ronnie sat
away from them in a mismatched hunter-green, wing-
back armchair. She was in no mood to sit shoulder-to-
shoulder and be all buddy-buddy with the other two, not
when they'd proven themselves to be the least trustwor-
thy friends on the planet.

She'd been in no mood for a knitting session at all,
really, but when she'd called Grace to read her the riot
act, her friend had informed her that they were all

needed at Charlotte's house to knit like the wind and fill an order for twenty dishcloths that had been placed through the older woman's craft booth.

Normally, Ronnie would have been happy to help. Normally, knitting relaxed her. But today she felt brittle enough to snap, and she was actually afraid that if she didn't get her temper under control, she might very well break the size seven metal needles clutched between her fingers.

"Oh, what are you complaining about?" Grace retorted. "You should be *thanking* us for providing you with the opportunity to have a dozen orgasms in the same night. My God, do you know how amazing that is? Even Zack has never accomplished that, and he's like the Energizer Bunny in the sack. That man just goes and goes and goes."

The slightly glassy-eyed expression on Grace's face and the breathy sigh that passed her lips did nothing to dispel Ronnie's annoyance. After all, she was having her skull pounded into the headboard on a nightly basis by a man she loved and was engaged to marry, whereas Ronnie now had to live with the knowledge that she'd repeatedly boinked her worst enemy.

She wondered how long it would take him to throw *that* up in her face. To brag about it with his friends, to try to humiliate her or use it against her. If he hadn't already.

It was enough to make a girl want to gouge her eyes out with a nice, sharp stick . . . or a nice, sharp knitting needle.

A noise from the kitchen reminded Ronnie that Charlotte was just a room away, and she made sure her voice was low enough not to be overheard when she responded.

"How many orgasms I had is irrelevant. I shouldn't have had *any,* because *you* should have protected me from him. You should have driven me home instead of turning me over to him like some virgin sacrifice."

Grace snorted. "Oh, honey, you're no virgin."

"Shut up," Ronnie snapped. "You threw me to the wolves. Or in this case, wolf."

"My, what big teeth you have," Grace teased, her eyes bright with amusement. "My, what big hands you have. My, what a big dick you have. Bring that bad boy over here and take me like you mean it!"

At her side, Jenna laughed, then lifted her half-knitted, sun-yellow dishcloth in front of her face when Ronnie shot her a nasty glance. But while Jenna might have been the quietest of the three, she was by no means meek.

"So how big was it?" she asked, her green eyes sparkling mischievously, her needles only half hiding a devilish grin.

Narrowing her eyes, Ronnie refused to answer, so Grace answered for her.

"Big enough that she was walking funny when she arrived."

Charlotte appeared then to hearty laughter and a fair share of *ooooh*s and *whoo-hoo*s from two-thirds of the room's occupants. The other third was completely unamused.

The older woman set a tray bearing teacups, a teapot, milk, sugar, and lemon wedges on the low coffee table in front of the settee before tugging at the hem of her brightly flowered polyester blouse and taking a seat directly across from Ronnie. Her big beehive poof of hair was as orange as ever, her lipstick thick and bubblegum pink even at eight o'clock at night.

"What's so funny?" she wanted to know, leaning forward to pour tea into the delicate china cups.

"Ronnie's mad at us for dumping her on Dylan Stone last night," Jenna supplied. "She had a little too much to drink, and Dylan offered to drive her home."

"That was awfully nice of him," Charlotte said, passing Jenna one of the cups, then lifting the milk, sugar, and lemon to silently question which she might like to add to her tea.

"That's what we thought," Jenna agreed.

"Once they got there, though," Grace said, "they spent the night doing the wild thing."

Charlotte's thin, brown, stenciled-on brows—which were a startling contrast to her Lucille Ball, carrot-red 'do—drew up in confusion. "What's the wild thing?"

The three younger women exchanged glances before Grace said, "They slept together."

"Well, they didn't exactly *sleep*. At least not much," Jenna teased.

"They went at it like a couple of horny howler monkeys."

Ronnie cast a dirty look in Grace's direction. "Thanks for the vivid imagery."

"You're welcome," Grace beamed.

"My goodness," Charlotte said. "A lot certainly has happened in a short amount of time. I'm so glad you girls came over so I didn't have to wait until next week's meeting to hear about it."

"Yeah, none of us want to wait a whole week to hear the juicy details," Grace added sweetly. "So come on,

Ronnie, spill. Was Dylan as sexy-hot naked as you'd expect given how good he looks in a pair of jeans?"

Ronnie cocked a brow at her too-curious friend. "What are you doing checking out how another man fills out his Levi's? Wouldn't Zack be annoyed if he found out?"

Given her current state of mind, Ronnie would be only too happy to rat out Grace to her fiancé. It would serve Grace right for getting her into this mess in the first place, and at the very least, it would draw the woman's attention away from Ronnie's fucked-up relationship with Dylan and onto her own.

Granted, Grace and Zack's relationship seemed to be functional and normal and healthy, and would probably last forever. Damn them.

"Zack knows that I occasionally check out other men's butts and packages. The same way he checks out other women's boobs. We may not be able to *order,* but we can still look at the menu," she said, voice cheeky, nose pointed slightly in the air.

It was all Ronnie could do not to stick her tongue out at her impertinent friend.

"Come on," Jenna wheedled. "We've all been dying of curiosity where Dylan is concerned. Zack and Gage are no mystery; Grace and I have been involved with them, so we've discussed them *ad nauseam* over the years. You and Dylan were the only unattached members of our little group, but now that you've hooked up, we want the scoop."

"You can't tell me you tried to picture Dylan naked," Ronnie challenged, astonished by the very thought. She wouldn't have expected something so impish of her friend. Especially when, for the majority of the time Jenna had known Dylan, she'd been a semi-happily married woman.

Without a hint of self-consciousness, Jenna replied, "Of course. Didn't you?"

Strangling on her own breath, Ronnie found herself unable to answer. Because the truth was, she *had* pictured him naked. Many, many, many, many, many, *many* times since she'd first met him.

She wasn't proud of it, but she'd certainly done it, and she suspected every warm-blooded American woman who'd ever come within ten yards of him had, too.

Now, though, she didn't have to use her imagination or fantasize the perfect physique beneath those soft, worn jeans and comfortable buttondown shirts. She *knew*.

Knew that his butt was, indeed, as tight and round and perfect as it looked beneath a thick layer of denim.

Knew that his chest was broad and smooth and would send professional trainers running for the gym to put in a few extra hours with the weights.

And she knew what had been hidden behind the seam of his zipper and how potent that particular appendage truly was.

Thanks to last night, she had a constant, full-blown, Technicolor instant replay of every single aspect of Dylan's naked, amazing, mouthwatering body seared into her brain.

The image flashed across her mind's eye, and she went hot and achy all over. She thought of him and knew that if he were in the room at that very second, she'd be all over him like rats on cheese.

She nearly groaned, realizing what sorry shape she was in. And her friends weren't helping matters.

"That's the problem," she told them. "I *shouldn't* have been picturing him naked. Ever. And I sure as hell shouldn't have slept with him. *Oh, God.*"

Bending double, she buried her face against her knees and groaned. Her stomach was a mass of tightly coiled knots. And not the good kind. Not the tight knots of awareness and longing Dylan had evoked last night. The bad kind that made her feel like throwing up. That reminded her of exactly what she'd done, and how wrong it had been, and just how many horrible repercussions there would be in her future because of it.

"I don't know what you're so upset about, dear."

Ronnie raised her head just enough to peek through the fall of her bangs and across the coffee table at Charlotte, who was sipping a cup of hot tea and munching on pretzel sticks like she didn't have a care in the world.

"You spent the night with a man you like and have known for quite a while, and find very attractive. You're both young and single. I don't see the problem."

"But I *don't* like him," Ronnie stressed, her voice muffled by her legs. "I hate him."

Charlotte didn't respond for a moment, and then she said, "I've always found that there's a thin line between love and hate."

Ronnie made a face where Charlotte couldn't see it. She knew the older woman was only trying to help, but *there's a thin line between love and hate* didn't.

"If you want my opinion—and I know you do," Grace said, "I think this has been a long time coming. You and Dylan have been dancing around each other, tossing out challenges and taking part in an old-fashioned pissing contest for months now. If you ask me, all that misdirected passion was bound to come out eventually."

Ronnie lifted her head to stare at her friend, blinking as though she'd never seen the woman before in her life. When had the pod people taken over Grace's body? When had they started turning her brain to soup and making her think these crazy, demented things?

"Granted," Grace went on, "I wouldn't have expected it to come out twelve or thirteen times in one night, but hey . . . more power to you, girlfriend. I say if you can find a guy who can keep it up that long, you should hang on tight. To him or it, whatever works."

Jenna and Charlotte both chuckled, but Ronnie remained unmoved. By the joke, anyway, not by the rest of Grace's little speech.

"Are you insane? Did you fall on your head in the shower this morning? And what do you mean, *it's been a long time coming*? You *expected* this?"

"Expected, no. Hoped, yes."

Unable to sit still any longer, Ronnie tossed her knitting on top of the table and shot to her feet to pace.

"I don't believe this! I thought you were traitors for sending me home with him last night, but apparently you turned traitorous long before that. Did you set me up? Was this all part of your evil plan to ruin my life and send me into a room with padded walls?"

Grace rolled her eyes. "Oh, don't be so melodramatic. Of course there was no plan. An opportunity presented itself and I thought it would be interesting to see how it played out."

"So I was just part of your little experiment," Ronnie accused.

"Yes," her friend replied with heavy sarcasm, "you've

been an excellent test study, and now we can put the finishing touches on our cure for HBS. That's Horny Bitch Syndrome, for you laypeople."

Ronnie narrowed one eye, annoyed at the implication.

"You have been a touch uptight lately," Charlotte volunteered.

"We thought rolling around in the sheets for a few hours with Dylan—or any half-decent man, actually— might relax you."

"And did it work?" Ronnie wanted to know, cocking a hip and crossing her arms. "Do I *look* more relaxed to you?"

"Definitely not," Charlotte said, and Jenna shook her head in agreement.

"Who knew that even a dozen big Os wouldn't dislodge the stick from your butt?"

After blinking a few times and letting the shock of that statement wear off, Ronnie replied, "I think I'm offended. I think I'm wondering at my choice of friends. Because believe me, if this is your idea of being a pal, I'd be better off buddying up to Jack the Ripper."

"Most of the time, you act like Dylan *is* Jack the Ripper," Grace said. "He's a nice guy, Ronnie. Given some of the Y chromosomes walking around out there, Dylan may even be one of the best. But you treat him like he's the Antichrist or something, sent to suck the soul from your body."

Ronnie knew she was overreacting, knew that her emotions and state of mind were always in chaos where Dylan was concerned. But after last night, Grace didn't know how close her comment came to the truth.

She *felt* as though Dylan had the power to suck out

her soul. And he'd most certainly turned her world upside down.

"We let him take you home because we thought that maybe if the two of you spent some time alone, you'd get to know each other better and maybe even start to like each other," Jenna interjected. "We didn't do it as an act of sabotage or because we thought you'd end up sleeping with him. Please don't be angry with us."

Jenna's soft plea and the genuine concern in her green eyes took the wind out of Ronnie's sails as nothing else could have. She stopped pacing, let her arms fall to her sides, and dropped back onto her seat.

"I'm not angry." Not anymore. She'd feel like a jerk if she kept her mad on now. "I'm just . . ." Confused. Frustrated. Petrified. Annoyed.

She took a deep breath, then a long swallow of her now tepid tea, and shook her head. "What am I going to do?"

"What do you want to do?" Charlotte asked.

"Go back in time and change what happened. Kill Dylan before he can breathe a word of it to anyone else. Crawl into a hole and die."

"All good ideas," Grace said flippantly.

"What about giving him a chance?" Jenna suggested. "Spend a little more time with him and see where things take you. You may end up liking him, and not just in the bedroom."

Ronnie scowled, not liking that suggestion at all. "Well, I *have* to see him again, whether I want to or not" she admitted, rubbing the pad of her thumb over the spot between her eyes where a headache was beginning to throb. "That's the problem—or one of many, anyway. I agreed to continue with our private knitting lessons."

Jenna and Charlotte raised brows, but remained silent at that bit of news. It was Grace who let out a loud guffaw.

"Oh, boy, you really are screwed."

With a groan, Ronnie reached for her abandoned knitting and flopped back in her chair, slowly wrapping the tomato-red yarn around one of the needles to form the first stitch of a new row. Then another and another as she eased back into the routine and stopped slacking off on her offer to help Charlotte fill her craft booth order.

She was getting nowhere in her quest to make sense of her actions last night. Just thinking about it was giving her an ulcer.

But Grace was right; she was screwed. Big time.

Her fear, though, was that very soon she would find herself once again in Dylan Stone's company, once again suffer a moment of weakness, and once again find herself screwed, both figuratively and literally.

A shiver raced down her spine. While the former made her break out in a cold sweat, the latter certainly did not. It made her feel warm and twitchy.

And that's what scared her most of all.

Row 12

Charlotte stood just inside her front door, watching as the girls climbed into their respective cars. Tiny moths and other nighttime bugs fluttered around the single bulb that illuminated the small porch and part of the yard. She lifted a hand to flick them away when they got too close, then kept her hand up to wave good-bye as the women drove off.

They'd gotten a lot done tonight, but her pleasure at filling the large dishcloth order was secondary to what she'd felt when she'd heard the news that Ronnie had succumbed to that nice young man, Dylan.

She was nearly giddy with excitement, realizing that the yarn she'd spun with the family spinning wheel was working. It really was enchanted. It really did possess the power to bring two people together in true love.

Oh, the happily-ever-after was still far off on the horizon, with Ronnie fighting it every step of the way. That girl was nothing if not stubborn as a barnyard mule.

But things had definitely been set in motion. After all, a night of wild, passionate lovemaking was a far cry from the snarking that usually took place between those two—even if Ronnie was trying her level best to go back there. She would just have to hope that the yarn was powerful enough to break through all that poppycock.

Turning to go back inside, Charlotte flipped off the porch light and locked the front door behind her. Not that it was necessary. She lived at least a mile from her nearest neighbor, on a very lightly traveled gravel road. But a woman alone couldn't be too careful.

Her fingers itched to go upstairs and spin another skein of yarn on the magic spinning wheel. To test its powers even further and see if she could manage another love match.

But just because Ronnie and Dylan *seemed* to be moving in that direction didn't mean the outcome was guaranteed. Better, she decided, to wait awhile longer and see how things truly worked out. There would be time later to do more spinning and matchmaking.

With a sigh, she shuffled back into the living room and began to clear the coffee table, stacking used dishes onto the serving tray and boxing up the finished dishcloths to transport to the craft booth.

The Knit Wits' next meeting was nearly a full week away . . . so long to wait for an update on the Ronnie and Dylan situation. She wasn't sure she could wait that long to find out, and wondered if there was some excuse she could concoct to contact Jenna or Grace again and maybe finagle a few juicy tidbits ahead of time.

Then again, good things came to those who were willing to wait, and she had a feeling that if she could be patient as this one played out, the results would be very good, indeed.

Row 13

Juggling bags of Chinese takeout and his ball of yarn and needles, Dylan made his way down the hallway toward Ronnie's apartment. He was whistling, he realized, and was further surprised when it dawned on him that he was in an exceptionally good mood.

He was actually looking forward to seeing Ronnie again—and not for the reason he would have expected.

She'd made it clear there would be no more slap and tickle between them. And while he was disappointed—what hot-blooded American male wouldn't be, after a night like the one they'd spent together?—he was also okay with her hands-off policy.

He figured he'd gotten luckier in the twelve hours he'd spent making love to Ronnie than he was likely to get in the next twelve years, so he would just have to save up those pleasures like some kind of sexual hermit, storing them away until he could come out of hibernation and go looking for a good time again.

Besides, having a one-night stand with the Queen of Mean was one thing. Going for a two-night stand, or anything more substantial, would put him at risk of getting *involved*. Of creating a . . . relationship other than the one they'd already established. And that was something he definitely didn't think he was man enough to handle.

Trading snipes and dares was easy.

Trading snipes and dares by day, then rolling around on the floor by night, would put him too close to a line he'd rather not cross.

Reaching her door, he lifted the hand that held his ongoing attempt at knitting and rapped with his knuckles. He waited, ready to greet her with a grin and a quart of the best egg drop soup Cleveland had to offer.

A minute later, when she still hadn't answered, his smile began to slip.

He checked his watch. Yeah, it was Saturday, but it was also after 10 PM, and judging by her routine in the past she should be here.

Knocking again, he crouched to see if there was any light showing under the door. But either the apartment was dark or the door was tight enough on its frame that it wouldn't have shown anything even if high-powered floodlights filled the room.

"Ronnie?" He tapped more loudly a third time, and leaned close to the door to listen for noise or movement inside. "Ronnie, it's Dylan. Are you in there?"

He thought he heard shuffling from the other side, but couldn't be sure. And then Ronnie removed all doubt.

"Not tonight, Stone. Go away."

She sounded odd, her voice thick and shaky.

"Are you all right?"

"Yes, now go away."

Tossing the needles and yarn on top of one of the bags of food, he tried the knob, but found it locked. With a low curse, he called out, "Open the door, Ronnie. I'm not leaving until I'm sure you're okay."

More noise from inside—some banging, grumbling, and a muted stomping that grew louder as she neared the door. The dead bolt twisted and she yanked the door open, but only the inch or two allowed by the still-caught chain.

A slim portion of Ronnie's face appeared, but even in shadow, her skin looked pale, her eyes puffy, her mouth drawn.

"I'm fine," she bit out. "See? Good-bye."

She moved to slam the door closed again, but Dylan was quicker. He shoved the toe of his shoe—which happened to be his favorite pair of year-round hiking boots—into the narrow opening, keeping her from shutting him out.

"Let me in, Ronnie," he murmured softly.

"Not tonight, Dylan, okay?" Resting her forehead against the edge of the door, her eyes fluttered closed. "Just go away and leave me alone."

Now she was downright scaring him. He'd never seen her like this. Hadn't known she *could* be like this, all subdued and vulnerable looking. And he'd never heard her voice sound so thin and strained, as though she'd taken more than she could handle and was ready to give up.

"If I go, it'll be straight to the nearest phone to call Grace and Jenna to come over and check on you. That's two buttinskies instead of one. Unless, of course, they decide to bring Zack and Gage along, which would make it four. And since I'm already here . . ."

He shrugged a shoulder, trying for his best harmless-human half smile. "Plus, I brought enough Chinese for a three-day sit-in. So who would you rather have bugging you tonight—a sexy, blue-eyed journalist who comes bearing lo mein and General Tso's chicken, or a couple of rolled-out-of-bed, let's-share-our-woes, empty-handed girls and their misbegotten significant others?"

Was that a quirk he saw tugging at the corner of her lips? He sure hoped so.

"They're not girls," she responded almost by rote, "they're women."

"They're women without wonton."

Her lashes swept upward and she studied him for second. Then she sighed with her whole body, closed the door thanks to his removed foot, and slipped the chain lock free. By the time the door opened again, wider this time, she was already turned and walking in the other direction.

She was dressed in pajamas already, but not the hot pink basset hound ones he'd been treated to on his first visit to her place. Tonight's set was canine-free, the pants a solid tangerine with no pattern or decoration, the long-sleeved top a swirling, whirling mix of mismatched but somehow well-blended colors. Blue, green, pink, yellow, beige, orange . . .

But it wasn't the roller coaster of colors that caught his attention so much as the pert roundness of her ass as it sashayed away from him. One thing was for sure, Ronnie Chasen looked as good going as she did coming. And he meant that both figuratively and literally.

Kicking the door closed behind him, he followed her into the living room and dropped the bags of takeout on the long mahogany coffee table. Ronnie was curled up in the corner of the couch, turned slightly away from him, inconspicuously trying to dab her eyes and wipe her nose with a tissue.

She'd been crying, just as he'd suspected. The question was, why?

She'd also been sitting practically in the dark, the only light in the apartment coming from a tall lamp in the corner with a low-watt bulb and an old-fashioned, muting shade edged with ugly olive-green fringe.

Her uncharacteristic show of emotion put him on rocky ground. Her flashes of temper and brittle personality, he could handle with his eyes closed. But tears, sadness, vulnerability . . . he could feel his palms turning damp, a trickle of cold sliding down his spine.

Buying them both some time, he slowly started removing Chinese carry-out containers from the bags and setting them on the table.

"Fork or chopsticks?" he asked, knowing it was probably the stupidest and least important dilemma in her world right now.

She tipped her head slightly, balling the tissue in her hand and lowering her arm so he wouldn't see what she'd been up to. "Chopsticks, I guess," she said in a watery voice.

He moved around the table and plopped down in the center of the sofa, close to her, but not touching. Flipping open containers and removing lids, he jabbed a set of chopsticks into a serving of shrimp lo mein and passed it to her.

"I'm really not hungry," she said, but he noticed she didn't refuse the noodles.

"Try to eat just a little. You look like hell, and getting some food in your stomach might help."

Eyes narrowing, she glared at him. He'd been telling the truth, though. Her eyes and nose were both puffy and red, her cheeks blotchy. She'd removed most of her makeup, but traces of eyeliner and mascara had run and smeared a bit beneath her lower lashes.

Funny how looking like hell could still look damn good, though. Just because she was all soggy and blanched didn't mean his little soldier wasn't willing to wake up and stand at attention.

"You don't know much about comforting someone in their time of need, do you?" she asked, poking around inside the square white carton.

He blew out a breath and shook his head. "Glad you noticed. No, guys don't have much experience with random displays of emotion. We're more the get-pissed-and-punch-something or get-drunk-with-friends-and-complain-for-a-few-hours types."

Popping a chunk of General Tso's chicken into his mouth, he chewed and swallowed before saying, "So do you want to talk about it? Whatever has you so upset?"

"And if I say no?" She lifted a small portion of noodles to her mouth, then seemed pleased with the taste and went back for more.

"Then we'll sit here eating Chinese takeout until our stomachs explode, wait an hour, and eat some more. Maybe we'll even find a movie on the boob tube to fill the empty silence."

And for the next several minutes, silence was exactly what he got. He ate a few more pieces of chicken before nudging her in the leg with the container and wordlessly suggesting they trade. She took the chicken and handed over the lo mein.

When he realized they didn't have drinks or spoons

for the egg drop soup, he got up and went to the kitchen for both. She didn't ask him what he was doing, didn't chastise him for poking around in her cupboards and drawers, didn't seem to care one way or the other. It was definitely spooky, considering the old Ronnie—or at least the less upset one—would have had her dander up a good ten or twenty minutes ago.

She even took one of the spoons and shared the soup with him straight out of the same container. It was *I see dead people* spooky.

Halfway through the fried wonton, she finally spoke. And Dylan nearly jumped out of his shorts because in the deep, dark silence of the room, he'd begun running the most bloodcurdling horror-movie scenes he could think of through his head for entertainment. Her low voice breaking into his thoughts was a little too *the call is coming from inside the house* for his peace of mind.

"I got some bad news today," she said.

After his heart returned to a normal rhythm, he wiped his hands on one of the paper napkins the Jade Garden had thrown in with their meal, balled it up, and tossed it among the rest of the mess on the table in front of them.

"I'm sorry to hear that. Do you want to tell me about it?"

A beat passed, and he started to think she was going to refuse. Then she took a deep breath, set her own food aside, and twisted on the sofa so that her back was against the arm, her legs drawn up to her chest, her feet flat on the floral cushion.

"Not really, but since you're here and you were nice enough to bring dinner . . ." Reaching behind her, she retrieved a sheet of trifolded paper and handed it to him.

"I applied for a position at another paper. A better

paper and a better position," she said while he unfolded the letter and read. "I didn't get it."

"I'm sorry," he told her, handing the letter back. "But you already have a decent job. Why are you so upset about not getting this one?"

Her eyes filled with moisture again, her lips quivering as her cheeks turned pink. "Because the job I have now isn't good enough. The salary isn't high enough. If I get fired tomorrow, I only have enough money to survive five, maybe six months."

Dylan blinked and then let out a laugh. "That's what you're worried about? Geez, Ronnie, I thought you were going to say you're practically destitute. A lot of people live from paycheck to paycheck, you know, and would be lucky to make it a month or two if they got fired. Sounds to me like you're doing pretty well if you could go six months with no income. Not that you couldn't find another job at the drop of a hat. You're a damn fine writer, Ronnie."

That was about as close to complimenting her as he'd ever gotten, but it just sort of slipped out. And he didn't regret it—it was true, and seemed to be what she needed to hear.

Only, apparently it wasn't. Instead of cheering her up, his comment seemed to distress her all the more. Her entire body tensed and she sat up even straighter.

"You don't understand!" she charged, vibrating with the intensity of her emotions. "Six months is nothing. What about the rising cost of living? What about the rate of unemployment in this country? There are no guarantees, Dylan. Every minute you can afford to buy groceries and pay your rent could be the last."

"Don't you think that's a bit extreme?"

"You have no idea," she charged, hopping off the couch to storm around the open area on the other side of the coffee table. Her posture was rigid, her movements jerky with agitation. "You talk about living from paycheck to paycheck. Try living with *no* paycheck. You have no idea what it's like to not know where your next meal is coming from, or if you'll get to eat at all that day."

He didn't miss the frantic glint in her eyes or the desperation in her quavering voice, and he was beginning to appreciate that whatever concerns she had about keeping her current job or finding a new one ran much deeper than just an impressive addition to her résumé.

"You're right, I don't," he said softly.

He was afraid that if he spoke too loudly or made any sudden moves, she would spook and revert back to her Iron Maiden persona. She was just beginning to open up, and he was just starting to get a peek beneath her thick, solid armor. He didn't want to do anything to screw that up.

"Do you?"

She laughed, a high-pitched, near-hysterical sound. If he hadn't had a couple of chopsticks in his hand that could double as defensive stabby devices, he might have been concerned.

"Boy, do I. I may look like I've got it all together, without a care in the world, but I've been fucked up since the day I was born. For most of my life, my family wasn't just poor, but impoverished. I don't know what my parents were thinking, having children when they could barely support themselves."

Long strides eating up the neutral, tan-crossed-with-mustard-yellow carpeting, she wrapped her arms around her waist as though trying to keep herself from twisting inside out with uncontrollable, renegade emotions.

"My father was injured on a factory assembly line, and my mother simply had too many babies tied to her apron strings to work outside the home."

"Not big believers in birth control, huh?" he asked quietly.

She snorted. "Definitely not. I'm not even sure they knew about the rhythm method. I mean, my God, who continues to bring children into this world when they can't support them? When they don't have a steady job, and have to live in a car three or four months out of every year."

Dylan's heart hitched at that disclosure. Was she serious? Had she really had to live out of a car as a kid?

It was almost too incredible to imagine. He understood that poverty existed, knew that not everyone was as lucky as he was to come from a fairly happy, average, middle-class family. There had always been food on the table when he was growing up. A roof over his head, a pool in the backyard, Christmas presents under the tree.

They hadn't been rich, but they hadn't really wanted for anything, either. He wouldn't say he or his brothers had been spoiled—his parents would have neither tolerated nor contributed to that—but their toy boxes had certainly been full.

Ronnie must have spotted the look of astonishment on his face because she paused in her pacing to confront him. "That's right, I lived in a car. Six or seven of us squeezed into this old, beat-up station wagon that had seen better days. Most of the time, there was no money for gas, so my father would park somewhere out of the way where we wouldn't be noticed. We went to the bathroom in the woods, bathed in creeks or streams, ate whatever we could find. My father worked odd jobs when he could find them; and when we had enough money, we would rent a run-down house or apartment somewhere, but that never seemed to last very long."

Tapping her foot, she stood just on the other side of the coffee table, staring daggers at him, her brows drawn tight over her blazing, coffee-brown eyes.

"So now you know," she told him, the words both watery and scalding at the same time. "Are you happy?"

Why in God's name would she expect him to be happy? Did she think he was some kind of soulless, demonic bastard?

Well, okay, up until recently, she probably had thought that, and for good reason. They'd both worked hard to put their very worst feet forward where the other was concerned.

But a lot had happened in the last few weeks, including a long, tooth-rattling bout of truly incredible sex. They may not have parted the next morning with hugs and kisses and whispered endearments, but he'd like to believe they hadn't fallen right back into their old, back-stabbing, hiss-and-spit routine, either.

"Of course not," he said carefully. "Why would I be?"

"Because now you know that I'm a complete fraud. The clothes, the attitude, the self-confident air. It's all an act, and I'm sure you'll have a jolly good time outing me to everyone in Cleveland in your next column."

He had to admit that for a brief second, he imagined doing just that. The journalist gene of his DNA itched at the prospect of revealing a secret . . . any secret, about anyone. But regardless of her apparently low opinion of him, he had no intention of repeating what she'd told him.

It explained a lot, though, now that he thought about it. The secondhand furniture, the generic drugs in the medicine cabinet, the do-it-yourself hair color and manicure set.

She was a woman who had grown up with nothing, or close to nothing, and still pinched pennies to keep from ever having to experience that sort of lifestyle again. A woman who, amazingly enough, managed to look like a million bucks every single day without spending loads of cash on herself.

Did he know anyone else who'd be able to pull it off so well with so little? He doubted it.

"I'm not going to write about this," he assured her with a small shake of his head. "And I don't think that being frugal and living within your means makes you a fraud. Way more people would go in the other direction, spending more than they could afford on clothes and shoes and trips to the salon, digging themselves into such a deep debt pit, they'd never get out."

She studied him for a moment, her mouth turned down in obvious doubt.

"You're just saying that," she told him. "As soon as you leave, you'll run to your computer and whip out a great big belly-laugh piece about poor, pathetic Ronnie Chasen, growing up like the Boxcar Children."

He chuckled at that. Arms on his knees, hands clasped between his legs, he shook his head again. "No, I won't. What happens in knitting group stays in knitting group, right? Didn't I hear one of you ladies say that at the last meeting? I figure it applies to private knitting lessons, too."

She eyed him warily, her gaze sweeping over the plethora of open Chinese take-out containers and his pile of yarn and needles resting at the edge of the table.

"We haven't done any knitting yet," she pointed out, and he could hear the doubt in her voice.

"No, but that is why I came over, so I suppose it counts."

Leaning back, he lifted his leg to rest one ankle on the opposite knee, and stretched his arms along the back of the couch. "Would it make you feel better if I told you something personal and private that I'd prefer didn't get out? That would make us even, and if I ever told your secret, then you could get back at me by telling mine."

She thought about that for a minute, and he could see the tension leaking from her limbs. Her eyes softened, losing their sharp intensity. Even her pale skin seemed to be less taut over her bones and muscles.

"All right," she agreed slowly. "But it better be good."

Hiding a grin, Dylan turned slightly, patting one of the cushions beside him. It took her a minute, but finally Ronnie made her way around the table and sat cross-legged against the far arm of the sofa.

Taking a deep breath, he admitted, "It seems we're both working at jobs that are less than our ideal, just waiting for a better one to come along."

She tipped her head to the side, her straightforward gaze meeting his own. Only the twist of her bubblegum lips alerted him to her rising ire.

"Are you saying you took the position at the *Herald,* stole it away from me, when you didn't even *want* it?"

He bit back a grin. Her reaction was so Ronnie-typical, he could have scripted it.

"Yeah, I guess I did. Do you want to hear this, or not?"

The fire in her eyes banked, but only slightly. "Keep going."

"I want to be a sports reporter. Have since I was a kid. Baseball, basketball, football, hockey, tennis, soccer, golf . . . I love them all. I've got stats whipping through my head twelve hours a day."

"What do you think about the other twelve?" she asked.

"Sex," he deadpanned.

Her mouth quirked up at the corner and he found himself almost smiling in return.

"I keep interviewing and putting in my résumé for sports positions. The only reason I moved to the *Herald* is because the old sports reporter was set to retire, and I figured if I was there, as soon as his job opened up, I could slip right in and take over."

He made a face, the annoyance at being shut out once again as fresh as it had been the day it happened.

"Makes sense, right? Except the old guy had a nephew, and they gave him the job instead. This bean-pole geek with flood pants and tape on his glasses, who wouldn't know a layup from a slam dunk, has my column. Every single time I come close to catching a break and getting the chance to write what I really want, I get knocked on my ass."

Reaching out, he snatched his glass of soda—generic, of course; after all, he'd gotten it out of Ronnie's fridge—and took a long gulp. He was just swallowing when his head snapped forward, nearly causing him to choke *and* break a tooth on the rim of the glass.

Pulling back, he turned to look at Ronnie, who'd leaned forward and was even now pulling back for another slap.

"That's for stealing my job," she told him.

Whap! to the back of his head a second time.

"And that's for being an idiot."

"Geez," he said, rubbing the stinging area. "Thanks for being a sympathetic listener."

"What's to sympathize with?" she demanded. "You took a job you didn't want—that I not only wanted, but needed, you dumb jerk—because you're too stupid to go after what you really *do* want more directly."

"Okay," he said slowly, ticking items off on his fingers. "Idiot, dumb jerk, stupid . . . You forgot dim, dense, slow, moronic, doofus."

"I didn't forget them, I just haven't worked them in yet."

"What's so stupid about trying to climb the ladder, trying to get closer to your dream?"

"Nothing. Nothing at all. But that's not what you're doing."

She was worked up again, but this time with a passion for her subject rather than shame and upset over her own circumstances.

"You're hiding. Playing it safe. Rolling over and playing dead just because things haven't worked out exactly the way you'd hoped."

"Well, what the hell am I supposed to do?" he charged back, starting to get riled up himself. "Walk into the paper of my choice and demand the sports-writer position at gunpoint?"

"Of course not, but am I the only one who's noticed that one of your best friends happens to be the star goalie of the Cleveland Rockets?"

He held her gaze for a moment, then blinked. "So?"

Her eyes went wide and she sat up straighter on the sofa, leaning forward to give him another whap. This one wasn't as hard, though, and caught him on the shoulder because he saw it coming.

"*Sooooo,*" she stressed, as though he was, indeed, slow on the mental uptake. "Zack is your best friend. He's known for being tight-lipped with the press. Imagine the attention you would get if you convinced him to give you an exclusive interview. You could take it to any paper in the city . . . any paper or magazine in the country, and they'd trip over themselves to hire you."

Feeling like he'd just been smacked between the eyes with a two-by-four, he stared at her, dumbfounded. He'd honest to God never considered such a thing before, but now that she'd verbalized it, it sounded so simple, so sensible, so *obvious*.

If there had been a brick wall nearby, he'd have jumped up and started pounding his brain against it. *Duh, duh, duh.*

Ronnie was right, he was an idiot. He'd always planned to get the ideal job, *then* take advantage of his friendships, not the other way around. And though Zack was his closest professional athlete friend, he had others. Some he'd met through Zack, some he'd met on his own simply by virtue of his huge love of all things sports-related.

The idea was so phenomenal, he wanted to rush out, track down Zack, and talk him into doing an interview right then. But of course it was late, Zack was likely busy with something else—even if it was only heating up the sheets with Grace—and he didn't have a single question in mind for his friend yet.

He would have to go back through past articles and interviews with Zack. There weren't many, but if he could hit on some questions and areas that hadn't been covered by anyone else, it really would be exclusive enough to garner major media interest. And as long as he didn't print anything too personal, he was almost certain Zack would agree.

It wasn't until he came back down to earth that he realized Ronnie hadn't moved. He hadn't, either, actually; he'd been too busy mapping out his future now that he was no longer burdened by Dumb Fuck Syndrome.

A slow smile spread across his face and he started to lean forward. He couldn't help himself. Even when she pulled back and wariness crept into her eyes, he didn't stop.

Reaching out, he cupped the back of her head in the palm of his hand, his fingers weaving into the silky strands of her chestnut hair. He pulled her toward him, and despite the guardedness in her expression, she didn't balk.

His lips brushed hers, feather-light, once, twice, three times. Her lashes fluttered closed and a breath of surrender rushed from her lungs.

He was pretty close to surrendering himself. She tasted of the Chinese buffet they'd gobbled down earlier, and the gentle mix of sweet and spicy made him hungry all over again—but not for food.

"Thank you," he whispered against her mouth.

His words must have surprised her because she went slack beneath him. Silently and with great reverence, he opened his mouth over hers, slid his tongue between her warm lips, and kissed her until steam poured out both their ears.

Row 14

Ronnie couldn't decide if she was more shocked by Dylan's whispered thank-you or by the unexpected kiss that was even now turning from soft and easy to firm and intense.

It felt so peculiar going from being completely distraught over having lost this latest job opportunity to having her pulse kick up and all pertinent hormones make a run for the southern border, but that seemed to be the effect he had on her.

One minute, tears and fury, next minute, *Ride me, cowboy!*

She moaned beneath his mouth, letting her arms wrap more securely around his shoulders and unlocking her ankles from their crossed position to open wider and invite him into the cradle of her thighs.

This was a bad idea. She knew it. Her brain was telling her to stop, to shut him down and hustle him out the door before things went any farther.

But her body . . . oh, her body was a weak, treacherous bitch. It wanted more of exactly what Dylan was giving her. What she knew from delightful experience that he could give her again and again all through the night.

His hand crept up to cup her breast and fondle the swelling point of her nipple through the soft cotton material of her pajama top.

And there went all of that nice, rational lucidity. Blip, bloop, blam, gone were all of her lovely sense and sensibilities, flying right out the window.

So what did it matter? One more night. One more bout of rock-my-world, trip-the-light-fantastic sex. She could totally put her foot down tomorrow and call a stop to any further intimate relations with the man she loved to hate.

She could.

She would.

But for now . . .

"Mmm, that feels good," she murmured as he released her mouth and began kissing a path down the side of her throat. At the same time, his fingers continued to flutter and tweak the tips of her breasts.

"How about this?" he asked, sliding the hand that had been at the back of her head down between her legs. He cupped her mound and applied a gentle pressure that had her wiggling in place.

It felt better than good . . . amazing, fantastic, phenomenal would have been a better description . . . and she wished for magical forces that would have allowed her to blink or snap or wiggle her nose and render both their clothes nonexistent.

But he'd done this to her before . . . stroked and caressed, kissed and enticed. Basically swept in, stunned her with his astounding powers of foreplay, and left her dazed, sated, and confused.

Time for a little payback.

It wasn't easy, what with his hand buried in her crotch and his fingers starting to dance in a way she *really* wanted to beg him to stick with until the bitter end, but she took a deep breath, pulled back as far as the arm of the couch would allow, and said, "Wait."

The speed with which he stopped was almost amusing. It was like one of those "sex on campus" instructional videos where they showed examples of green-light/red-light behavior.

"Something wrong?" he asked, and only the heaving of his chest and tautly defined muscles of his throat belied just how much control he was exerting to *not* continue touching her.

Oh, she was going to enjoy this.

"Yes, as a matter of fact, there is," she told him, straining not to grin, even though one was struggling to get loose.

Giving his chest a little shove, she pushed him away, then swung out from under him and got to her feet beside the couch. Dylan's face fell, and he turned to collapse against the sofa back.

He perked up, though, when she crossed her arms in front of her and tugged the hem of her pajama top straight up over her head. A second later, she shrugged out of the bottoms and kicked them aside, too.

Completely naked, she stood in front of him, watching his eyes darken with desire and the already impressive tenting behind the zipper of his jeans swell even larger.

"I thought . . ." His voice cracked and he had to stop, swallow, and start again. "I thought you weren't interested."

"What gave you that idea?" she asked cheekily, resting a hand at her waist and cocking her hip to one side.

His brows rose. "You. You said stop."

"No," she corrected him, striding the step or two forward to reach him and climbing onto the couch, straddling him with one knee on either side of his thighs. Her fingers tunneled through his hair as he lifted his head slightly to meet her gaze. "I said wait. There's a difference."

He sat motionless, obviously viewing her as a predator and himself as the prey. The image—a lioness stalking a gazelle—amused her, bringing a smile to her lips.

"Okay, what are we waiting for?"

"Nothing now." She tugged his head back, leaning forward to press her bare breasts to his chest while her mouth began to gently peruse the strong, masculine lines of his face.

"I wanted you to wait because it's not fair for you to be in the driver's seat a second time in a row. If we're going to do this again—" She wiggled her hips, grinding herself over the solid ridge of his trapped erection. "—and it certainly feels like we're going to, unless you have some objection, then I want to be in charge for a change. I want the chance to make you come twelve or thirteen times in one night."

A huff of stale air burst from his lungs. "Sorry, babe, I can pretty much guarantee that's an objective you're not going to reach, no matter how hard you try. The mind is willing, believe me, but the body is far from able. I may be as young and randy as the next guy, but even I can't get it up a dozen times in one night."

She slipped a hand down between their bodies and

rubbed him suggestively and with great purpose. "Mind if I give it a try?"

The muscles in his arms, thighs, and abdomen all went tight as elevator cables. "Be my guest."

She grinned. He sounded nonchalant, but she could feel the heat and tension rolling off him in waves.

She could leave him now, worked up, desperate, ready to chew nails for the chance to get off. It would be such poetic justice in so many ways.

And a few weeks ago, she would have done it. She would have gloried in the ability to get him all lathered up, then walk away, leaving him hard and aching, panting for more.

Now, though, her vindictive streak when it came to Dylan Stone seemed to have disappeared. Or at least taken a short jaunt down to Jamaica while the rest of her stayed behind to get her groove on.

And just like the last time she'd been naked with him, she decided to block out any pesky everyday concerns. Her underlying hatred for him, their ongoing battle of one-upmanship, whatever realities might come crashing down in the bright light of day.

She was like a junkie jonesing for a fix. Just one more hit and she'd be okay. Just one more hit and she'd quit, give it up forever, check herself into rehab. Honest. Just one more hit . . .

She only hoped that after tonight, after she'd let herself chase down this one last high, she would have the strength to say no from now on. Because he was a bit like a drug: slowly but surely becoming addictive and necessary to keep her body functioning. To stave off the tremors and anxiety and sickness of withdrawal.

But call her a junkie, an addict, a glutton for punishment. Like Dylan, sitting immobilized beneath her, she was more than willing to go with the moment and follow where her raging hormones were leading. And like Scarlett O'Hara, she would think about the consequences tomorrow.

Sliding her palms down the long, sleek line of his chest, she curled her fingers into the material of his shirt and tugged it from the waistband of his jeans. He moved slightly to help her pull the fabric free, but otherwise let her do all the work.

She was fine with that . . . after all, she was the one who'd insisted on taking the reins this time around . . . but still she took her time releasing the row of tiny white buttons running down the front. Slipping her hands inside to caress his warm, smooth skin, she pushed the edges of fabric away, revealing more of his chest inch by glorious inch.

She could feel him vibrating with unleashed arousal, his teeth grinding as he fought not to reach out and take over, to simply take what he so obviously wanted. The knowledge of just how strong that urge was in him made her thighs clench and weakened her resolve to go slow and draw out the agony for both of them.

Licking her lips and swallowing past the lump of dry desire in her throat, she pushed the shirt over his shoulders and down his arms, waiting for him to sit up just a bit so she could pull it free and toss it aside altogether. While she went to work on the snap of his jeans, his hands came up to toy with her breasts. Cup them, squeeze them, circle and tease her nipples with the sides of his thumbs.

She moaned and arched her back, enjoying his ministrations even as she considered shutting him down. Was she still in the driver's seat if she let him take the wheel now and again?

Did she care?

At the moment, no. Right now, she was much more interested in getting them both naked so she could *really* start making him squirm.

The metal rivet of his jeans popped open and she very carefully began to lower the zipper. It wasn't easy, considering the pressure of his erection pressing against the other side.

To keep tender flesh from getting snagged . . . because she couldn't think of anything that would put an end to an intimate encounter quite as quickly—or painfully—as getting a guy's cock caught in his zipper . . . she slipped her free hand inside, behind the denim closure.

Although the thin barrier of his underwear protected her from direct contact with his goods, they didn't keep him from groaning or his dick from twitching. His grip on her breasts tightened as his head fell back and he let his eyes drift closed.

"Don't fall asleep on me yet," she teased softly.

"Trust me," he said, eyes still closed, "I'm wide awake."

She could feel that. He pulsed beneath her hand, and she was flooded with exquisite memories of having him inside her, so long and thick and relentless.

When the zipper was as low as it would go, she trailed her fingers under the waistband of both his pants and briefs as far as she could.

"Lift up," she told him, flexing her hands so that her nails dug gently into the tender flesh of his hips and upper buttocks.

He did as she asked, and she wasted no time skimming the jeans down his legs. But to get them all the way off, she had to slide off his lap and onto the floor. Once there, she made short work of removing his boots and socks and, finally, his pants.

"That's better," she murmured, taking a moment to admire what a gorgeous male specimen he was.

All hard planes and smooth lines. Rakish, windblown hair and a hint of stubble covering his jaw. Hairy legs and a less hairy chest. Less hairy, but with an alluring trail of light curls leading down, down, down in a pleasure path to his most masculine asset.

He had perfect shoulders, perfect biceps, perfect pecs, a perfectly mouthwatering set of six-pack abs . . . and that was only above the waist. Below, he had the potential to raise a woman's core temperature by at least ten degrees for every second she spent admiring him. It was like looking into the sun, blinding in its intensity.

She felt the tip of her tongue dart out to worry the center of her upper lip. It didn't help, either, that she knew exactly what that piece of equipment could do. She knew its potential, its staying power, and the amazing skill of the man who wielded it.

From his deceptively relaxed pose, Dylan's eyes fluttered open, flickering like blue flame as he stared down at her. "Keep doing that with your tongue," he warned, "and you won't be in charge much longer."

Tilting her head to one side, she said, "Oh, really? You got a problem with my tongue?"

It was the worst *Godfather*/*GoodFellas*/*Taxi Driver* impression ever, but it brought a smile to his face nonetheless.

"Yeah, as a matter of fact, I do. I can think of much better things for a naked woman to do with her mouth."

She arched a brow. "A naked woman who's already on her knees, you mean?"

His smile transformed into a full-fledged leer. "Yeah."

Oh, he had some nerve. What part of *woman on top* did he not understand? She should punish him for his insolence, really she should.

A shiver of excitement stole through her at the memory of the first time he'd shown up at her apartment, and his discovery of her Domiknitrix screen name, which had led him to openly wonder what hid inside her bedroom closet.

Leather bustiers? Fishnet stockings? Thigh-high vinyl boots with razor-sharp stiletto heels? Riding crops and full-length whips?

She wished now that he'd been right. If she'd had a few pleasure-and-pain sex toys tucked away, she would retrieve them and show him exactly how a dominant/submissive relationship was supposed to work.

But since she'd pretty much been thinking along the same lines as he was, she decided not to punish him. Yet.

Then again, a good blow job—if done right—could be a decent form of punishment, too.

She decided then and there to suck him until he begged, cried, whimpered . . . and came like an unmanned fire hose. That would teach him who was boss.

Rising up a little straighter from her crouched position, she placed her hands on his bare knees and applied pressure, causing him to splay his legs farther apart. Then she moved between them until her belly bumped the edge of the sofa. At the same time, she let her fingers dance over the tops of his thighs, enjoying the crisp, rough texture of the tiny hairs there.

She could feel his muscles like steel beams beneath his skin, and the slight, occasional tremor of need that ran through him from head to toe. The brisk, wintry fragrance of his cologne mixed with the headier trace of his own testosterone-laden scent, and she breathed deep, inhaling every musky molecule.

His fully erect cock, surrounded by a bed of tight, light blond curls, strained upward and nearly bent far enough away from her to touch the flat surface of his belly. The soft, walnut-sized spheres of his balls were already drawn up with arousal and in anticipation of even greater pleasure.

She licked her lips again. He wasn't the only one thrumming with expectancy. The upbeat strains of "Lollipop, Lollipop" started rolling through her brain, and she found herself silently humming along.

From the moment she'd stripped him bare and gotten her first really good look at him (her apartment had been much darker the first time they were together, with only the occasional ray of moon glow to illuminate their respective bodies), she'd been wanting to lick him like a lollipop, so it was no surprise the song had popped into her head.

Her gaze rose one more time to his. His clouded, blue velvet eyes were watching her through hooded lids. With a smile, she leaned forward, opened her mouth, and ran the flat of her tongue along the bottom of his thick, velvet-over-steel length from base to tip.

Dylan let out a hiss, his hips rising slightly from the cushion of the sofa of their own volition. For a brief second, his eyes fluttered completely closed and the cords of his neck went taut as his head tipped back.

But then he seemed to get himself under control, nostrils flaring and chest rising as he breathed deep. A second later his eyes were open and riveted back on her. The only outward sign of his continued eagerness was his fingers clenching and unclenching in the sofa cushions on either side of his hips, as though trying to keep himself from reaching out to grab her and force her mouth to go exactly where and how he wanted it.

She might have grinned if her lips hadn't been otherwise occupied. Then again, she thought, as she swirled her tongue around the plum-shaped tip, it turned out to be pretty easy to smile around a guy's cock, as long as she was careful with her teeth.

And she was . . . very careful. Careful to use just the right amount of pressure, just the right amount of suction. She licked and nipped and treated him just like the lollipop she'd been humming about, and then tilted her head to take him inside.

Within her closed lips, her tongue swirled around the rigid length, her hand clasped him near the base. Every once in a while, her fingers gave him a squeeze and she made a concerted effort to change up the motion of her mouth, to never continue the same action for long.

"God, you're good at that," he said in a thin, tight voice that made him sound as though he were being strangled. "Whatever happens, don't stop. Fire, flood, earthquake . . . keep going, just like that, and I'll die a happy man."

Since she couldn't speak at the moment, she responded by fluttering her lashes in what she hoped was a coquettish and seductive way. If not . . . well, giving head caused bizarre enough facial expressions to begin with; she didn't want to look like she was being struck by ocular Tourette's at the same time.

Under her elbows, which rested on his long, hard thighs, she could feel Dylan flexing, struggling to control his breathing, trying to hold back his body's sharp response to what she was doing.

But she didn't want him to hold back, didn't want him maintaining control. She wanted him sweating out of every pore, teetering on the edge of the most excruciating orgasm he'd ever experienced, and breaking apart like a meteor rushing to earth.

While one hand continued to apply on-and-off pressure at the base of his cock, her other slipped down between his legs to cup his balls. She both heard and felt him inhale sharply at the added caress, and tasted the salty evidence of his impending climax on her tongue.

Slowly, as the hand on his testicles grew more active, squeezing and rolling the small globes around and against each other, the hand on his penis loosened so that she could take all of him into her mouth. That caused him to shudder again, and she increased the tempo of her suck-and-slide routine to keep him right there, right on the brink.

"Ronnie, that's enough. I'm gonna blow," Dylan rasped out, apparently changing his mind about his previous order to keep sucking no matter what.

She could tell he was almost beyond speech, hopefully beyond rational thought. But despite his request, she didn't stop, didn't even slow her pace. She merely gave his sac a gentle pinch and shook her head as best she could.

With a groan, his abdomen went rigid, his shoulders pressed farther into the sofa back, and his hands finally came up off the couch to grasp her skull. His fingers tangled in her hair, digging against her scalp to both hold her in place and aid her movements now that he realized she was in it for the long haul.

She continued to suck with her entire mouth and circle inside with her tongue for several minutes more, until he was panting for breath, his hips thrusting off the couch faster and faster. The head of his cock hit the back of her throat, but she didn't care. She didn't let up on her speed or pressure.

She could hear the heavy scratch of his breathing and feel the tension building in his long frame. Then he bit out a harsh, "Jesus, I'm coming!" and his whole body went stiff in a wash of release.

She swallowed rhythmically, taking all of him, everything he had to offer, not pulling back until he was completely drained and his entire body had gone slack.

Pushing herself up with her hands on the tops of his thighs, she crawled onto his lap and leaned against his still-heaving chest. His head was tipped back, rolling bonelessly on his neck as his eyes cracked open to meet her gaze.

With the pinkie of her right hand, she slowly reached up to wipe the corners of her mouth.

He grinned at the wicked display, one arm coming up to curve around her back and tug her closer. His other hand rose to brush the hair away from her face and tuck a loose strand behind her ear.

"That was amazing, thank you. And feel free to do it again, any ol' time you like."

She thought about telling him he'd be lucky if she ever did it again—at least with him—but she was feeling too darn passive and pleased with herself to be snarky. Even with him.

So she settled on a noncommittal, "Mmm."

The tips of his fingers skimmed along her skin. Down the side of her throat, over her shoulder, past the curve of her breast and waist, then back up.

It was gently arousing. Not the hot, fast, race-toward-completion sort they'd both experienced and shared so far in this . . . whatever it was they were doing together.

And though she thoroughly enjoyed the wham-bam stuff, this was nice, too. In fact, she thought she might be happy sitting here, just like this, for a good, long while.

At the same time he stroked her up and down, his lips began a light, pleasurable tour of her cheek, her jawline, her earlobe. She moaned softly, feeling her limbs go supple like taffy and a slow warmth build low in her belly.

"I suppose you'll expect me to repay the favor," he said softly against her throat.

Normally, she probably would have, but he'd caught her in a weak moment. She was feeling complacent and generous and not so much like keeping track of who did what to whom or whose turn it was to come next. Besides, the night was young, and if the last time Dylan fucked her was any indication, he wouldn't leave her hanging.

"Nope," she said, shifting slightly on his lap and letting her own fingertips trail through his soft blond hair.

"I'm in charge, remember? You don't have to repay any favors, you only have to do what I tell you."

His mouth quirked up at the corners, and a spark of humor lit in his eyes. "Are you going to tell me to repay the favor?"

An unexpected laugh rolled up from her diaphragm. "No. You did plenty the other night. I'm just waiting for you to revive a little . . ." She wiggled suggestively on his lap, delighted when she felt a telltale stirring on the underside of her thigh. "And then I thought I'd climb on board and ride you like a bronco at a rodeo."

His lips twitched and a brow arched upward. "Done a lot of bronc bustin', have you?"

Shifting back a few inches, she continued to straddle his hips, resting her butt near his knees and her hands on his smooth, broad shoulders.

"By the time I'm finished, you'll be giving me an award for Cowgirl of the Year."

At that, his cock gave a mighty jerk and shot up about forty-five degrees. She chuckled and slid forward to trap the growing appendage between their two bodies. His hands shot out to grip her hips and hold her even closer.

"Have you got a hat?" he asked. "Or maybe some boots and spurs."

Once again, keen disappointment washed over her at her sorely lacking wardrobe. If she spent much more time with this man, she might just have to find a local costume shop and stock up on some tried-and-true favorites. A cowgirl outfit, a dominatrix outfit, maybe a cute little French maid uniform.

She'd never felt compelled to do that sort of thing for any other man, and she *shouldn't* want to do it for

this one. But with his hands on her rear, his cock pulsing between them, and a look of hot, sexual awareness
in his eyes, she almost did.

"Sorry," she told him with a small shake of her head,
giving him no clue of the thoughts muddling her brain,
"you're going to have to settle for me in the buff."

"This is something I think I can handle."

He straightened away from the back of the sofa,
bringing his chest into contact with the tips of her
breasts. His hands squeezed her buttocks, then slid along
the sides of her waist until they reached the undersides
of those breasts. He cupped them and moved so that the
solid plane and wiry hair of his chest tickled her nipples,
which were already beaded but tightened even more at
the contact.

"I won't be sure, though, until after this bronco riding thing you've teased me with." He lifted his head to
nip her chin and then her lips. "Care to saddle up and
show me what it's all about?"

Boy, howdy, was she. His mouth was hypnotizing
her. His hands at her breasts were sending currents of
desire coursing through every cell of her body.

Heat pooled at her center, and her inner muscles
pulsed with need. She wanted nothing more than to grab
his joystick, slide down on the solid, substantial length,
and work them both into a lather.

But she held herself back, concentrating on her
breathing and the axiom that good things come to those
who wait. She didn't just want good, though; she was
holding out for freaking fantastic.

Tipping her head to the side, she narrowed her eyes
and said, "That sounds a bit too much like you being in
charge. You aren't trying to take over, are you?"

"No, ma'am. Not if it means the difference between getting inside you and going home with a raging hard-on."

She smirked, running her hands along the sides of his head to grip his hair.

"Good answer."

Then she lowered her mouth and kissed him.

Row 15

"I think I'm getting the hang of this," Dylan said.

He was sitting on her bed, back propped on pillows that were stacked against the brass headboard, his long legs stretched out in front of him. He was still blessedly naked, but the twist of her snow-white sheets covered him from waist to midthigh.

Ronnie was tucked up to his side, her legs curled beneath her. She was wearing his earlier-discarded shirt, buttoned all the way down, but only halfway up her chest.

After a rather steamy session in the living room that had left her limp as a dishrag, he'd played Prince Gallant by picking her up, carrying her into the bedroom, and setting her carefully on the bed. They'd lain together for a while in the dark silence, and then Dylan had gotten it into his head that he still deserved a knitting lesson.

A naked knitting lesson.

She was surprised by how much he'd gotten done on his project since she'd last seen it. What "it" was, she wasn't entirely sure, but the length of black yarn still seemed to be coming along well.

Though the ratty, mangled end was still there, his stitches were becoming neater and more uniform, and he seemed to be more confident about what he was doing.

"You know what helped me?" he said.

"What?"

She was plastered to his side, her right breast pressed to his left bicep, her right arm draped over his shoulders and back. Every once in a while, she'd reach out to aid his motions, help him with a stitch or a yarn over, but otherwise he was doing fine on his own.

She didn't know whether to be pleased or concerned over that, so she chose to simply ignore it for the time being.

"Realizing that knitting is a lot like sex."

It took a minute for his words to sink in, but even then, she didn't think she'd heard him correctly.

"How in God's name do you make a connection between sex and knitting?" she asked incredulously.

"Well, number one, I'm a guy." He tipped his head in her direction and gave her one of his charming, boy-next-door grins.

"And number two, look at it." He lifted the yarn and needles in his hands, drawing her attention to the long line of his fingers, the light dusting of hair along his knuckles, the firm competence as he looped the soft black yarn around the sturdy white needle.

Okay, so maybe she was starting to see it. Her skin tingled just watching him, and knowing what other delights those big, strong hands were capable of.

"You've got your long, hard stick slipping into the soft, open hole of the yarn. Then back out. Then in. Then out. Then in." He said it all very slowly, using the yarn and needles and those bronzed fingers to illustrate his words.

She had to swallow twice before she felt steady enough to say, "I guess I see your point."

"Yep. As soon as I started thinking of knitting as just another form of making love and realized the whole thing just required a bit of finesse, it all came together for me."

"I see that. After you lose the challenge, maybe you could write a book about knitting just for men. *How to Get Your Yarn Off in Ten Easy Steps.*"

"I'm not going to lose the challenge," he retorted, "but I do like the book idea. It needs a better title, though. *The Joy of Knitting,* maybe."

"Or *Sex and Stitches.*"

"*Knit Your Way to the Perfect Orgasm.*"

"*Two Needles Are Better than One.*"

"Hey." His brows drew together, and he gave her a disgruntled look.

She shrugged, feigning recalcitrance even though she was fully enjoying their little sparring match. "It's a good title."

"Not as good as *Sex and the Single Knitter.*"

"Oooh, that is a good one," she agreed. "You could include all kinds of tips for flying solo. Just a man and his knitting, home alone night after night, the motion of the yarn and needles getting him all hot and horny."

"Are you implying that a man who knits must be lonely and lacking companionship with the opposite sex?"

He didn't bother looking at her this time, but continued his slow, deliberate movements with the needles and yarn.

"Because if you were, I would be forced to point out that the same might be said of women who knit."

"Oh, really? Is that why you were so overjoyed when I publicly challenged you to learn to knit? Because you were eager to show the world what a manly pastime it is?"

"Yep, that's it exactly."

She gave an unladylike snort. "Right."

"It is. See, knitting might have been considered a women-only hobby once upon a time, but now that I've taken it up, I've obviously proven it's a leisure pursuit that crosses the gender line."

With a chuckle, she said, "I can see how you managed to finagle your job at the *Herald*. You're very good at piling on the bullshit."

"It's not bullshit. I'm showing people that real men have needles and they know how to use them."

"I can definitely see that on the dust jacket of your book."

He gave a solemn nod before the room fell into several minutes of heavy silence, the only sounds those of their breathing and the soft click of his needles stitch after stitch.

She didn't know why their easy back-and-forth had suddenly come to an end, but now a heavy tension seemed to hang in the air, stealing any chance of further friendly repartee.

When Dylan did speak, though, she almost wished he'd kept his mouth shut and left them in strange but companionable silence.

"I've been thinking about that discussion we were having earlier," he murmured.

Her legs were falling asleep, so she squirmed a bit

on the mattress to find a more comfortable position. "Men who knit getting laid more often than those who don't?"

"No, although I'm sure there have been studies done to prove that that's true."

She nodded but didn't bother to hide the sarcasm in her voice. "Oh, I'm sure. That's why you see all those yarn groupies hanging around outside craft stores."

He made a face but didn't rise to the bait. "No, I mean what we were talking about way earlier, when I first got here."

The reminder made her tense. In the past few hours, she'd done an admirable job of blocking out the mood she'd been in when he'd arrived and what had caused it. She'd especially been blocking the fact that she'd cried and wailed and all but had a nervous breakdown right in front of him.

Was this the point when he'd throw it back in her face? Rub it in and start heckling her, or bribing her with the threat of making her private life public?

If so, she seriously thought she might maim him with his own knitting needles. Tie him up with that black yarn and spend a couple of hours treating him like a life-sized voodoo doll.

Heart pounding in her chest, she quietly asked, "What about it?"

"Well, if you ever tell anyone I said this, I'll of course deny it, but you're a damn good writer. Sometimes, I think you could write rings around me."

She blinked, remaining so still, she wasn't even sure she was breathing. Never in a million years would she have expected a statement like that to pass Dylan Stone's lips. Not even after what they'd shared.

Hot, sweaty, teeth-rattling monkey sex was one thing.

Complimenting a rival journalist was something else entirely.

She felt tears prick at the backs of her eyes, and then felt them prick harder as the oddity of being moved by his words caused even stronger emotions to well up.

Normally, her patent response would have been *Damn straight*, and then perhaps a tirade about all the reasons she should have gotten his job, and all the reasons he was underqualified for the position. But she couldn't seem to rouse the proper level of ire or disdain for either.

Instead she managed a shaky "Thank you" after two failed attempts and one embarrassing clearing of her throat.

"You're welcome." If he noticed the threadiness of her tone or her statue-like stiffness at his side, he didn't let on.

Setting his knitting aside, he shifted on the mattress so that they were facing each other. Her arm fell from his shoulders and she moved a little away, only to have him hitch closer once again.

Meeting her gaze, he said, "I'm not sure if you realize this, but people *love* your column in the *Sentinel*. Women, especially. It's hip and edgy, sometimes laugh-out-loud funny, and offers practical advice for the city's residents."

The only thing she could think to say was *thank you*, but she was afraid of sounding like a broken record, so she said nothing.

He lifted a hand to stroke her hair, the other rubbing gently along the fabric of his shirt that covered her arm.

"My point," he continued, "is that you might not see that as being big enough or important enough, but it is. It's a reflection of you, something that comes to you naturally and that you have a real talent for. And money and prestige aren't everything. Sometimes just having a job that pays the bills, lets you live comfortably, maybe help your family or splurge on yourself once in a while, is enough. You don't have to kill yourself to make and do more, more, more. You don't have to make yourself sick worrying about what you'll do in five or ten years."

She understood what he was telling her, but she'd spent so long worrying over every penny, feeling like no matter how much she earned, it was *never* enough, that she wasn't sure she could believe him.

She had a stable, well-paying job, one that would leave most people living a contented, stress-free life. But still she clipped coupons, bought her clothes and furniture and tableware at secondhand stores, turned in her recyclables for cash. She read newspapers and magazines at work so she wouldn't have to pay for her own subscriptions. She drove an ancient Chrysler that still looked good but had well over a hundred thousand miles on it because it had been considerably cheaper than newer models. And she'd never owned a VCR, a DVD player, or even a stereo because it seemed like a waste of money when she could simply watch basic cable or listen to the radio.

Most people would probably consider her antiquated or out of touch.

She considered herself somewhere between down-right cheap and shrewdly frugal.

But when people grew up the way she had, the fear

stayed with them, and they would do whatever it took to avoid living at that level of poverty again.

She'd never discussed this part of her life with anyone else before. Not even her parents. But for some reason, she felt safe talking about it with Dylan. He was being so kind and accepting, and seemed to be genuinely trying to help.

Though it nicked her pride to put voice to her thoughts, she knew that if anyone would have answers for her, it would be Dylan. In so many ways, he was a mirror image of her. The other side of her coin.

They were different in a lot of ways, but they were alike in many, too. They were both stubborn and arrogant and ambitious and competitive. They were both damn good writers, attractive, and fantastic in bed.

Hey, if a girl was being honest with herself, then she might as well be honest about everything.

And where they differed . . . him being laid-back while she was sometimes incredibly uptight . . . well, maybe they could help each other. Maybe she could convince him to lean into certain aspects of his life more, and he could teach her how to relax and stop obsessing about every little thing.

"So," she said slowly, using the tip of one perfectly rounded, paint-tipped finger to draw patterns on the bit of sheet that covered his upper thigh, "hypothetically speaking, if one wanted to loosen her grip on the purse strings slightly, how would one go about that?"

He grinned at her, apparently amused by her complicated phrasing of what was in essence a simple question.

"Well," he said, mimicking her serious tone, "one could start by sitting down and figuring out how much one spends on the necessities each year, and then

comparing that with one's annual income. I think you
would be pleasantly surprised to realize you're probably a lot better off than you believe. Then, one might
hire a financial planner to help squirrel away some
money . . . maybe open some investments, buy into
some mutual funds, start contributing to a retirement
fund of some sort."

A sparkle lit his eyes as he continued. "You may be
interested to note that you aren't even allowed to take
money out of a Roth IRA until you turn fifty-nine without being penalized, which means that any money you
contributed would just be sitting there, earning interest,
and you couldn't touch it. If you opened an account
now, think of how much money you'd have saved up
when you finally did retire."

His brows were waggling now, and she found herself nearly smiling, nearly feeling lighthearted about
her finances, which wasn't a sensation she could ever
remember experiencing before.

She had a savings account, of course, but she'd never
thought about some of the things he'd mentioned.

Finding a financial planner whose job it was to see
that she stayed afloat, didn't spend beyond her means,
and would always have enough to fall back on in case
of a rainy day . . . even if that rainy day turned into a
full-blown tsunami season.

And the stock market . . . she'd always been too nervous about money, wanting to keep it with her—as
close as possible to being right there in her hand—to
actually buy into something like that. But if she started
small and got involved in some low-risk investments,
she thought she could let go of her white-knuckled grip

long enough to see if they actually worked out to her benefit.

She liked his last suggestion best. She'd never thought of starting a retirement fund outside of the one provided by her employer, but it made total sense. Not only would she have more control over it, but it would be that much more of a cushion to fall back on later, as well.

She considered it all for a moment, wondering if the modicum of tension she felt loosening near her stomach and leaching out of her body through the soles of her feet could become a permanent sensation. Could maybe even grow and expand until she didn't need an entire roll of Tums to get through the bill-paying process each month.

Meeting his gaze, she said, "I find your philosophy interesting and would like to subscribe to your newsletter."

He threw back his head and laughed. "You've got it. I may have to stop at the library on the way home, though, to read up on some of this stuff. Or, you know, talk to my dad, who happens to be a CPA."

Her eyes widened and her mouth fell open. "You're kidding me! So you really do know about all this financial planning stuff."

He shrugged one strong, bare shoulder. "Some, yeah. What I've picked up from him over the years, and then if I have any specific questions, he's happy to answer them. He's always after us kids to do this, do that—prepare for our financial futures, sock something away for a rainy day."

"You jerk," she rapped out, socking him lightly on the chest. "You had me believing you were some kind of financial whiz kid trapped in a jock's body, and here you have an inside source. You're a money tease!"

His amused expression deepened, and he rubbed at the spot near his shoulder where she'd punched him, acting like the light tap had actually hurt.

"Look who's talking. I offered you a thousand dollars to teach me to knit and you've been taking your own sweet time about it. Do you think I don't know you've been farming it?"

Her cheeks flushed at being called out, because that's exactly what she'd been doing.

"I had to. Otherwise you might have zipped ahead to win our wager, and I couldn't let that happen. Just be glad I didn't teach you to knit rows of knots or something equally devious. I may not have been the best teacher, but at least what I've shown you so far *is* the proper way to knit. Besides," she told him, keeping her face tipped away, "that makes me a yarn tease, not a money tease."

"A tease is a tease, babe, no matter how you slice it. Lucky for you, I like that in a woman." He waited a beat, and then added, "And I think it's about time for me to be in charge again."

A wicked glint slid behind the lapis blue of his eyes a split second before he sprang forward, knocked her to her back, and pinned her to the mattress. She gave a shriek of surprise before the air was driven from her lungs.

Holding her arms above her head, he grinned down at her, his body pressed to hers from breast to ankle. His scratchy legs tickled her own, and only his shirt on her body kept them from touching skin-to-skin from the waist up.

It did nothing, though, to keep intense, immediate awareness from swamping her senses and sending a shock of hot, demanding desire straight to her core.

Lord, what this man did to her with just a touch, and sometimes just a look, should be illegal. What they did together probably *was* illegal in twenty-five of the fifty states.

His face hovered centimeters from hers, his warm breath washing over her, raising gooseflesh along her arms and chest. Just below the hem of the shirt, the proof of his arousal nudged at her, and she wanted nothing more than to spread her legs and invite him in.

"I've got you, my pretty," he murmured in a soft, mesmerizing voice, tracing his lips along the line of her jaw. "And your little dog, too."

"Sorry," she said in an equally low voice, "there are no dogs here, only one lonely little pussy in need of some petting."

To emphasize her words, she opened her legs and let him fall even farther into the cradle of her thighs.

Heat like that from an atomic explosion filled his countenance, and she thought she actually heard a snarl roll up from his throat. His teeth latched on to her neck, gently nipping at a line of muscle that ran all the way down to her clavicle. At the same time, he lifted her legs straight up along the line of his chest so that her ankles rested near his shoulders.

"It's deeper this way," he hissed in a strained voice, "and I've been dreaming about having your ankles up around my neck since the first time we met."

"Just as I thought," she huffed, finding it none too easy to speak with her body twisted awkwardly, and desire humming in her veins. "You're a perv."

"Not perverted. Just horny, and intelligent enough to notice a smokin'-hot woman when I see one."

Grasping his cock, he found her opening and drove inside, sending the oxygen from both her lungs and diaphragm like a balloon with a slow leak.

One thrust and he was buried to the hilt. No preliminaries, no foreplay. But then, none were necessary. She was as hot and ready for him as though he'd spent hours priming the pump. Maybe more so.

Her blood pounded through her veins, sizzling like live wires and sending hot rushes of sensation to all the right places. Her skin tickled in anticipation. Her legs, sticking straight up in the air, shook with need.

And between her legs, where Dylan was stuffed tight, filling her almost to overflowing, she was swollen and wet and desperate for satisfaction.

His rough palms ran up and down her legs, grazing her thighs both inside and out, her bottom, behind her knees, her taut insteps. And he pounded into her, long, hard strokes meant to bring her to orgasm in record time.

"What about you?" he asked, his words broken by the slam of their bodies and the exertion of energy. "What did you think about me the first time you saw me?"

"I thought . . . too bad I hate this guy; he looks like he'd be a really great lay."

His lips twitched, even as sweat dotted his face and chest. "Oh, yeah?"

She rolled her eyes, recognizing a worm in the water when she saw one. He might be fishing for compliments, but that didn't mean she had to bite.

"Don't push your luck," she warned. "And stop talking. You've got work to do!"

He didn't stop grinning, but he did shut up and turn his attention back to curling her toes and sending steam shooting out her ears.

While her fingers curled into the sheets and she arched her back, panting as excruciatingly pleasurable sensations began to build, his slow stroking of her lower body turned into a strong, solid grip. First at her knees, then her thighs, and finally her hips. He held her tight, bringing her forward and back to meet his powerful thrusts.

In only seconds, their movements grew faster and more frantic. Their mingled gasps and groans, along with the low creak of the bed rocking beneath them, echoed through the room.

She bit her lip to keep from whimpering, but couldn't remain completely silent. "Yes," she breathed. And then again and again, the soft words slipped from her mouth, "Yes, yes, *yesssss*."

Dylan held her gaze, his arm, chest, and abdominal muscles pulled taut, his face flushed with the need for release.

"Come for me," he commanded, his words punctuated by low grunts and the rhythmic slapping of their bodies. "Come now."

He was at the very edge of exploding, but he needn't have worried, and no orders or requests were necessary, because she was right there with him.

Heat flooded her system until she thought she might spontaneously combust. Her nerve endings were alive with need and awareness, rising to the very surface of her skin so that even the air around her felt like a caress.

Around his cock, her internal muscles fluttered and

spasmed with approaching climax. It was there, shimmering, vibrating, hovering just out of reach.

And then, with one hand still digging into the flesh of her hip, Dylan reached between her legs and over her mound to slide his thumb into her plump, wet folds and press firmly against her clit. That was all it took to send her screaming, bucking, shuddering into orgasm.

She would think later that it was a wonder her neighbors didn't call the police and report a murder taking place in her apartment, but at that moment she couldn't have held back if a thousand deadly vipers had been poised to strike at the slightest provocation.

Her mouth was barely open, ready to voice her completion, when Dylan followed her over. His thumb stayed on her clitoris, circling, rubbing, and he continued to both thrust into her and yank her against him as he gave a harsh shout and ground out a crude, "Fuck, yes" just before his body went rigid and he poured himself inside her.

He collapsed atop her, nearly folding her in half, but it took a good five minutes for the discomfort to even sink in.

"Um . . . Dylan?" she managed, and only had to clear her throat and lick her dry lips twice to get it out.

"Hmm?"

"You're crushing me. Not to mention turning me into a cheap card table." Her legs were still caught inside his arms, against his chest, her ankles pushed practically to her ears.

"God, I'm sorry," he groaned. His movements were stiff and slow, but he hoisted himself off her, gently lowering her legs back to the mattress before rolling to his side and propping himself on an elbow to gaze down at her.

Reaching across her near-comatose form, he used the tips of two fingers to toy with her loose and now-damp curls. He tugged a thick strand over her shoulder and dusted the nipple of her left breast with the ends. She wouldn't have thought it possible after what they'd just done, but the tip began to bead and tighten in response to the direct stimulation.

"You probably don't want to hear this from someone you consider to be your archnemesis," he murmured in a distracted tone, "but I think you may be ruining me for other women. If we keep this up, my dick is going to shrivel up and fall off."

An image of that unlikely turn of events flashed in her head and she gave a soft snort of amusement.

"That would definitely be a shame," she replied. And she meant it. He was so damn good with that thing, it would be a shame to deprive the women of the world of such an amazing and impressive instrument.

But what circled even more menacingly through her brain was his previous statement about being ruined for other women.

A part of her hoped he was right, which was bad enough.

The really scary thing, though, the part that froze her blood and sank to the bottom of her stomach like a stone, was her growing suspicion that he may have ruined her for other men.

Row 16

Dylan stayed at her apartment until early Sunday morning. He cooked breakfast for her, which she found both sweet and disconcerting.

She didn't want him being nice to her, doing things for her, slipping under her radar and nestling beneath her skin, somewhere close to the region of her heart. That would be bad, bad, bad, bad, bad.

So even though she ate his fluffy scrambled eggs and light, airy buckwheat pancakes—and enjoyed listening to him whistle while he worked, and watching him move around her tiny kitchen in nothing more than a pair of loose, faded Levi's—she wouldn't let it get to her, wouldn't let it mean anything.

They'd had amazing sex six or eight or twenty times, and he was simply feeding her to keep up her strength. No big deal.

It didn't mean anything, and neither did the naked knitting lessons he'd insisted they continue, which *always* led to much more fun and creative things to do while naked.

But when he scribbled his father's phone number on a slip of paper and pressed it into her hand, she could only stand there, dumbfounded while he leaned in to place a soft kiss on her lips, whispered good-bye, and closed the door behind him.

He was only going back to his own apartment. He had some work to get done by morning, he said, and she was sure they'd see each other again soon. If not at The Penalty Box, then when he next showed up at her door looking for more knitting instructions and hot jungle lovin'.

It wasn't permanent, and every time she came down from a Dylan-induced orgasm she thought had to be the biggest, brightest, best, most amazing she would ever experience—at least until the next one came around— she swore it would be the last time she'd let him touch her. That she would get up, get dressed, kick him out, and tell him never to return.

And every time, she let herself capitulate, let herself play along for just a while longer, let herself bask in indescribable pleasure and enjoy the company of a man who turned out not to be the world's biggest jackass, after all.

She planned to keep that little nugget of truth under wraps for the time being, though, especially considering she'd based the better part of her career *and* personality on shouting it from the rooftops and disparaging him every chance she got.

But no matter what they did behind closed doors, or how well they got along when no one was looking, it wasn't going to last.

She was sure he knew it, too. That as soon as . . . whatever was going on between them . . . ran its course, they would go back to hating each other.

So why, then, had he given her his father's phone

number and whispered, "Call him. He'll help you out," before he'd left?

Why was he so willing to help her overcome her fears of never having enough, and let her be in contact with his family when he knew she would be referring to him by any number of unflattering, thinly veiled four-letter descriptions in future columns and dares?

Staring down at the piece of paper in her hand, she debated calling Dylan's dad right that minute to pick his brain about her financial future. She really wanted to talk to the man and find out what she was doing right, what she was doing wrong, and what she could be doing even better.

But she didn't think that simply talking to a knowledgeable accountant would fix her problems. Not all of them, anyway. She had a feeling—heck, she *knew*— that her anxieties ran deeper than just how many savings accounts or mutual funds she tucked money into.

Until she dealt with the underlying cause of her personal demons, she thought, feeling like she was channeling Dr. Phil, she didn't think she would be able to take positive steps, move forward, and truly breathe easy.

Crossing the living room, she tucked the phone number beneath the edge of her cordless phone base, then continued on to her bedroom, where she changed out of her Austin Powers *Do I make you horny, baby? Do I?* shorty pajamas, which she'd finally had the courage to wear in front of Dylan.

Courage—ha! She'd had the time of her life donning them in the dark while he was sound asleep and snoring lightly in her bed, then rousing him with kisses and making sure he saw the lime-green message on the tank top's iron-on front.

He'd wasted no time in answering the groovy question, either . . . by pressing the proof of his randiness against her hip, stripping Austin and his shag-o-rific slogans from her body, and then spending the better part of an hour kissing her from head to toe. Licking her from head to toe. Making her whimper and beg and shiver with ecstasy from head to toe.

Yes, these were good, good pajamas. She might never wear another pair again, at least not when Dylan was around.

Slipping into comfortable blue jeans and a burgundy knit pullover, she pulled her hair into a loose ponytail, grabbed her purse, and left her apartment.

The trip to her parents' house in Mercer, Pennsylvania, wasn't one she made very often and took longer than she remembered. Still, it was a nice, relaxing drive, and once she got out of the city, the traffic thinned out, the roads turned more rural, and she was able to enjoy the changing leaves on the trees and the brisk autumn morning.

Her parents lived in a small town, in a moderately sized, two-story house that sat a few yards back from the road. There was a medium white birch in the front yard, a couple of pines in the back, and flower beds lining the porch and driveway that—thanks to her mother's green thumb—bloomed into wild bursts of color during the spring and summer months.

She pulled into the gravel drive and parked behind her mother's tan, two-door sedan. Getting out of the car, she took her time walking around to the narrow walkway as her gaze landed on a new wooden swing sitting motionless beside the thin, leafless trunk of the birch.

It was a beautiful, golden oak with rounded edges

and hearts cut out of the backboards, hanging from a matching frame. Her father's handiwork, no doubt.

While she'd been growing up, he'd worked as a carpenter and handyman whenever he could, and when they'd bought this house, he'd spent a good deal of time fixing it up and getting it to where he wanted it. Now it seemed that he'd moved on to the aesthetics.

Taking the two wide steps up to the front porch, she used the brass door knocker to announce her presence, then turned the knob and walked in.

She would never dream of leaving her apartment unlocked in the heart of Cleveland, even though the city's crime rate was down significantly over previous years, but her parents felt completely safe in Mercer. They locked their doors at night, but left them open during the day so they could come and go as they pleased, and so that neighbors could get in to borrow something if they needed it, whether her folks were home or not.

It was a nice attitude to have. A little naive, maybe, but nice. And a part of small-town living that Ronnie only now realized she missed.

"Mom? Dad?" she called out, closing the door behind her and kicking off her shoes in the entryway. She left them on the brightly colored mat that already held a pair of her father's work boots and her mother's tennis shoes.

"Veronica?" She heard her mother's muted voice a second before she appeared in the hallway from the direction of the kitchen.

"Veronica! What a surprise." Wiping her hands on the apron that hung around her neck and tied at her waist, she came forward to give Ronnie a big hug.

Seeing her mother was like looking into a mirror

twenty years in the future. They had the same build, the same smile, and the same brown eyes and wavy brown hair, though her mother's was a tad lighter these days, colored to hide the gray.

"I must have sensed you were coming. I just put a batch of chocolate chip cookies in the oven."

"My favorite," Ronnie said with a smile.

Her mother smiled back. "I know. So what are you doing here?" she asked, taking Ronnie's hand and pulling her farther into the house, toward the kitchen.

With a shrug, Ronnie said, "I woke up this morning with no last-minute work that needed to be done by to-morrow and decided I wanted to see you."

"Well, you should have called first. I'd have fixed lunch and made sure Daddy was home."

"He's not here?"

"No, but he should be back soon. He went over to the Wilsons' after church to help them put up the rail-ing on their new deck."

While her mother moved around to the side of the center island nearest the stove, Ronnie sat on one of the stools on the other. She hoped her cheeks weren't visibly red with the knowledge that while her parents had been in church, praying and asking forgiveness for their sins, her body had been twisted like a pretzel around Dylan and they'd been willingly beating a path straight to Hell.

Thankfully, her mother didn't seem to notice that her thoughts had turned decidedly un-holy. She set a glass of milk in front of Ronnie and then returned to filling a cookie sheet with dollops of sweet, buttery dough.

Both the cookies in the oven and the raw dough in

the large mixing bowl smelled delicious, and Ronnie
was reminded of those rare times as a child when her
mother would splurge on the ingredients for cookies
and let them all help mix the batter and plop it onto the
sheets. Only about half of it ended up as actual cookies,
though, since the kids tended to eat the dough straight
out of the bowl before it ever made it to the oven.

That was a happy memory from her childhood, and
she found herself smiling. Maybe Dylan was right. Not
everything she'd been through growing up had been
bad, and she'd do well to spend more time remembering the good stuff than worrying about the bad repeating itself.

For old times' sake, she reached out and ran a finger
through the glob of raw cookie dough in the center of
the bowl, then brought it to her mouth. Her eyes drifted
closed in ecstasy as sugar and flour and butter and semi-
sweet chocolate chips melted on her tongue and slid
down her throat.

Her mother laughed, leaning out of the way when
she went back for another swipe. "I remember when
you kids used to do that. I let you because you liked it
so much, but I was always worried one of you would
get sick from eating all those raw ingredients."

"None of us ever did," Ronnie mumbled around her
sticky index finger.

"No, but it's a mother's job to worry."

Ronnie finished licking her finger, a ball of tension
starting to form low in her belly. It was a mother's job to
worry—though she didn't necessarily think that should
be the case—but was it also a daughter's?

The oven timer began its annoying beep, and her
mom turned to remove the first sheet of cookies, done

to a perfect golden brown. She slipped them off the parchment paper and onto a rack.

"Don't burn yourself," she reproached as Ronnie immediately reached out to snitch one.

But, of course, she did, and she didn't even care. Burnt tongue or not, she didn't think there was anything in the world better than homemade chocolate chip cookies hot out of the oven.

After polishing off two, she brushed her hands on the legs of her jeans and took a sip of milk to wash them down.

"Mom, can I ask you something?"

"Of course." Without bothering to look up, she slid a fresh sheet into the oven, then started filling another.

"How are you and Dad doing these days? Financially, I mean."

A quizzical expression crossed her mother's face. "Fine, sweetheart, why?"

Ronnie was surprised that her mother didn't understand, didn't immediately sense what she was after. "Because, you know . . . of the way things were while we were growing up."

That seemed to give her mother pause, her brows knitting in a bit of a frown while her hands slowed their repetitive motions.

"What things?" she asked.

Again, Ronnie was startled by her mother's response. She sat back on her stool, her fingers tightening imperceptibly on the edge of the island.

Softly, with her heart pounding in her chest, she said, "Everything, Mom. We had nothing growing up. There were times we lived in the car, times we went without enough food to eat or shoes that fit. How can you not be afraid of that happening again every day of your life?"

Finally grasping the gravity of the conversation, her mother set aside the bowl and spoon. When the oven timer went off again, she quickly punched the button to silence it and removed the tray of baked cookies, placing them on the stovetop to keep them from burning. Returning to the island, she shed the pair of oven mitts and slid onto the opposite stool, holding Ronnie's solemn gaze.

"There's no doubt that your father and I were too young to get married and start a family. If we'd known in the beginning how difficult things would be, I'm sure we both would have chosen to wait a few more years before jumping into anything. But we loved all of you kids very much, and did the best we could."

"I know that," Ronnie acquiesced, feeling a pinch of guilt. "But, Mom, we had *so little*. There were times when we literally had nothing. And now . . ."

She swallowed, her throat growing tight with tears and long-suppressed emotional trauma.

"And now, I find myself constantly worrying about money. I clip coupons like I'm on a fixed income. I buy generic *everything,* brand-name *nothing*. I buy all my clothes and shoes at thrift shops. When it comes time to pay bills every month, I practically have to load up on Xanax and cheap wine to keep from having a panic attack, and I have plenty of money in the bank, so I *shouldn't* be panicked. I live with this constant sense of foreboding, scared to death that I'm going to wake up one day to find myself with nothing, needing to live in my car, eat out of Dumpsters, beg on the street . . ."

"Oh, darling." Hopping off the stool she'd only

climbed onto a minute before, her mother came around to wrap her in a giant bear hug. Holding her tight, she rocked Ronnie back and forth, pressing her cheek to the side of her head.

For long moments, Ronnie let herself absorb her mother's warmth, float in the comfort and security of her embrace.

"I had no idea you felt this way, sweetheart. Times were tough when you were little, I know, but I didn't realize you'd carried that all the way into adulthood."

"How could I not?" Ronnie asked in a watery voice. "I remember how cramped that car was when the seven of us had to squeeze in and sleep there every night. I remember how often we went to bed hungry, or you and Daddy stayed up into the wee hours worrying about how far you could stretch his pay from one odd job or another."

Pulling back a fraction, her mother ran her fingers through Ronnie's hair. Both their faces were lined with tears. With the hem of her apron, her mother dried Ronnie's cheeks first, then her own.

"I'm so sorry, sweetheart. I wish I could go back and change things for all you kids . . . for myself, too, sometimes."

"I know. I know that. And I'm not blaming you or Dad. That's not why I brought it up," Ronnie rushed to assure her. "I just . . . I guess I wanted to know how you and Dad are doing now. If everything is okay, if you're hurting for money at all, if you worry about your future or paying your bills or one day ending up on the street again."

When Ronnie once again started to cry, her mother went for a box of tissues for them both.

"Your father and I are doing just fine now. I love my job at the bakery, and your father never seems at a loss for work. We've got a nice nest egg tucked away, and this beautiful house you helped us buy is ours now, free and clear."

"And you don't worry?" Ronnie pressed. "At all?"

"I don't. Oh, I won't say the thought doesn't occasionally cross my mind—or your father's. After all, no one knows what tomorrow might bring. But I don't let it keep me up at night or stop me from enjoying my life to the fullest."

She placed her hands on either side of Ronnie's face and looked her straight in the eye. "And you shouldn't, either."

Blinking rapidly, Ronnie wished she could take her mother's words to heart. They sounded nice, so sensible. But saying was easier than doing, and while Ronnie might agree, might want to throw herself into that approach enthusiastically and without reservation, she wasn't sure she knew how.

"As hard as things were while you were growing up," her mother continued, "the most important thing to remember is how we stayed together and worked together to get through it. We were a very strong, loving family, and those years weren't all bad. We may not have had money, but we loved and supported each other."

That was certainly true. She didn't think of it very often, but now she recalled just how much laughing they'd done when she was a kid. There had been sing-alongs and campfires, long walks along dirt roads and in the woods, and trips to the creek where they'd spent hours swimming and splashing and swinging from tree branches into the water. Her parents had always done

their best to make things fun and try to help them forget that they didn't always have a roof over their heads
or enough food to fill their bellies.

They had been *close* when she was a child. She and
her brothers and sisters had been inseparable, and God
help anybody who messed with them. Mess with one
Chasen, you messed with them all; it had practically
been their family motto.

Until that moment, Ronnie hadn't realized just how
far she'd drifted from everyone. She visited her parents
only once or twice a year, even though she lived only a
couple of hours away. She exchanged the occasional
letter or phone call with her brothers and sisters, but
didn't really keep up with their lives. She couldn't even
remember where they all lived—states, yes, but town
names? Actual addresses or phone numbers by heart?

Had she let her fear of going back to living hand-to-
mouth cause her to push her own family away, when
they were the ones she could count on most in the
whole world, no matter what?

What a dolt she'd been. She had nieces and nephews
she barely knew, but suddenly, she *wanted* to know
them, very much. She felt almost desperate to contact
her siblings, to not just make an obligatory phone call,
but to *really* find out how everyone was doing and
make a point of staying in better touch.

As soon as she got home, she would dig out her address book, *memorize* every single one of their addresses
and phone numbers, and call them all. She would find out
how they were doing, make sure they knew she loved
them and didn't want to keep her distance any longer, invite them all for Christmas.

Given the size of her apartment, that last might not

be feasible, but maybe she could put the wheels in motion for a big family gathering at her parents' house over the holidays.

She could bring Dylan and introduce him as the man who routinely made her eyes roll back in her head. Tell everyone that while she didn't necessarily like him, she no longer *despised* him like a bad case of poison ivy on her no-no area.

Okay, that probably wasn't such a good idea. By Christmas, she and Dylan probably wouldn't even be heating up the sheets anymore.

Since she hadn't come to her parents' house to contemplate her nonrelationship with Dylan, she shrugged off the small niggle of regret that tugged at her insides at the thought of them going their separate ways, and instead tried to focus on what her mother had said.

"I loved it when we used to make those mountain pies out of white bread and cheap pie filling," she said, surprising herself with the cheerfulness in her voice.

She *did* have happy memories of her childhood, and she wasn't quite sure why—or how—she'd stuffed them down so far and let the bad memories and the fears they generated take over so thoroughly.

Her mother smiled. "And catch crawfish in the stream."

"And frogs, and newts, and sometimes a water snake, but that was more Joe and Mike."

With a shudder, her mother said, "One of the many delights of raising boys."

They laughed, and a few minutes later were back to baking cookies. While her mother slid a new, full sheet into the oven and reset the timer, Ronnie picked up the wooden spoon and started dropping dollops of dough onto another.

This was nice—being home, helping her mother in the kitchen, simply relaxing and enjoying herself. She couldn't remember the last time she'd done something like this without feeling as though the weight of the world balanced on her narrow shoulders, and it made her all the more determined to get past her own insecurities so she could start making new, worry-free memories. With her family, her friends, and in every aspect of her life.

While they baked and chatted, keeping the conversation light, Ronnie made a mental list of what she needed to do when she got back to Cleveland.

She would call Dylan's father, for one. If he was as financially savvy as Dylan claimed, she wanted to talk to him and get some advice about handling her own money, and it would probably be smart to do that before she and his son went their separate ways.

Depending on what he suggested, she suspected she would also look into hiring a financial adviser to help her put her money here, there, and everywhere in order to be safe and grow as much as possible, whether it was through earned interest or intelligent investments.

By the time the sound of crunching gravel alerted them to her father's return, she felt lighter and more relaxed than she could ever remember. Her mother was drying her hands on a dish towel, preparing to meet him at the front door, but Ronnie stopped her.

"Let me surprise him," she said, wiping her own hands, then picking out the biggest fresh-out-of-the-oven cookie she could find.

With a grin, she skipped out of the kitchen and down the hall in time for the door to swing open.

"Hi, Daddy," she singsonged, bringing her father's head up.

His eyes went wide for a startled moment before he spotted the cookie she held out. Reaching for it, he smiled and opened his arms, and she wasted no time launching herself into his welcoming embrace.

Row 17

"So how's your knitting coming along, Aunt Bea?"

"Bite me, Hoolihan."

Sitting in the center of Zack's deep, soft, over-stuffed leather sofa, Dylan scowled and continued to concentrate on his stitches.

He already felt like a pansy, sitting here with his testosterone-laden friends, watching the Steelers game and *knitting,* for God's sake. He should be perched on the edge of the sofa, tipping back a brewski, and shouting at the screen like Zack and Gage.

But his deadline for making it or breaking it on this latest challenge was fast approaching, and he wasn't about to let their usual Sunday get-together set him back and cost him his prized Harrison Award. Not to mention the humiliation he would suffer when the entire city discovered he'd been unable to complete a simple task that every high school girl and her grandmother knew how to do.

So he'd bitten the bullet, packed up his needles and yarn, and come over to Zack's to watch the game and take his licks from two guys who'd never had to check their balls at the door just to keep from getting their asses handed to them by a woman.

Even if that woman was Ronnie, and she happened to be smokin' hot when he got her alone, winning this challenge was for the greater good. For his job, his pride, and the pride of every red-blooded male walking the streets of America.

And if that meant taking some ribbing from his supposed best friends, so be it.

He finished a row, dragged another length of yarn from the rolled-up black ball, and turned his needles to start back the other way.

He would be glad when he won this bet and could once again turn the tables on Ronnie. What he would make her do, he wasn't quite sure.

He'd been contemplating it ever since she'd dropped the knitting bomb on him, but now that they'd started sleeping together, things like collecting litter along major freeways in a string bikini in the dead of winter, or shaving her head and dressing like a Hare Krishna to distribute pamphlets outside the bus station, had morphed into decidedly more sexual tasks.

Entering the Miss Ohio pageant and requiring her to use her amazing mouth for the talent portion. Working at a strip club and doing a little pole or lap dancing— provided his was the only lap she gyrated on. Dressing in skintight black leather and spending a day with him at the *Herald,* keeping him on the straight and narrow, and putting him to work and treating him like the bad, bad boy he was if he slacked off on the job.

It didn't take much of that for his Johnnie Walker to sit up and begin to beg, and he moved the length of his knitting down a few inches to cover his crotch. If Zack

or Gage noticed his boner, they would no doubt think
he got off on playing with yarn, and that was something they'd *never* let him live down.

Until the end of time, anytime they passed by a
scarf, a hat, a pair of gloves or mittens, it would be,
*Ooh, Stone, does this make you hot? Would you two
like to be alone?*

No, thank you.

When another commercial came on, leaving Zack
without active play to distract him, he took a long pull
on his bottle of beer and turned back to Dylan. Reaching
for the end of the knitting connected to the needles—
and entirely too close to the bulge behind Dylan's
zipper—he said, "It doesn't look like you've gotten very
far. What's it supposed to be, anyway?"

"A scarf," Dylan replied shortly.

Though he wasn't sure it looked much like one at
the moment. The end was a mishmash of stitches, too
tight and then too loose as he'd been struggling to
learn, struggling to do everything right.

A few inches up, he'd gotten the hang of things . . .
give or take. At any rate, the last few inches he'd done
looked better than those first several rows.

But if it was going to be a scarf, he'd better get a
move on to finish it. At its current length, it would
probably do better as a bib.

"I've only got a week left to get this done and show
Ronnie that I learned to knit, or my ass is grass. I'm
going to work on this thing every waking minute until
it's done, and get my Harrison Award back."

"Hey, you know us," Zack replied with a shrug.
"We're just kidding around."

"Yeah," Gage said. "I'm kind of impressed myself.

You don't work those things quite as fast as Jenna, but you're not doing half bad."

"And you know we always want you to win these competitions, too," Zack put in. "It wouldn't do to let the ladies pull one over on us men. Shit, we'd never hear the end of it if they did."

A moment passed in silent agreement as Zack and Gage both took a sip of their beers and all three of them nodded in deep male accord.

Dylan had every intention of winning this bet, even if Ronnie was doing her level best to distract him with slick, sweaty, mind-numbing sex.

That was something his friends weren't yet aware of, and he intended to keep it that way for a while longer. The knitting thing was bad enough; he didn't need them ragging on him for falling into bed with his archnemesis, too. He preferred to take his lumps one at a time, thank you very much.

But without letting them know *why* he was bringing it up, this did seem like the perfect opportunity to follow through on Ronnie's suggestion that he try to get an exclusive interview with Zack.

He'd been thinking about it all day, ever since she'd brought it up and the lightbulb had gone off over his head flashing, *Duh! I can't believe it took* Ronnie *to point out what was in front of my face the entire time! Bang, bang, bang.*

That last was the sound of him mentally smacking the heel of his hand against his own forehead.

"Actually," he said, choosing his words carefully, "I've been thinking maybe it's time to put an end to this one-upmanship business with Ronnie."

Zack froze with his beer bottle halfway to his lips, and Gage turned his gaze almost in slow motion from the TV to Dylan.

"Come again?" Gage said.

Lifting a shoulder, Dylan kept his attention on his needles and yarn. "It's getting a little old, don't you think? We've made each other do just about all the zany, ridiculous, humiliating things we can. If we keep this up much longer, I'm afraid we'll cross the line into true degradation or even something seriously dangerous. I think it might be time to wrap it up and move on."

"Move on to what?" Zack wanted to know.

I'm so glad you asked, Dylan thought somewhat wryly.

"Well, you know this columnist gig isn't my idea of a dream job. It pays the bills, and the challenges with Ronnie have kept things interesting, but I've been thinking lately that I should maybe make more of an effort to start doing what I really *want* to be doing before it's too late."

"The sports reporter thing, right?" Zack asked. He was nodding, his elbows balanced on his splayed knees. "You'd be damn good at it. I always wondered why you settled for writing about other stuff when your heart wasn't in it."

"I guess I figured writing was writing, and that eventually I'd luck into exactly the job I wanted. But since that hasn't happened quite as easily as I'd hoped, I've been thinking I might need to go at it from a different direction."

"And that would be . . . ?" Gage prompted.

Dylan spared a glance for one friend before turning

to the other—the one who could make or break this brilliant idea of his. Or of Ronnie's, really, but that was a detail he didn't intend to share at the moment.

Taking a deep breath, he shoved the row of stitches he'd been working on farther down the needle so they didn't slip off, then set the whole wad of yarn and plastic beside him on the couch.

"It sort of involves you," he said, holding Zack's gaze.

"Me?" his friend asked, straightening a few inches as his eyes went wide. "Why me?"

He looked part startled, part guilty, and Dylan wondered what he'd been up to that being singled out worried him.

"Well, you are the hockey star."

His expression turned even more wary as he glanced back and forth between his two friends, the football game in the background now completely forgotten. "Yeah. So?"

"So . . . ," Dylan dragged out, "you're also known for being closemouthed with the press, but since you happen to be one of my best friends, I was hoping you might be willing to bend your rules a bit and grant me an exclusive interview. It could really open some doors for me."

When Zack didn't react, Dylan started to worry he'd made a colossal mistake. He wanted to be a successful sports reporter, and his best friend did happen to be one of the biggest stars in the NHL, but he wasn't willing to risk that friendship just for a glowing addition to his résumé.

"Look," he said, holding up his hands and leaning back against the sofa, "maybe it was a bad idea. Forget I mentioned it. I—"

"Je-zus," Zack swore, cutting Dylan off as he fell back into his own chair.

Across the room, Bruiser jerked awake at Zack's heartfelt exclamation. He looked around, realized nothing of interest—at least to him—was going on, and went back to sleep on his giant red-and-blue Rockets dog pillow that was roughly the size of a toddler's first mattress.

Driving his fingers through his blond hair from hairline to nape, Zack said, "You really know how to shrink a guy's tea bags, buddy. For a minute there, you had me thinking you were going to ask me to pose nude for *Playgirl*, or tell me you were gay and wanted to be my love bunny or something."

Dylan didn't know whether to be relieved or offended by Zack's reaction.

On the other side of the couch, Gage was chuckling and using the lip of his longneck in a poor attempt to hide his amusement.

"Sure, I can do that," Zack continued. "There will have to be some ground rules. You know there are things I'm not going to talk about with a reporter, even if he happens to be one of my best friends. But aside from that, I'd be happy to sit down with you for an interview."

"Great, man. Thanks, I appreciate it."

A jolt of achievement and no small amount of excitement rolled through Dylan. And he wanted more than anything to pick up the phone and tell Ronnie the good news, tell her she'd been right, and that quite possibly she was the most brilliant person in the entire state of Ohio.

Better yet, he'd like to tell her in person, see her face and that thick mane of soft chestnut hair falling around her face.

But he might be smarter not to mention the Mensa IQ thing. After admitting how he felt about her writing, he didn't want to stroke her ego any more.

Besides, if he was going to stroke her, he could think of about a dozen other places he'd rather focus his attention on.

With a grin, Dylan imagined how hard Ronnie would punch him if she could read his mind right now. Not that he wasn't strong enough to take it . . . and then wrestle her to the ground and kiss the mad right out of her.

"You got something else on your mind, man?" Gage asked, interrupting his thoughts and the mini fantasy that had begun to play out in his head. " 'Cause you look way too happy about a lousy interview with 'Hot Legs' over there . . . unless, of course, he's right about you buttering him up to be your boyfriend. No pun intended."

"Well, pooh," he said, making his voice go high and slightly effeminate. "You found me out. It's true, I've got a huge crush on this big galoot." He tipped sideways just enough to curl his fingers around Zack's knee and give a squeeze.

"Whoa!" Zack jumped up like a diamondback had just shaken its rattles underneath his chair, and put an extra couple of feet of space between them. "Keep your hands to yourself. It's not funny anymore."

Dylan laughed and gave his own knee a hearty slap. Even Gage was getting a chuckle out of Zack's over-the-top reaction.

"Sit down, you homophobic pussy."

It took a minute for their laughing to die down. When it did, Zack slowly returned to his seat and mumbled, "I'm not homophobic. Or a pussy."

"Oh, come on," Dylan said. "If we were in the locker room after a game, you'd let me slap your bare ass and think nothing of it."

"Yeah, well, we're not in the locker room," Zack retorted, brow creased in discomfort, "so hands off my knee, my ass, and everything else."

Batting his eyes and putting a bit of sass into his voice, Dylan said, "All right, but you don't know what you're missing."

Zack flipped him the bird, drawing more loud guffaws out of Dylan and Gage both.

"So what was the grin about?" Gage wanted to know a few seconds later, after Zack had grumpily turned his attention back to the game and Dylan had once again picked up his knitting.

He shrugged. "Nothing in particular."

Gage raised an eyebrow and took a slow sip of his beer before leaning back against the soft. He crossed one leg over the other and held his right ankle where it rested on his left knee.

"A guy doesn't smile like that about nothing in particular," he commented drily, flicking at the label on his bottle with the side of his thumb. "Does it have anything to do with Ronnie?"

The soft question caused a clench low in Dylan's gut. But instead of being a clutch of fear or guilt or wariness, it seemed to feel more like possessiveness and . . . restlessness, desperation, even.

"What if it does?" he replied slowly, not meeting Gage's gaze, even though he could sense both of his friends watching him.

Gage shook his head once, with an indifferent twist to his lips. "Nothing. I was just wondering. We haven't heard you complaining about her the way you used to, so I thought maybe the two of you had come to an understanding."

"Or maybe that kiss a couple of weeks ago turned into more," Zack offered.

Dylan had been friends with these guys long enough to know they weren't ribbing him now, weren't looking for a weakness they could exploit. As with Miranda rights, anything he said could and probably would be used against him down the road, but at the moment they were open to a frank and earnest discussion.

It happened sometimes. When Gage was having trouble with his marriage to Jenna and going through his divorce, and again when Zack started toying with the idea of proposing to Grace. Dylan supposed it was his turn in the hot seat.

"This doesn't go any farther than this room," he qualified, waiting until he'd gotten the requisite nods—from his best buds, that was as good as a handshake or a blood oath—to continue. "We've been sleeping together."

Gage raised a brow and Zack gave a long, high whistle through his teeth.

"What?" Dylan prompted, a slightly defensive edge to his tone. "No catcalls or lewd comments? No *How was she?* or *Is she good with her mouth?*"

"I would, but I'm too afraid of getting a knitting needle to the 'nads," Zack said.

Dylan cocked his head, waiting for Gage's reply.

"Not me," the smart cop said, holding up his hands. "I know better than to flap my gums around a guy who's got a serious jones for a girl. Haven't you ever heard 'When a Man Loves a Woman'? Sam Cooke knew what he was talking about."

It spoke to the depth of Dylan's confusion about his relationship with Ronnie that he didn't correct Gage on his *serious jones* remark. A week ago, he'd have been all over that, insisting he didn't have a serious jones for her, didn't have any sort of jones for her.

But now . . . now, he'd be lying if he denied it. He did have a jones for her. A big one.

He had the hots for her, in ways he'd never had the hots for any other woman. She made him want to—and willing to—do things he'd never wanted or been willing to do before. Made him want her even when she was nowhere around, while he was with his buddies, watching basketball, drinking beer, and knitting, for God's sake.

At a time when he'd normally be thinking about those three things to the exclusion of everything else, she had his cock half hard behind the confines of his zipper and wondering how soon he'd get the chance to see her again.

But it wasn't just the sex. He wished it was. Falling for Ronnie had never been part of the plan, but he was very much afraid that's what had happened.

It wasn't just the sex he liked about her, it was her skin, and her lips, and her luxurious hair. Her voice, and her smile, and the soft sway of her hips when she walked.

He liked talking with her and listening to her defend her positions to the death, even if 90 percent of the people in the room disagreed with her.

She was one of the most passionate people he'd ever met—in bed, at home, at work, in every aspect of her life.

She was also smart, and witty, and funny, and though

it made him uncomfortable to admit it, he was pretty sure he wanted to be with her longer than just the next couple of days or weeks. Maybe even longer than a couple of months.

Scary stuff. And if Ronnie found out he'd been thinking along those lines, she'd either laugh in his face or use one of her ice-pick high heels to kick him in the ass and out of her apartment.

"So are things getting serious?" Zack ventured, tossing the remote control he'd used to turn the volume down on the TV back on the glass-topped coffee table, testament to the significance of their conversation.

"I don't know," he replied, rubbing his jaw. "No doubt about it, the sex is great. If you think Ronnie looks hot in one of her prim little dress suits, you should see her naked. She could peel the paint off the walls and turn it liquid again."

"Yeah," Gage said drily with a wry quirk to his lips. "It's probably not smart for us to be visualizing your girlfriend naked. That's an invitation to a bloody nose and loose teeth, if you ask me."

"And I can't spare either," Zack put in, covering the bridge of his nose, which had a small bump from the last time it had been busted by an opposing team member.

"Don't let her hear you call her my girlfriend or she'll skin you alive."

"She doesn't want to be your girlfriend?" Gage asked.

Dylan rolled his eyes and tapped the flat end of one of the needles he was using against his thigh. "She doesn't want to be in the same zip code with me. While we're going at it, she forgets she hates me like a cold sore, but as soon as she comes up for air she's back to thinking I'm the Antichrist."

Gage and Zack both chuckled.

"So how do you manage to get her into the sack in the first place?" Zack wanted to know.

"Stealth, misdirection, and heavy doses of cough medicine in her wine," he quipped.

The guys laughed at that, and the mood in the room lightened a few degrees.

"Frankly, I'm surprised to hear you've been tapping that. I didn't think anyone could melt the Ice Queen," Zack said with a smirk. "Not to mention, I thought you were one of the things that chapped her ass the most."

"I am," Dylan agreed, the corner of his own mouth lifting in amusement. "But you know what they say about there being a thin line between love and hate."

"You think she's in love with you?" Gage asked.

The question hit a little too close to home, and it took a second for Dylan's gut to unclench and his mind to formulate an answer.

"Definitely not," he responded slowly, remembering the number of times she'd turned away from him after they'd made love, in embarrassment and regret. The number of times she'd made a point of telling him it had been a mistake to sleep with him, and swearing him to secrecy so that no one would ever find out she'd let her guard down long enough to fall into bed with the enemy.

A twinge of disappointment seeped into his voice as he said, "It's just lust and the illicitness of a forbidden affair."

"One more reason for us to keep our traps shut, then," Zack said. "We wouldn't want to be the cause of you losing access to a regular supply of booty."

"Gee, thanks," Dylan quipped. The sex was good, no doubt about it, but that wasn't his main concern anymore.

Shifting in his spot on the sofa, he went back to knitting, carefully forming one stitch after another. After a couple of minutes had passed with no further questions or well-meant comments from Gage and Zack, Dylan quietly murmured, "I'm thinking of trying to talk her into sticking things out awhile longer, seeing where they take us."

Zack's eyes widened, but Gage's expression remained stoically unreadable.

A beat passed before Gage raised his bottle of beer in a mock salute and said, "More power to you, brother."

Zack's response was slower to come. Finally, he said, "Yeah, good luck with that," sounding none too convinced that Dylan would be successful. "And if it doesn't work out, you can always send her down to the rink to keep the ice from melting between games."

Row 18

When Ronnie walked to her desk at the *Sentinel* offices
Monday morning, she did it with a bounce in her step
and a smile on her face. She couldn't believe how good
she felt.

For the first time, she was happy to come into work.
She was looking forward to checking her messages and
e-mail, sitting in on the editorial meeting, and brainstorming ideas for new columns. It didn't all feel rote
to her anymore, like she was slogging through quick-
sand just trying to get to where she really wanted to be.

For once, she felt as though she was exactly where
she belonged, doing exactly what she was meant to do.

And her concerns about money . . . well, they were
by no means completely alleviated, but they had been
significantly reduced after a phone call to Dylan's father, who had talked to her for several hours about financial planning.

He'd also given her the name of a professional financial planner whom he seemed to think would help her
get everything organized to the point that she wouldn't
need to worry about money or her future at all.

Although she'd tried several times, she hadn't been

able to adequately express her gratitude to Mr. Stone for his help and advice. She had a feeling, though, that she would have to find a way to thank Dylan.

The only problem there was that she could very easily envision *several* hot and sweaty ways to express her appreciation to *him*.

Dylan was the one thing that tarnished her otherwise buoyant mood. She honestly didn't know what to do about him.

Did she want to keep sleeping with him?

Oh, yeah. Especially since no other man she'd ever been with had managed to curl her toes and send her eyes rolling back in her head as often as he did.

Did she want things between them to become more serious?

That she wasn't so sure about. There were moments she thought the answer was yes, and she could almost picture them going out on normal dates, hanging out with their friends, getting to know each other the way significant others did.

Other times, it was a definite no. It was ridiculous to think there would ever be more between them than the most superficial chitchat and tooth-rattling, seizure-inducing boinking.

Well, she didn't need to worry about that just now, she thought, punching the button to boot up her computer and dialing her voice mail at the same time. She probably wouldn't see him for a few days, which meant she didn't have to decide how to deal with him quite yet.

While clicking to check her e-mail, she automatically jotted down notes from two of her voice-mail messages. The third one, however, gave her pause.

It was an associate publisher of a newspaper in Chicago where she'd sent her résumé the month before and then flown out to interview with a few weeks earlier. For a second, her heart jolted to a stop. Then it picked up again with a too-rapid beat.

She paid careful attention, hearing the words she'd always dreamed of, listening to the man make her the offer she'd always prayed for—a better job at a bigger, more prestigious newspaper than the one she was working at now.

Half in a stupor, she wrote down the man's name, his number and extension, and the details of the offer he mentioned in his message, then replaced the handset and sat back in her squeaky desk chair.

The irony of the situation slapped her in the face and caused a near-hysterical giggle to roll up her throat and pass her lips before she realized she'd made a sound.

Oh, this was rich. *Be careful what you wish for,* her father would say in that low, intelligent manner of his, *you just might get it.*

For so long, she'd been working toward this very thing . . . the promise of a better job. Higher pay, higher stature, more editorial freedom, a chance to climb the journalistic ladder, maybe one day write for the *New York Times* or work for CNN.

So why wasn't she still clutching the phone, frantically punching numbers and praying the *City News* publisher would already be in his office to hear her jubilantly accept his offer?

Because what Dylan had said the other night was playing through her head instead, louder and more insistent than the knowledge that she could pick up and move to Chicago, if she wanted. Louder, even, than the idea of one day winning a Pulitzer or becoming a household name.

Maybe because, deep in her heart, his words rang true. She did like her job at the *Sentinel*. She enjoyed having her own column and being able to write about almost anything she wanted.

She realized, too, that he was right about people— women, especially—taking her advice to heart. There were piles of letters in her bottom desk drawer and closet at home attesting to that, and more pouring into the mail room every week.

Some even came from areas outside of Cleveland, proving that the popularity of her column was spreading. Without realizing it, or even intentionally moving in that direction, she'd somehow become the city's Dear Abby or Ask Heloise. And one day, if she stuck with it, her column might even go into syndication and end up in national papers no matter where she lived.

That would be a form of achieving her dream, wouldn't it? Never mind that it hadn't happened exactly as she'd planned or expected.

Success was success, right? And everyone had to find their own path, their own happiness.

Fingering the slip of paper with the *City News* publisher's information, she folded it in half and slipped it into the front pocket of her Hermès knockoff handbag.

Kicking it back under her desk, she actually considered calling Dylan to tell him about this new turn of events and ask his advice.

Which only went to show how wrapped up she'd become in him in such a short amount of time. He was in her thoughts, in her head, under her skin . . .

And at home, he seemed to have permeated every inch of her apartment. Everywhere she looked, there was some memory attached to him . . .

Standing in the kitchenette Sunday morning, his hip cocked against the counter while they sipped glasses of orange juice and his gaze raked over her from head to toe, tempting her to drag him back to bed.

Making out once, twice, a dozen times on the living room sofa. Doing things she'd previously thought were reserved only for the Kama Sutra or the freakishly limber.

Lying in bed or moving around the apartment, listening to the water run in the bathroom while he'd showered. Imagining him standing stark naked beneath the hot, steady stream, all sleek lines, smooth skin, and hard, bulging muscles.

Whew. Was it getting hot in here, or was it just her?

She grabbed a folder from the corner of her desk and waved it in front of her suddenly overheated face and neck.

And her bed . . . She'd had a hell of a time falling asleep last night with his scent on the sheets. It permeated every fiber of the bedclothes, wrapping around her, making her feel safe and warm and incredibly horny all at the same time.

She'd tossed and turned like crazy, fighting the urge to reach for the phone. To call him to come over and relieve the ache building in her breasts, between her legs, and over every other inch of her body, as well.

Finally, she'd slipped a hand beneath the covers and taken care of business herself. It hadn't been nearly as satisfying as when Dylan touched her, but it was enough to help her drift off to sleep.

The only problem with that was the erotic, extremely realistic dreams that had plagued her the rest of the night. Even her subconscious, it seemed, was hot for Dylan's bod. She may have been asleep, but the hours until dawn were filled with images a thousand times more blistering than flying solo.

She was pretty sure she'd continued to toss and turn, at least judging by the state of her bedclothes when she'd awakened to the annoying buzz of the digital alarm. The pillows had been tossed to the floor, one tipped sideways against the bed frame, the other somehow ending up halfway across the room.

But this time, instead of being caused by the struggle to fall asleep, the unusual activity had stemmed directly from her temporary stint as a triple-X actress and her quadruple-X co-star.

Flicking the folder back and forth, she created an even stronger breeze in an attempt to lower her rapidly rising internal temperature. Outwardly, it worked, but fanning herself did nothing to squelch the sensual tension pulsing between her thighs.

All right, so it was clear that today was in no way going to be a typical, boring, play-catch-up Monday. It might actually turn out to be the most important Monday of her life.

She had two giant dilemmas yawning in front of her, and two monumental decisions to make.

Number one, what was she going to do about the *City News* job offer in Chicago?

Was she going to quit her job here, pack up everything she owned, and move halfway across the country? Away from her friends and family?

Or was she going to continue at the *Sentinel,* working her way up as best she could, or perhaps simply being content with where she already was?

And number two, what was she going to do about Dylan?

Should she end things now, make a clean break, and insist they go back to the way things had been, with the two of them being at each other's throats most of the time? Or should she stick it out awhile longer, maybe see where the future led them?

At the very least, she might get a couple of months of great sex from the deal.

Of course, that was the crux of the predicament, wasn't it? She wasn't sure great sex was the issue anymore. She was afraid her feelings for Dylan had gone a little beyond that, and that she maybe wanted more.

And that scared the Chocolate Chestnut, Clairol #392, right off her lighter brown roots.

What she needed, she decided suddenly, tossing aside her makeshift fan and reaching for the telephone, was advice from certified professionals.

And girlfriends and martinis were as professional and reliable as it got.

"So we're talking *reeeally* good sex, right?"

"Yes," Ronnie responded to Grace's eloquently phrased question. "But sex isn't everything."

Grace snorted. "No, but depending on the guy, it can be a hell of a lot."

"Do you think he's the guy?" Jenna asked quietly, her green eyes widening slightly as she tucked a loose strand of short black hair behind one ear. "That he's the one?"

Toying with the cherry stabbed through with a tooth-pick in her Hpnotiq martini, Ronnie shook her head. "I don't know about that. I just think . . . I'm not sure I'm ready to put an end to things. It feels like there may be more to experience with Dylan, more to explore."

"And you're willing to put aside your differences, your very public competitions, to do that?"

Hmph. Well, apparently she hadn't thought that far ahead.

"I don't know. I hadn't considered that," she admitted. "I guess I sort of assumed that we'd go on the way we have been professionally while carrying on a hot and steamy *un*professional affair behind the scenes."

"One that no one would ever discover, right? No one would ever see the two of you together, no one would ever notice that maybe the insults you toss back and forth weren't as harsh as they used to be."

Ronnie's brows knit. Dammit, Grace had a point.

"And what if you do take the job in Chicago?" Jenna asked. Sadness tugged at the corners of her mouth. "I know I should be happy for you, but I hate that you're even considering it. I would miss you like crazy. But if you go, you'll never know what might have happened with Dylan because there's no way he'd go with you."

Ronnie hadn't considered that, either. Raising her drink to her lips, she drained the last of the turquoise-blue cocktail and let the glass slam back on the table. If the conversation continued in its current vein, she might need another to get through the rest of this lunch.

"I can't make life decisions based on what may or may not develop with some random man."

"But Dylan isn't random," Grace pointed out. "He's someone you've known for more than a year now, someone you've battled with and shared passionate lovemaking with. Someone you're considering becoming more serious with. That might be worth tossing into the equation."

"Are you sure there's alcohol in your appletini?" Ronnie asked with a scowl. "Because you're making entirely too much sense at the moment."

"You should make a Pros and Cons list," Jenna suggested diplomatically. "That's what I do when I have a big decision to make."

"Pro:" Grace said, her long, pink perfectly manicured nails wrapping around her glass as she took a sip of her drink, "He makes your teeth sweat and can bring you to orgasm with a heavy blink."

Ronnie scowled. "I wouldn't go that far," she mumbled. Although her friend wasn't terribly far off the mark.

"Con: Since you're both in the public eye, if things don't work out, there could be a nasty breakup involved," Jenna added.

"Pro: Dylan is a good guy. I know you've spent the last year devising painful and imaginative ways to make him beg for death, but from being around him and hearing Zack talk, I can tell you unequivocally that he is not a total jerk. He may have the usual personality defects common to the entire male species, but he's not going to lie to you, cheat on you, or treat you like crap."

Jenna nodded in agreement. "That's true. You could definitely do worse."

"I have," Ronnie quipped, rolling her eyes and thinking back to some of the jag-offs she'd dated over the years.

"Con: Getting serious with a guy changes everything," Grace continued. "Your life would no longer be your own. You'd have to plan things together, ask for his input, take his feelings and opinions into account. And it's not easy, believe me."

"Pro: Having someone to come home to, to love you and hold you and support you in everything you do, is priceless," Jenna whispered almost wistfully.

Though neither Ronnie nor Grace would say anything, they knew Jenna had been happiest when she'd been married to Gage . . . at least while things had been good . . . and that she missed him now that they were divorced.

It was also clear to Ronnie that they weren't getting very far with the Pro/Con list for Dylan. Both sides evened out, leaving her in the exact same spot as before . . . confused and completely undecided.

"All right, we've established that the thing with Dylan could go either way. What about the job offer in Chicago?"

"Chicago is a nice city," Grace said. "You can add that to the Pro column."

"You could eventually end up working at the *Tribune* or *Sun-Times,* which would be right up there with writing for the *New York* or *L.A. Times,*" Jenna told her. "Pro."

"You'd be getting more money, maybe have more opportunities than you would here."

"You've been wanting to change jobs for a while now," Jenna added. "For as long as we've known you, you've wanted bigger, better, more, and this might just be it."

"Chicago is farther from my family than Cleveland,"

Ronnie pointed out, knowing her friends would under-stand, since she'd already filled them in on feeling as though she'd just rediscovered her family and being ea-ger to reconnect with all of them. "And from you guys."

"That's a big one," Grace admitted quietly. "There's always e-mail, phone calls, and the occasional visit, but it isn't quite the same."

Running the tip of her perfectly manicured index finger around the rim of her martini glass, Grace didn't make eye contact for a second. Then she lifted her head and glanced at Ronnie head-on.

"You may not like this suggestion," she said slowly, "but I think you should sleep on it. Don't decide any-thing just yet. Go home, go to bed, let it all sink in, and then follow your gut. Think about moving to Chicago, and if a zip of excitement goes through you, then you know it's the thing to do. Think about waking up beside Dylan for the next year or two, and if it feels like that's the next best thing to having bamboo shoots shoved un-der your fingernails, then kick him to the curb."

"So basically," Ronnie drawled, "you're saying you don't know what the hell I should do now any more than you did two hours ago."

One corner of Grace's mouth tipped in a crooked smile. "That's about the size of it."

Spreading his feet, Dylan shifted into a broader stance and raised his fist to rap on Ronnie's door.

There were only a few days left until he would ei-ther do or die on this knitting challenge, and he should really be at home, working on the scarf he was still about three feet from finishing.

But instead, here he was, standing outside Ronnie's

apartment with some sort of sharp, radiating ache in the center of his chest driving him to see her.

Maybe because of the challenge deadline, because he knew there was a good chance that as soon as he succeeded in beating her at her own game—and he still fully intended to win this thing, even if it meant taking time off work and knitting twenty-four hours a day to get the job done—their time together would end.

Whether because she'd be pissed he'd managed to learn how to knit, after all, or because she didn't want to run the risk of anyone seeing them together in a way that could be even remotely presumed to be intimate, he could feel in his gut that she planned to break things off.

And he was okay with that.

He was a big boy. He'd been involved in affairs that had come to an end before, and it wasn't like she was the only woman in Cleveland. Give him a day or two and he'd bounce back.

But there was still time left before the ax fell, and he found himself compelled to be with her as much as possible until it did.

How Ronnie would react to his unexpected arrival, however, was left to be seen.

To his surprise, she didn't start breathing fire the minute she opened the door. If anything, she looked almost pleased to see him.

"Dylan," she said breathlessly. She was carrying a dish towel and drying her hands, leading him to believe she may have been washing dishes or fixing dinner for herself. "What are you doing here?"

"Can I come in?" he asked, avoiding giving a direct answer to her question.

"Of course." Stepping back, she opened the door

wider, then closed it behind him as he moved into the entryway.

A glimpse into the kitchenette area proved him right on the dishwashing guess. The sink was full of sudsy water, a few mismatched plates and glasses were drying on the folding dish rack, and Maroon 5 played softly from a small radio set up on the countertop.

"I talked to my dad today," he said, moving farther into the apartment, stuffing his hands distractedly into the front pockets of his well-worn jeans. "He said you called him last night."

"I did." Dipping into the kitchen, she hung the damp towel on the handle of the oven door, then returned to the living area, sauntering over to the sofa and folding a leg beneath her before she plopped down on one of the overstuffed cushions.

He watched her, his mouth growing increasingly dry with every swish of her hips, every flick of her bare feet, every flutter of the stray curls that framed her face, falling loose from the twist of hair clipped at the back of her head. His palms itched to touch her, and the monster in his pants reared its head, desperate to get out, go on the hunt, and bring down its prey.

"He was wonderful, thank you for giving me his number."

This was, without a doubt, the least prickly he'd ever seen her. She looked positively inviting; comfortable, relaxed, claws retracted.

Taking it as a sign he wouldn't be maimed and dismembered if he moved closer, he slipped between the coffee table and couch and sat down beside her. They touched from knee to hip, and the same heat that was always there when they got within six feet of each other blazed to life, scorching his insides and leaving them a bubbling, molten mess.

"I'm glad. You're welcome." Leaning forward, he rested his elbows on his knees, twisting his hands together in front of him. "He enjoyed talking with you, too. Said you sounded like a smart and very pleasant young lady."

His lips tipped at that, and he turned his head just enough to see her smiling in return. "I told him he didn't know you very well or he wouldn't have been crazy enough to believe the *pleasant* part."

"You did not!" she gasped.

He was surprised the exclamation didn't come with a hearty slap to his shoulder or the back of his head. "Nah. But I was tempted."

Not nearly as tempted as he was, though, when she uncrossed her legs and stretched them out across his lap. For a minute, he sat frozen, not sure how to react.

In all the time he'd known her, or even that they'd been sleeping together, she'd never made a move like this. Jumped his bones once or twice, sure. Gone for the jugular . . . that, too. But to touch him voluntarily, without the intention of sliding immediately into raunchy, toes-to-the-ceiling, ass-in-the-air sex, was something entirely new.

Of course, being a guy, the fact that she might not have toes-to-the-ceiling, ass-in-the-air sex in mind didn't mean it wasn't swimming around in *his* overactive, erotically charged brain. And it was quickly making itself known in other parts of his body, as well.

There was no way she couldn't feel his boner pressing against the back of her knee, but she pretended not to, scooching closer and swinging her feet, drawing his attention to her bare, red-tipped toes. He swallowed hard, picturing those toes wiggling above his shoulders while he made her scream in ecstasy, and tried not to follow suit.

Instead of resting back against the arm of the sofa, she stayed sitting upright, one hand behind his neck, toying with the ends of his hair, the other flicking a button at the front of his shirt.

She might as well have been licking him straight down the center. His balls tightened and his cock gave a wicked twitch behind the fly of his jeans, while she seemed calm as a cucumber, completely oblivious of the lust burning through his system like a brushfire.

"I suppose I should thank you," she said softly.

"For what?"

He hadn't done anything to earn her appreciation yet, but the night was still young.

Her brow furrowed as she shot him an odd glance. "For putting me in touch with your dad. And making all those suggestions about how to handle my finances so I don't have to worry about them anymore. I took your advice on both counts, and I'm feeling less stressed already."

"So I done good?"

She chuckled. "Very good. Thank you."

She shifted her hips, bringing the side of her thigh into direct contact with his straining erection.

In a gravelly voice, he said, "I can think of better ways for you to show your appreciation."

Her eyes went wide, but there was a twinkle in the deep brown pools, and one corner of her mouth twitched. "Is that why you came over tonight? To get lucky?"

At the moment, he couldn't remember his own name,

let alone what had driven him to her door. "You got a problem with that?" he volleyed back.

The fingers at his nape tugged more firmly at his hair. The ones at his shirtfront made quick work of popping the top button, then the next one down, then the next . . .

Blood sped through his veins faster than NASCAR qualifiers. She wasn't pushing him away and hadn't knocked him on his ass yet. That had to be a good sign.

Or not. With Ronnie, it was hard to tell.

Her face, with its high cheekbones, lush lashes, and full, bow-shaped mouth, moved in until he could feel her warm breath dancing over his skin.

With her lips hovering just above his, she whispered, "No, I don't suppose I do."

And then she was kissing him.

Row 19

Given the steel pipe trying to force its way out of his pants and the pent-up need swirling into tsunami proportions just beneath the surface, he expected the first touch of her mouth to be an explosion of passion. To waste no time in flipping her onto her back, stripping her bare, and sending them both to the naughty side of Heaven.

So it came as a bit of a shock when he found himself enjoying her soft, tender kiss, the feather-light brush of her lips, and the warm flood of sensations washing over him.

If this was their final time together, the last time he would ever stroke her hair, feel her pressed tightly against him, run his fingers over her supple flesh, then he wanted to remember everything. He wanted to take it slow and enjoy every touch, every taste, every breathy sigh.

At that somber realization, the raging inferno of lust beating through his blood banked to a low simmer. His grip on her waist loosened. The press of his mouth on hers softened and the pressure in his lungs and chest returned to almost normal.

He brought a hand up to cup her face and deepened the kiss just slightly, running the tip of his tongue along the line of her closed lips until she opened and let him in. Her own arms wrapped around his neck and shoulders, pressing her breasts flat against his chest.

The kiss went on for what seemed like hours, slow and languorous, tender and yielding. So much of the passion that had passed between them had been hot and fast and earth-shattering that the dichotomy of what was taking place now felt almost surreal.

It was nice, though. Different, but nice. He even thought that he might be able to get used to this sort of thing . . . Long, lazy lovemaking sessions on a Sunday afternoon when they had nowhere else to be. Slow, leisurely petting that maybe didn't even go anywhere but was satisfying all on its own.

Oh, yeah, he could get used to this—as long as she was the one draped across his lap, gently kneading his biceps, squirming like a kitten trying to find the best position for an afternoon nap.

But that wasn't an option, was it?

Tonight, this very moment, might be all they had left.

The pads of his fingers skimmed her cheek, the line of her jaw, the long column of her throat. And then, never taking his mouth from hers, he scooped her up and carried her to the bedroom.

She didn't fight him, didn't even ask what he was doing. Of course, her mouth *was* otherwise occupied, but he liked to think she'd have been pliant and agreeable even if it hadn't been.

Laying her down across the neatly made bed, he stretched out atop her and continued kissing her, continued stroking her, continued filling his mind and soul with every memory and sensory perception possible.

A part of him suspected that ten, twenty, fifty years from now, he would still be thinking back to his time with Ronnie with a smile on his face and a chubby in his pants.

Ronnie kept her eyes tightly closed and schooled her breathing as she felt the mattress shift beneath her. Brushing the hair away from her face, Dylan placed a soft kiss on her brow and then climbed out of bed.

Though he made barely a sound, she could hear him padding across the carpeted floor, gathering his clothes, and moving toward the door. Cracking a lid, she watched his deliciously tight backside in the shadowed darkness as he slipped out the door.

Her stomach might have lurched at the sight of those perfect buns of steel, except for the fact that it was currently quite full and weighted down by her heart, which had taken a serious dip when he'd pressed his lips to her forehead.

That wasn't something casual lovers did. Was it? Or was she reading too much into it?

If she was, though, then she must also be reading too much into their lovemaking last night. Not the urgent, flash fire of passion she'd grown used to with him, but a slow, sweet, tender joining of their bodies that she didn't think she'd ever experienced before with anyone.

He'd kissed her and held her and touched her forever before beginning to slowly undress her or himself. Even then, he'd seemed in no hurry to be inside her, continuing his calculated exploration.

And while she'd enjoyed every second of his languid attentions, she'd also felt like a pan of water working its way to a hard boil. Bubbles of excitement had popped and rolled through her bloodstream, tickling under her skin.

She'd tried several times to speed things up, to urge him along so he would just take her already, but he'd held his ground. She didn't think there was a millimeter of flesh he hadn't caressed, kissed, licked, or suckled. Some parts had been lucky enough to get the full, four-course treatment.

He'd curled her toes, weakened her knees, and all around made her feel like the most beautiful, treasured woman on the face of the earth.

When he'd finally slipped inside her, it had sent her over the brink into immediate orgasm. Not a gasping, writhing, tooth-rattling orgasm, but one that was slow and gentle and rippled through her in one long, ongoing cascade of pleasure.

Though he'd managed to hold himself together rather than following her over into instant satisfaction, she'd been pleased to feel the steel-cable tension in his tall frame and see a muscle tic in his jaw as he'd clenched his teeth against coming too soon.

But even then . . . even after enough foreplay to get him into the *Guinness Book of World Records* . . . even after making her climax at the first touch of his penis inside her . . . still he seemed in no rush to hurry things along.

He continued to tease her—face, throat, breasts, belly—with his hands and mouth. And when he finally began to move, it was with slow, sure strokes designed to build the excruciating pressure all over again.

He let her come twice more before giving in to his own pleasure, and after regaining his strength he'd done nothing more than roll to the side, yank the bedspread around to cover them both, and then hold her as they both slipped into a safe, comfortable sleep.

She could hear Dylan in the bathroom, and turned her head to glance at the glowing red numbers of the digital clock on the nightstand. No wonder he was leaving . . . they both had to be at work in only a couple more hours, and he likely planned to run home and change clothes before heading for the office.

Since her entire closet of fresh outfits was only a few feet away, she could afford to lie in bed and feign sleep a bit longer—at least until Dylan was gone.

Not that she wanted him to go. Oddly, she found herself wishing he'd come back and climb into bed for another round of pop goes the weasel.

Only a week ago, he'd have done just that. He'd have held her wrists above her head, covered her with his body, and used every seductive skill in his extensive arsenal to convince her to blow off her responsibilities for the day and stay in bed with him doing the nasty.

She'd have probably gone for it, too.

So why wasn't he doing that today? Why had he sneaked out of bed instead of waking her with kisses and his already rigid erection pressing into her hip? Why had he let her sleep through the night instead of rousing her again and again the way he would have only days ago?

It all felt very peculiar to her, and she couldn't decide whether to be nervous or relieved by his behavior.

She heard the front door click and let out a sigh. Throwing back the covers, she padded naked across the room.

Her mind was the same maelstrom of confusion it had been before she'd opened the door last evening to find Dylan on the other side—looking sexier than any man had a right to—and lying in bed contemplating the mess her life had become wasn't going to help her figure things out any sooner.

Grabbing her robe, she went to the bathroom to shower and dry her hair, then started fixing her makeup and getting dressed.

She was no closer to having answers to her problems than she had been yesterday. If anything, she had more questions . . . and more emotions welling up to get in the way.

This wouldn't have happened a month ago. Before she'd made the colossal mistake of challenging Dylan to learn how to knit, and then compounded that colossal mistake by agreeing to help him learn, her life had been fine.

With the exception of a few minor personal issues, her life had been freaking perfect, and she'd have had no trouble deciding whether or not to take the job in Chicago. In fact, she probably would have had her bags packed before the associate publisher had even finished making his offer.

But now . . .

Now she'd resolved a few of her original personal issues, only to replace them with a big, honking buttload of new ones. Ones that had her doubting her own desires, questioning her own judgments, and wanting things she had no business wanting.

Grace's brilliant suggestion that she "sleep on it" and let her subconscious find the right answers for her hadn't done a whit of good, unfortunately. Probably because she and her subconscious had both spent the night sleeping *on Dylan* instead of her current pile of moral dilemmas.

And moping around her apartment, wishing solutions would magically appear before she left for work, wasn't going to get her anywhere, either. Finishing her last bite of toast, she shrugged into her coat, grabbed her purse, and took off.

Things were getting down to the wire, and if she didn't figure out what to do soon, about all of it, she was afraid her head would explode. She'd tried talking to her friends, searching her heart, making a list of Pros and Cons . . . next up: a Lucky Eight Ball, Ouija board, and maybe Pin the Tail on the Donkey.

Surely one of them could give her a definitive answer about whether she should turn her back on Dylan and take the job in Chicago or stay in Cleveland and take a chance on a man who made her laugh, made her *crazy,* kept her on her toes, and could give her a dozen big Os in a single night.

A few days later, on Friday, Ronnie held her breath as the latest issue of the *Herald* hit her desk. It was late, almost time to head home, and today was the day Dylan's column came out The day she would discover whether he'd succeeded in his knitting lessons or not.

She almost hoped he had, even though it would mean she'd lose and would have to return his beloved Harrison Award.

Flipping through the pages, she found his column, her eyes immediately locking on the grainy black-and-white photograph of a long, dark, hand-knit scarf above the text.

Well, good for him. It wasn't good for her reputation or her end of their supposedly bitter rivalry, but she was actually proud of him. He'd accepted her challenge and worked hard to learn how to do something he never would have tried to do on his own. Something other guys would probably rag on him about, if they hadn't already.

A few weeks ago, she wouldn't have thought he'd have the balls for it. Now she knew he had the balls for that, and a heck of a lot more.

While this sort of news would have had her frowning before, this time it made her feel warm and content. She didn't need to read the article to know he'd succeeded, but her gaze scanned the words, anyway.

In his easy, flowing prose—which she'd always secretly admired—he chronicled her throwing down the knitting gauntlet, and how easy he'd thought such a challenge would be . . . only to find himself aggravated and perplexed when his yarn and needles wouldn't get with the program. Though he didn't mention her by name, he did confess to seeking one-on-one instruction, admitting to how helpful the lessons had been . . . especially those that had stretched into the wee hours and kept him *up* much longer than anticipated.

Anyone else reading his article wouldn't have thought twice about his description or word choices, but she recognized the innuendo and knew he wasn't referring so much to their knitting lessons as to what usually developed during them. The sly dog.

Once again, something that would have driven her crazy before didn't bother her in the least now. Instead, it brought a smile to her face and pleasant memories to mind that made her tingle in all the right places.

Unlike most of his other I-did-it-so-there-take-that
articles, though, this one didn't present a counterchal-
lenge at the end. It surprised her a little . . . they'd been
playing the back-and-forth, anything-you-can-do-I-can-
do-better game for so long, she'd almost braced herself
for whatever he would dare her to do next . . . and yet it
didn't. For some reason, after all they'd been through together, everything they'd done and discussed, it seemed
natural for their competition to come to a quiet and
peaceful conclusion.

Or maybe he didn't intend for it to be over; maybe he
hadn't come up with anything just yet and would publi-
cize her next challenge in a subsequent column. But by
then it might very well be too late. She might be gone.

With the proof of his accomplishment tucked under
her arm and a wide smile on her face, she made her
way out of the *Sentinel* building. She still hadn't made
a final decision about the new job, but she'd dropped
the associate publisher an e-mail thanking him for the
offer and letting him know that she would have an answer for him first thing Monday.

A week should have been more than enough time to
decide, but since she was still on the fence, she'd created
a do-or-die deadline in order to force herself to go one
way or the other.

And come Monday morning, she would. Yes or no.
Go or stay. She had the weekend to decide, and what-
ever came out of her mouth then, she would stick with.
No waffling, no going back.

She only hoped that two days was enough time for
her topsy-turvy stomach and roller-coaster emotions to
settle down and pick something already.

Letting herself into her apartment, she deposited the

paper and her other items on a beaten-up credenza just
inside the door, readjusting the matchbook from under
one of the legs when it wobbled slightly.

She bypassed the kitchen and walked directly to her
bedroom, where she stripped out of her restrictive dress
clothes and changed into a pair of comfortable Bobby
Jack pajamas. The monkey was picking his nose in the
center of the gray, short-sleeved top, and hanging from
a vine with a bunch of bananas in his hand over and
over and over again on the matching bottoms.

Making her way to the bathroom, she swept her hair
away from her face, twisted it into a makeshift bun at
the back of her head, and held it in place with a giant
clip. Then she washed the makeup off her face and
headed back to the kitchen to find something to eat.

Thanks to the upheaval of her life the past several
weeks, her cupboards were frighteningly bare. A trip to
the grocery store would definitely be required over the
weekend if she wanted to eat at all next week.

Turning on the radio for a bit of background noise,
she shimmied and sang along to Shakira's "Hips Don't
Lie" while she searched for nutrients. She may have
only understood every third word of the song, but she
liked the beat.

She found a package of saltine crackers and a can of
vegetable soup in one of the cupboards, and half a
block of cheese in the refrigerator. Not exactly her idea
of a gourmet meal, but beggars couldn't be choosers.

Dumping the soup into a saucepan and setting it on
a stove burner to heat, she piled the cheese and crackers and a small knife on a cutting board and carried
them into the living room. She hit the remote to turn on

the television, then returned to the kitchen to shut off the radio.

She had just turned, ready to go back to the sofa, when there was a knock at the door. Her stomach immediately took a nose dive as she pictured Dylan standing lazily on the other side.

She wasn't expecting him, and in fact there was no reason under the sun that she could think of for why he'd be dropping by. He certainly didn't need another knitting lesson; his column in today's *Herald* had proven that the few they'd shared had paid off handsomely.

But before she'd challenged him to learn how to knit, she'd rarely gotten visitors. Even Grace and Jenna hardly ever dropped by her apartment; they tended to all meet elsewhere unless something specific was planned, like movie or home spa night.

For the past few weeks, though, she felt as though her apartment had turned into Grand Central Station. There was always a knock at the door, whether she was expecting it or not, and it was always Dylan.

On the up side, when he did show up, he tended to bring food.

Her spirits rose and her belly grumbled.

Then again, the last time he'd shown up without notice, it had been for sex and sex alone. And though she hadn't complained—still wouldn't, considering the pleasant ache he'd left between her legs—if he was showing up now to gloat over his slam-dunk win or for a post-win booty call, she swore she'd strangle him with his newly knitted scarf.

With a wary scowl drawing her brows together, she

made a point of turning the fire off under her soup so it wouldn't burn, then went to the door, peered through the peephole, and slowly opened it to exactly the sight she'd expected.

He looked as good as ever, standing there in worn jeans and a soft maroon buttondown shirt. Also as expected—or rather, *hoped*, she was loath to admit—he held two brown paper bags of takeout.

"Dylan," she said cautiously, trying not to let the delicious smell of Chinese influence her one way or the other. "I didn't expect to see you tonight."

"I thought you might be hungry," he said, lifting the bags a couple of inches in case she'd missed them.

So hungry, her mouth watered just imagining what might be in those bags. But she bit her lip to keep from licking them, and prayed her stomach wouldn't pick that moment to growl and give her away.

"You didn't come here just to bring me dinner," she told him. "And you're not here for a knitting lesson. I saw your column, and you obviously don't need them anymore."

Eyes narrowing, she folded her arms under her breasts and widened her stance. "You're not here to gloat, are you?" she asked in an accusatory tone. "Because if you are . . ."

She couldn't think of anything suitably threatening, but give her a minute . . . or a bite of moo goo gai pan . . . and she'd have a *list* of painful ways to punish him.

"I didn't come to gloat," he said with only the hint of a grin on his smug face. "I don't need to. My finished product speaks for itself."

That sounded a little too much like gloating for her tastes, but since he wasn't sticking out his tongue and dancing a jig, she supposed she'd have to give him his brief moment in the sun.

And then it dawned on her. "You came to collect your Harrison Award."

God, how she was going to hate giving that up. The idea of actually physically handing it over to him gave her chills.

His eyes filled with surprise for a second. "No," he responded slowly. "Although now that you mention it, I would like it back. Let's leave that for later, though," Dylan said when she remained silent. "Can I come in?"

For a long minute, she stood there, undecided. On the one hand, he did come bearing Chinese. On the other, history had proven that any time he entered her apartment, she had a tendency to end up naked, with her legs pointed straight up in the air.

And she needed to maintain a clear head this weekend so she could decide whether or not to completely alter her life. Sleeping with Dylan again would only fog her brain and make that decision more difficult.

Dylan sauntered into the living area and made himself comfortable on the sofa, spreading out the small, white Chinese take-out containers on the low coffee table just as he had so many times before.

Drawn by the mouthwatering aromas, she joined him, sitting close and reaching for a set of chopsticks. He handed her an entire container of sweet-and-sour pork, having discovered it was her favorite, then picked up a box for himself.

After they'd eaten in relative silence for several

minutes, the sharp edge of Ronnie's hunger was satisfied, and her mind rolled back to his reason for once again showing up at her door uninvited.

"So what are you doing here?" she asked, dipping her chopsticks into his container and grabbing a mouthful of noodles for herself.

He did the same, his arm brushing hers as he pilfered a chunk of orange-glazed pork.

"I came to thank you," he said, after he'd finished chewing.

Of all the things he might have said, that was one she never would have expected. "Thank me for what? And please don't say for teaching you to knit. You know I didn't help you any more than I had to, and I wouldn't even have done that if I'd known you were going to pull this one off."

His mouth quirked in a hint of a smile. "I know. But thanks, anyway. The naked knitting lessons, especially, really paid off."

A flush of heat suffused her cheeks at the reminder. She'd known that would come back to bite her in the butt someday—and not in the good way.

"Yeah, yeah," she replied, rolling her eyes and hoping he wouldn't notice her blushing. "You're lucky I didn't take the opportunity to do a little amateur acupuncture with the needles. And you still owe me that thousand bucks."

He gave a bark of laughter and slapped her on the thigh. His touch alone sent her temperature rising by a good ten degrees. Having him treat her with such familiarity, as though they were buddies—or lovers—shocked her into losing her breath altogether.

"That's my Ronnie, always quick with a comeback

and ready to do bodily injury, if necessary. Don't worry, you'll get your money."

He continued talking . . . she knew this because she watched his lips move . . . but for a moment, all she could hear was a loud ringing and the echo of him saying, *That's my Ronnie.* Over and over, the comment played through her head like a scratched record. And her heart skipped a beat wondering if he meant it, or if it had been merely an off-the-cuff figure of speech.

As her hearing began to clear, he said, "No, I want to say thank you for suggesting that I ask Zack about an exclusive. I don't know why I didn't think of it myself a lot sooner. He agreed, though, and we conducted the interview earlier this week."

He shifted beside her, his leg bumping into hers as he leaned his arms on his knees and rubbed his hands together almost nervously. "I've already been shopping it around."

This was good news, right? Ronnie's nose wrinkled. It *sounded* like good news, but then, why was he fidgeting and acting so uncomfortable?

"I'm glad," she said carefully. "I hope you get some good nibbles."

Pushing up from the couch, he stalked across the room, digging his hands into the back pockets of his jeans as he began to pace.

"That's the thing," he muttered, pointedly avoiding her gaze. "I already got some nibbles. More than nibbles—I got huge, marlin-sized yanks on the line. As soon as word got around that I'd gotten an exclusive, candid interview with the Rockets' star goalie, my phone started ringing off the hook. At work and at home."

As the speed of his words increased, so did his strides.

And then suddenly, without warning, he stopped and spun in her direction. Eyes locking on hers, he said, "I got an offer from *Sports Weekly*."

She was still digesting that information when he rushed forward and plopped down on the sofa beside her again, this time on her other side, forcing her to shift to hold his gaze.

"*Sports Weekly*, Ronnie. Can you believe that? They're only, like, the most popular sports magazine after *Sports Illustrated*."

A smile spilled across her face before she could think to stop it. Not that she would have; she was truly happy for him. It seemed they'd both been offered their dream jobs in the same week.

"Congratulations," she said, and meant it. Then, even though she suspected she already knew the answer, she asked, "Are you going to take it?"

He'd be crazy not to. The same way she'd be crazy not to take the job in Chicago.

His head bobbed in a nod. "I already gave my two weeks' notice at the *Herald*."

Her grin broadened and she leaned in to hug him. He felt amazing—hot and hard and oh, so inviting.

She tried not to let her hunger or her growing sense of loss slip into her voice when she said, "Good for you. You deserve it, and I know you're going to love covering all those games and interviewing all those sports figures. It's what you've always wanted, right?"

His arms around her back tightened and she closed her eyes, swallowing hard as emotions threatened to overtake her.

"Yeah," he whispered softly just above her ear. "It's

going to mean a lot of traveling, though, following different teams through each sports season."

"You'll get used to it," she told him, forcing a brusqueness into her voice that she didn't particularly feel. "And after a while, I'll bet you even start to like it."

She gave his shoulder a firm pat, pulling away before she did something stupid like spill her heart out or jump his bones for one last ride on the train to O-town.

"I've got some news, too, actually," she continued, tucking a strand of hair that had come loose from its knot behind one ear.

She hadn't actually made up her mind until that very moment, but now that she knew Dylan would be out of town more often than he was home, that he was about to embark on the career he'd always wanted . . . she couldn't stay here and watch that without either going insane with jealousy or succumbing to her need to throw herself at his feet, so it was better to follow his lead and get the hell out of Dodge.

Pasting a wide smile on her face, she pitched her voice an octave higher than her mood would naturally convey and announced, "I'm moving to Chicago."

Row 20

Dylan felt as though he'd been dropped from a very tall building and had yet to land. His vision narrowed, going dark at the edges while his hearing went haywire, fading in and out like a hard-to-tune radio station.

Ronnie was moving? To Chicago?

Since when?

"I got a new job offer, too," she said, doing that eerie thing where she read his mind. "At the *Chicago City News*. It's a more prominent paper, better money, will provide me with better career opportunities. So it's, you know . . . good. Just what I've always wanted, too."

Yeah, it was just freaking fantastic. Just what she'd always wanted.

Except that she wasn't supposed to want to leave Cleveland.

Okay, he'd known that was part of her agenda practically from the beginning because it went hand in hand with climbing the ladder to success, but still . . .

She wasn't supposed to want to leave Cleveland, because she was supposed to want to be with him. He was supposed to have won her over with his sophisticated charm and out-of-this-world sexual prowess.

Dammit. Hell, damn, shit, fuck.

This wasn't going at all the way he'd imagined. In fact, it was so far off track, he might as well be in Siberia.

Think, Stone. Get your ass out of the fire and back into the frying pan.

"This is great," Ronnie went on, bouncing to her feet. "We're both starting new jobs, turning new corners in our careers and our lives. It's amazing how things turn out sometimes, isn't it?"

She had her arms wrapped snuggly around her waist, emphasizing the generous curve of her breasts where some goofy-looking monkey had its finger stuffed up its nose.

How was it even possible for that to turn him on?

Maybe it had something to do with knowing the exact size and shape and feel of the breasts the stupid chimp was pressed up against, and being able to see the slightest hint of nipple through the gray cotton.

Taking a deep breath, he clenched his fists to keep from running a hand down the front of his trousers in an effort to rein in his raging libido, and forced himself to focus on the little fragments of his life that were currently breaking apart and spinning out of control.

Now, what had she been saying? Oh, yeah. That their lives were coming together so well, and they should both be so happy.

Screw that. A new job wasn't going to make him happy. It wasn't going to make her happy, either. Neither was moving across two states.

And if she *was* happy about it, then she wouldn't be standing there looking pale and pinched and hugging herself like her pet parakeet had just died.

He knew her well enough by now to recognize that the smile on her face was for his benefit, not her own. His heart lifted as that knowledge seeped into his bones, making him push back his shoulders, straighten his spine, and puff his chest out just an inch or two. He grinned, brimming with renewed determination.

"Actually," he said slowly, "I'm not sure it's as great as you think."

Her phony smile faltered. "What do you mean?"

"Well, see," he drawled, taking half a step forward to crowd her, "I didn't come over here just to tell you about *Sports Weekly*."

Her voice was soft and reed-thin when she said, "You didn't?"

"Nope."

Another step forward. She licked her lips and took a nervous step back. It took all the self-control he could muster not to flash a wide grin before grabbing her up and kissing her senseless.

Moving at the speed of molasses, he leaned in, amused when she leaned back, then over until he could reach the paper sack he'd left on the floor while they'd eaten. Straightening, he noticed that her chocolate-brown eyes had gone round in wariness.

God, she was just too adorable for words. And so easy, he could tease her for days if he weren't chomping at the bit to get this over with and move on to better, sweatier things.

The paper bag crinkled as he opened the top and dug inside. "I came to give you this."

Ronnie's heart froze in her chest and refused to beat as she watched him pull the long, black scarf he'd knit for their challenge out of the plain brown sack. She'd missed the extra bag when he'd first arrived, assuming it was more Chinese food. But now . . .

She swallowed hard, reaching out to touch the soft alpaca yarn he'd used to make the scarf. Her fingers skimmed the even stitches of the simple pattern.

It was beautiful. She knew how much trouble he'd had getting the hang of knitting at first and was sure if she looked closely enough, she would spot imperfect or dropped stitches here or there. But none of that took away from its inherent allure, made even more special by the fact that he was giving the scarf to her.

"For me?" she asked, embarrassed to hear the hitch in her voice and felt tears rising to the surface.

"For you," Dylan said gently, his own voice sounding less than 100 percent steady.

Raising her head, she met his gaze and prayed he wouldn't notice how close she was to a total meltdown. "Why?"

"Because I don't want you to move to Chicago. Unless you agree to let me relocate with you," he added almost as an afterthought. "Because I don't want what we have to be some forbidden, temporary fling that we have to keep a secret for fear of ruining our reputations as mortal enemies. I want to be able to walk into The Penalty Box and kiss the smart-ass attitude out of you any damn time I please, regardless of who might be looking."

His big, strong hands curled around her elbows and tugged her closer, until her breasts brushed his chest and her knees bumped against his. "I came over here to tell you about my new job because *you* made it possible. *You* drove me to do something I don't think I'd have done on my own. I didn't come to gloat, I came to . . . Well, to let you know that there will be a lot of traveling involved in working for the magazine, and to make sure that would be okay with you."

"Why . . ." The word came out as a squeak and she stopped to clear her throat before trying again. "Why would you care if it was okay with me or not?"

One corner of his mouth quirked up in amusement. "Hand-knit scarves obviously keep your brain from running on all cylinders. I'll have to remember that the next time I want to win an argument. It will also give me an excuse to continue with the knitting."

Her brows began to draw together, but he kissed her there before a full-blown case of annoyance could develop. "It matters because I was kind of hoping you'd move in with me. Or let me move in here. Either way, I want us to give this thing between us a go. See if our compatibility in the bedroom can carry over into everyday life."

Her heart had gone from a dead stop to beating almost out of control. It felt as though the organ was pounding its way up her throat, blocking both the air to her lungs and the blood to her brain.

"Are you asking me to . . ."

"Move in with me," he stressed, his expression going very serious and a little green around the gills for a second. "Be my girlfriend. Date seriously. See where things go."

Ronnie bit back a laugh, the sudden break of the pressure building inside her leaving her feeling light-headed and relieved for the first time in several long, excruciating minutes.

If ever there was a man determined to avoid the M-word, Dylan was it. Rather than being offended, though, as many women might be, she was happy to avoid it, too. Just finding out that he didn't want their time together to end was enough to make her want to jump up on the coffee table and do a little striptease.

And maybe later, depending on how the rest of this conversation went, she would.

"So you think we should bury the hatchet, both privately and publicly," she said carefully, still fingering the scarf in his hands. He'd added a bit of fringe at the ends, which was even softer than the rest of the more tightly knitted stitches. "Put an end to our competitions and stop making each other do crazy, embarrassing things just to prove who has the bigger set of brass ones."

"Yeah," he said, the ghost of a smile snaking across his face. "I gladly concede defeat in that department. We won't have much of an outlet for goading each other if we're both writing for different media, anyway. Besides . . ." His smile widened and he gave her a sexy, toe-curling wink. "It would probably be more fun to work out our aggressions in other ways. Say, like making our way through the Kama Sutra."

He wiggled his brows like a dirty old man, sending her into peals of laughter. Her head fell back and her arms came up to twine around his neck.

"That's a mighty tempting offer," she murmured, unable to keep the joy from spilling out of her heart and into her eyes, across her mouth. "But I have a confession to make."

His lips pressed against her own, their soft warmth tempting her even more than his previous suggestion.

"What's that?" he asked, continuing to rub and nibble.

"I don't want to move to Chicago."

His movements stilled and he pulled back to look her directly in the eye. "Are you sure?"

She nodded. She'd never been so sure of anything in her life. "I thought I did. Or rather, I thought I would if I ever got the chance. But I don't want to leave Cleveland if this is where you are, and you were right about my already having a great job. I really do like writing my column for the *Sentinel,* and I'm not sure I want to give that up anytime soon. And now that I'm not so worried about money or my financial future—also thanks to you," she added with a lopsided grin, "I don't feel as desperate to move on and do something else. I'd kind of like to stick around and see where life takes me."

He tugged her close, looping his arms around her waist and locking the black scarf between their two bodies. "Does that include moving in with me?" he asked, his tone low and scratchy with desire.

"Yes," she answered without thought, without hesitation. She didn't need to think about it; every cell of her being was standing up and doing a club version of the Snoopy Dance.

"But I'm not agreeing to move into your place until I've seen it," she qualified, poking him in the chest with the tip of her index finger. "I've never even been to your apartment. For all I know, it could be crawling with cockroaches and littered with stinky jockstraps."

"Hey, give me a little credit," he grumbled, his mouth drawing down in a frown.

"Nope. Not until I've checked it out thoroughly. And if it's unsatisfactory, then you can move in here or we can look for another place that's big enough for the both of us. Sound good?"

"On one condition."

His eyes narrowed, a wolfish, predatory glow glinting in the azure depths. A flash of apprehension skittered through her belly, and she knew instinctively that she was in trouble.

Flicking her tongue over her dry lips, she took a shallow breath and braced herself for whatever he might say or do next. "And that would be . . . ?"

"We keep this apartment until we're completely moved into the new one."

Okay, that hadn't been even close to what she'd expected to hear.

"Why?" she asked, thoroughly confused.

Tugging the scarf out from between them, he wrapped it around her neck and pulled her close for a long, deep, soul-shattering kiss. She barely noticed when he slid his hands down her arms, dragging the scarf along.

Coming up for air, leaving her gasping like a trout on a hook, he shot her a wicked smile. And that's when she felt the scarf at her wrists . . . both of which were now angled behind her, held together at the small of her back with the knotted length of soft black yarn.

"So we can do this," he said, giving the scarf an extra tug to test its security.

"And this."

He took her mouth again, tasting her, claiming her, ravaging her. By the time he lifted his head, she was putty in his hands, remaining on her feet only because he was holding her up.

His lips continued to dance along her skin, skimming her chin, her nose, the line of cheekbone just under her eye. "And, maybe, a few of the things that got you the name Domiknitrix to begin with."

A sharp stab of desire washed through her, pulling every muscle in her body into a tight knot of need.

"I don't know," she murmured, amazed that she was capable of functional speech at all. "I'm not sure you can handle what earned me that name. There may be whips and chains and the occasional act of submission involved."

One sandy brown brow shot upward, deepening her urge to knock him to the ground, climb on top of him, and put an end to the ache throbbing between her thighs.

"I can take anything you can dish out, babe," he responded, and there wasn't a doubt in her mind he meant what he said.

"Then it sounds like a plan to me."

A great plan. A phenomenal plan. The best plan ever to be concocted since the beginning of time.

"Good," he whispered matter-of-factly against her mouth. "We can do the other later, but for now, I'm afraid you're at *my* mercy."

Hooking the heel of his foot behind her ankle, he yanked her legs out from under her, toppling her gently to her back on the couch. Following her down, he proceeded to slowly, *agonizingly* strip her of her Bobby Jack pajamas and give her a prelude to what was to come now that they'd given up hating each other and were going to take a stab at loving each other instead.

Mmmm. She suspected she was going to thoroughly enjoy working *with* Dylan rather than against him for a change.

She was going to like it *a lot.*

Row 21

When Ronnie arrived at The Yarn Barn that Wednesday for the weekly knitting meeting, she was smiling from ear to ear. The same as she had been ever since Dylan showed up at her apartment and admitted that he wanted to work on building a future with her.

Neither of them had actually come out and said *I love you* yet, but they used the L-word in other ways that led her to believe the real thing was probably lurking just around the corner.

He often told her he loved her eyes, her mouth, her body . . . loved making love with her, loved her column, loved her sense of humor. And though it hadn't been easy for her at first, she'd begun to return similar sentiments of her own.

It was getting easier, too, and the more time she spent with him, the more she found to admire and fall in love with.

He made her smile and laugh more than anyone else she'd ever met.

He rocked her world in the bedroom like she'd never imagined was even possible.

But more than that, he supported her in everything she did.

Though he was giving up his job at the *Cleveland Herald,* she had decided to stay at the *Sentinel.* She'd not only decided to stay but was taking a renewed, energized interest in her job, brainstorming ideas for making her column even bigger and better and more exciting.

Since she no longer had the ongoing battle of the sexes between their two columns to fall back on, she needed something fresh and new to grab readers' attention and give them a reason to seek out her section of the paper each week. And almost every night, Dylan happily lay awake with her, letting her bounce ideas off him, and throwing in a few of his own.

She had a nice, long list started, and had already typed up a handful of columns to use in the future. Sometimes she got so jazzed about them, her fingers couldn't move over the keyboard fast enough to keep up with the words rattling around in her brain.

For the first time in a *long* time, her life seemed to be perfectly on track and running smoothly. She was happy in her career, and happy for the changes taking place in Dylan's career, even if she would miss him those times he was on the road.

Things with her family had never been better. She'd spoken with each of her brothers and sisters, and in some cases her brothers- and sisters-in-law and a few nieces and nephews, as well. She'd called her parents, too, and a big family get-together was planned for the holidays. She'd even offered to cook the bird, which was only now beginning to scare the turkey feathers out of her.

But it was her previously nonexistent love life that put the skip in her step and had her grinning like an idiot. The Ice Queen, as she was apparently known within certain circles—Zack was *so* going to get a kick to the kneecap for that one the next time she saw him—was definitely well on the way to melting into a puddle of warm and slippery goo.

She wondered if her friends would notice. As much as she'd wanted to, she'd resisted the urge to call them two seconds after Dylan had untied her wrists and she'd regained consciousness. She'd wanted a bit of time alone with him first, to get used to the idea that they were a couple now, and to enjoy his extremely determined, single-minded devotion to her pleasure.

Her heels clicked as she sauntered down the main aisle of the store to the meeting area in the back. Everyone else was seated already, knitting out and conversations going full-force.

They all glanced up as she approached and she greeted them with a smile that almost turned into a giggle before she tamped down the growing need to spill her guts.

Setting her purse and knitting tote on the seat of her chair, she carefully unwound the soft black scarf Dylan had given her from around her neck. She loved it, wore it everywhere, and was only sorry that soon enough the weather would turn warm again and she'd be forced to tuck it away with the rest of her winter wardrobe. Unless she could somehow find a way to make scarves in summer a hot new fashion statement.

Or maybe she could convince Dylan to knit her a tank top or a pair of hot pants to get her through the off season.

"You look awfully chipper tonight," Grace said in her usual blunt-as-a-razor manner.

Half a dozen gazes swung to Ronnie and latched on. For a second, she tried to look serious, but she didn't have enough guile left at the moment to pull it off.

Letting her joy shine through, she took a seat between Jenna and Grace and pulled out her yarn and needles.

"Yes, so?" she replied primly, avoiding her friends' stares.

"*So . . . ,*" Grace dragged out. "What's going on? Spill."

Feigning nonchalance, Ronnie murmured, "Oh, nothing much. Just that I've decided to pass on the job in Chicago and move in with Dylan instead."

The gasps and shrieks that met her announcement were earsplitting, and she finally gave in to the laughter bubbling in her throat.

"*Dylan Stone?*" Melanie all but squawked, eyes nearly bugging out of her head. "The 'ignorant, arrogant Jackass'? The one you once said you'd rather have a flesh-eating bacteria on your hoo-ha than be anywhere near? *That* Dylan?"

Ronnie flushed what she was sure was a bright crimson. She had a feeling a lot of the things that she'd said about Dylan in the past were going to come back to bite her in the ass.

And knowing her friends, they would take great glee in reminding her of them all, then bringing them up again and again and again and again . . . just to make sure she learned her lesson and ate a fair amount of crow.

But she was okay with it. Considering the current set of circumstances and how happy she was with how things had turned out, a little abject humiliation was a small price to pay.

"Yes," she said somewhat sheepishly, "that Dylan."

Still having trouble assimilating Ronnie's announcement, Melanie asked, "When in God's name did this happen?"

Which was the perfect opening for Grace to lavishly rehash the last several weeks of Ronnie's life. The knitting challenge turning into private knitting lessons . . . the private knitting lessons turning into hot, window-fogging, wall-climbing, howl-like-a-banshee sex . . . and finally the new job offer forcing her to reassess her career goals and feelings for a man who was supposed to be her sworn enemy.

But that was as much as Grace knew, so all eyes turned back to Ronnie.

Setting aside her knitting—since it was obvious no one would be getting much work done at tonight's meeting—she crossed her leg and let one of her fire-engine-red sling-backs dangle from the tips of her toes. Taking her time, and trying not to let her happiness tangle her words, she filled them all in on everything that had happened in the past week, from Dylan winning the knitting challenge to the moment he'd declared his undying lust for her.

She skipped the part where he'd tied her hands behind her back and showed her the meanings of the words *oh, dear God, harder, faster, yes, yes,* but from the sparkle in her closest friends' eyes and the sly expressions on the others' faces, everyone was already picturing how she and Dylan had celebrated their new-found fondness for each other.

Jenna reached across the arms of their chairs and gave her knee a squeeze. "I'm so happy for you, Ronnie. I knew you and Dylan would get along if you just took the time to get to know each other better. And I'm *really* glad you decided not to take that job in Chicago. I would have missed you too much if you'd moved that far away."

Murmurs of agreement followed Jenna's heartfelt speech. She thanked them all, letting her gaze move around the circle of friends until she spotted Charlotte's bright orange mop of hair.

The older woman's mouth, painted bubblegum pink with a lipstick that was *so* not her color, was pulled into a peculiar moue. Ronnie realized she hadn't heard a word from Charlotte, and she was the only one still studiously knitting, her needles clacking away as though nothing unusual was taking place.

And maybe as far as Charlotte was concerned, there wasn't. Just because Ronnie's life had been turned upside down—in the very best ways possible—didn't mean Charlotte had to care.

"What do you think, Charlotte?" she asked pointedly. "Am I making a mistake by turning down a job I thought I'd always wanted and agreeing to move in with a man I've always purported to hate?"

And if that wasn't an invitation to brutal honesty, she didn't know what was. She only hoped she could handle whatever response the older woman chose to give her.

"Oh, I think it's wonderful, dear. It's lovely that you and your young man have finally learned to talk out your differences instead of harping at each other through your newspaper columns."

The words were pleasant enough, sounded sincere enough, but the odd light in her eyes and strange twist of her lips never altered. Ronnie didn't know whether to be relieved or offended. She'd expected more from Charlotte, she guessed. A bigger, more exuberant, Charlotte-like reaction; something to go with the bright orange hair and mismatched polyester ensembles.

But then the others started chiming in again, distracting her and demanding more details about her time with Dylan. The PG- to R-rated version, anyway.

The hour passed quickly, and just as Ronnie had predicted, no one—save the unusually focused Charlotte—got much knitting done. They didn't seem to mind, though. They were women first, knitters second, and a good piece of gossip trumped the chance to make progress on a current project or share new patterns any day.

As they all got up to don their coats and gather their things, each of the ladies came up to give her a hug and wish her congratulations again. A few even offered bits of advice on living with a man . . . Start early on training them to put their dirty clothes in the laundry hamper. Threaten to withhold sex if they forget to put the toilet seat down more than three times in a row. Tattoo important dates like birthdays and anniversaries on her forehead, otherwise they were sure to forget.

Ronnie promised to remember and not let Dylan get away with watching too much ESPN or being too much of a slob, then asked who cared to join her at The Penalty Box for a drink.

For the first time ever, she and Dylan had agreed to meet there immediately after her knitting group. For the first time ever, she was looking forward to seeing him there, instead of praying he'd get hit by a bus on the way, or by some miracle leave before she arrived.

She almost didn't want to wait for anyone else to

decide if they were going or not; she just wanted to get there and see him again. See him, touch him, kiss his lips. Sit and have a drink *with* him instead of crawling off to the farthest corner of the bar and drinking to forget that he was in the room and likely ogling her ass.

These days, she liked knowing he was ogling her ass. Especially since it meant that before long, he'd be doing a lot more than just *looking* at that portion of her anatomy.

They'd been apart for almost seventy-five minutes now, and she *missed* him, God help her.

Lord, she was such a sap. She'd gone from being the Ice Queen to being a big jiggly pile of lemon Jell-O who practically couldn't function if she didn't get her Dylan fix every couple of hours.

Thankfully, she didn't think her pathetic-ness showed, which meant nobody needed to know just what a pushover she'd become because of a man.

But not just any man. *Dylan.*

Her heartbeat doubled just thinking about him, and she curled her fingers into the soft black alpaca wool of her scarf to keep from rushing the girls into making up their minds. As usual, Grace and Jenna were headed her way, but the others begged off with various excuses.

"Are you sure you won't join us, Aunt Charlotte?" Jenna asked, waiting for the older woman to gather her things and waddle along with them toward the front entrance of the store.

"Oh, no, no. I've got too much to do at home, but thank you for the invitation." She covered her head with a giant variegated hat she'd made herself, complete with earflaps and a pom-pom on top, and tied it beneath her chin. "You three girls have fun, though, and con-gratulations again, Ronnie. I'm very happy for you."

After thanking her, the three of them made their way to Grace's car. Since Dylan had dropped Ronnie off at the store for her meeting, she needed a ride to the bar.

Another first. Ronnie imagined there would be a lot of them from now on, and though she never would have expected it of herself, she was looking forward to experiencing each and every one.

On the ride to The Penalty Box, Grace and Jenna wanted the full scoop and all the details Ronnie hadn't divulged in front of the others. And while she filled them in on most of it, there were still some things she kept to herself. The sexier, kinkier, more private stuff that even her very best friends didn't need to know about. She preferred to keep that just between Dylan and herself.

And when they arrived at the bar, ducking inside quickly to get away from the wind and cold, her eyes immediately scanned the room for Dylan. She found him sitting at his usual table, along with Zack and Gage and three half-empty bottles of their favorite beer.

It might have been her imagination, but almost like a scene from a movie, the loud cacophony of the bar seemed to soften, and Dylan turned his head in her direction. As soon as he saw her, he pushed his chair back to stand, the legs scraping across the floor and adding an even sharper edge to the rope of tension arching between them.

All eyes tracked him as he moved toward her, his long strides eating up the space that separated them. He grabbed her around the shoulders, yanked her to his chest, and kissed her like a soldier just back from the war . . . a little more of a performance than she'd counted on, but definitely something she could get used to.

After sucking the air from her lungs and leaving her none too steady on her feet, he stepped back, stared at her a moment, then held a hand out in invitation.

She knew that just about everyone in the room, save her friends and his, expected her to deck him. They were waiting for it. A month ago, she wouldn't have left them hanging, but probably would have sucker-punched him in the gut before he'd gotten his mouth anywhere near hers.

But now, she simply linked her hand with his and followed him to the large round table where his buddies were waiting.

A second passed, and then the entire bar erupted in whoops and whistles, cheers and catcalls, and though Ronnie's stomach was tight in embarrassment over their public display of affection, she felt warm and contented, too.

This definitely beat a public pissing contest any day of the week.

From now on, if she felt like competing with Dylan, she would be *way* more creative in her dares, and do it in the bedroom where they'd already established that *anything goes*.

Bind Off

Charlotte watched her three favorite girls from the knitting group walk together to Grace's car while she remained on the sidewalk outside The Yarn Barn.

She kept her expression carefully blank until they'd rolled out of the parking lot . . . then a wide, beaming grin spread across her face. She picked up her sneaker-clad feet and did a little jig right there, singing along with her excitement.

She'd done it. Or rather, the spinning wheel had done it.

Even after that night at her house when Ronnie had confessed she'd gone to bed with her so-called enemy, Charlotte still hadn't been sure she should believe the stories she'd been told about the wheel being enchanted and bringing true love to anyone who used the yarns it spun.

She'd been hopeful, but not certain.

Now, though . . .

Oh, glory. The proof was in the pudding, and now she *knew* her mother and grandmother and all of her other little old ancestors had been right about the magic of the spinning wheel. Ronnie's happiness in finding love with a man she'd formerly professed to hate more than a case of the chicken pox was proof of that.

Charlotte could barely contain her glee as she pranced across the sloppy wet parking lot to her old but reliable Buick and climbed inside. She cranked the engine, then turned up the heat, eager to make her way home and get to work.

Now that she knew she could rely on the power of the spinning wheel, there was someone else she wanted to help find true love.

Spinning the yarn for this one would be tricky, since her niece enjoyed making fancy, fuzzy boas more than knitting just a run-of-the-mill scarf or hat.

But with the help of her enchanted spinning wheel, maybe she could help Jenna get over her failed marriage to Gage and once again find true love.

Ronnie's Scarf

(as knit by Dylan)

Materials:
Size 10 knitting needles
1 8-ounce skein of yarn (any color)

Special Instructions:
yo = yarn over
(bring the yarn over the top of the right hand needle)
k2tog = knit 2 together
*(insert the right hand needle into the front of the next two
 stitches on the left hand needle, then knit them together
 as one)*
( ) = directions in parentheses are to be repeated

Directions: Cast on 23 stitches
Knit first 5 rows
Row 6: k3, (yo, k2tog, k1) repeat 4 more
    times, yo, k2tog, k3
Rows 7 and 8: knit across
Row 9: Repeat Row 6
Rows 10 and 11: Repeat Rows 7 and 8
Continue pattern until scarf reaches about 4
    feet or desired length
Bind off

Fringe (optional):
Cut several pieces of yarn, about 5 inches long. (The more
pieces you use, the thicker your fringe will be.)
With a crochet hook, attach individual pieces of yarn to both
ends of scarf using a "cow hitch" stitch. (See graphic.)

Keep reading for a sneak peek at
Heidi Betts's next novel

*Loves Me,
Loves Me Knot*

Now available from St. Martin's Paperbacks

Cast On

With a final shove, Charlotte Langan managed to heave
the heavy, centuries-old spinning wheel up the last two
attic steps and onto the dusty floor.

When she'd hauled the thing down to her bedroom
six months before, she certainly hadn't anticipated the
need to carry it back up so soon—at least not by herself.
But with her niece due to arrive any minute, she didn't
have much choice. Jenna would be staying at the house
for the next two weeks while Charlotte was on the road
with one of the country's largest traveling craft shows.

She'd been preparing for this trip for years. Raising
and shearing her own alpacas—who had become practically like children to her, given the amount of time
she spent with them. Dying their fiber and spinning it
into yarn. Knitting scarves and hats and mittens and
sweaters—everything she could think of that might sell
until she had boxes upon boxes of items ready to go.

Some of her creations she sold at her booth in a local indoor craft and flea market, but since she spent
most of her time either knitting or spinning, she had
plenty left over for the traveling show. Or rather, she

had enough left over from her stockpiling for the traveling show to also keep the small local booth.

Breath wheezing from her lungs, Charlotte tugged the hem of her floral polyester top down over her wide hips and continued to slide the spinning wheel across the floor toward a far, shadowed corner. She planned to lock the attic door, and couldn't think of any reason her niece might have for poking around up here, but she didn't want to take chances.

If Jenna found the ancient spinning wheel in a corner of the attic, covered by a thick white sheet, she might wonder why Charlotte wasn't using it. Why she'd gone to the expense of purchasing a new one when she had a perfectly good and probably much more valuable one in her possession.

Oh, Charlotte could lie to her. She had no compunction about that sort of thing, not when it was for the greater good. She could tell her niece she hadn't wanted to risk anything happening to the family heirloom . . . or that it had a squeaky wheel . . . or that it didn't spin quite as well as the other one.

And Jenna would probably believe her. The dear, sweet child would never even consider that her eccentric old aunt might be up to something. Something secret, something devious, something . . . well, something Jenna would likely not appreciate if she knew.

Because the spinning wheel she was even now covering with the sheet, hiding like a fat kid squirreling away a last slice of birthday cake, wasn't just old. It wasn't just a family heirloom or a possibly priceless antique. It was magic.

Charlotte hadn't believed it in the beginning. When she'd first remembered the old spinning wheel in the attic, she'd also begun to recall the tales her mother and grandmother used to tell her during her youth about its enchanted properties. How it was a true love spinning wheel, and that the yarn it spun could bring two people together for their very own happily ever after.

At the time, she'd thought they were simply stories created to lull her to sleep or fill her head with Rose Red dreams. But when Ronnie Chasen, one of the young women in her Wednesday night knitting group, had found herself at sixes and sevens with a fellow journalist, Charlotte had decided to put the spinning wheel to the test.

As hopeful as she'd been that the soft black yarn she spun with Ronnie and Dylan in mind would work to draw the two together, she wasn't sure she'd actually believed it would. Not until the sparks had begun to fly and the animosity between the two newspaper columnists had turned into something equally combustible, but far more . . . naughty. The details Ronnie had since shared with the group were enough to turn Charlotte's hair carrot orange . . . if it weren't already, thanks to a copious supply of L'Oreal's limited edition "I Love Lucy" do-it-yourself hair coloring kits.

The good news, though, wasn't that Ronnie and Dylan were apparently extremely sexually compatible, but that the spinning wheel had worked! The yarn it spun really did seem to be magic and able to generate love where there hadn't been love before.

Of course, one positive result couldn't really be considered conclusive evidence, could it? No. As impressed as Charlotte was with the results of the first skein of yarn she'd spun on the antique wheel, she thought that another test or two might be in order.

And if anyone needed a little love in her life, it was her dear niece, Jenna. The poor girl just hadn't been the same since her divorce from Gage a year and a half before. The two had been meant for each other—or so Charlotte had thought. She'd been completely shocked when they'd split up, and she still wasn't sure she understood the reason for the breakup. Not all of it, anyway.

But just because Jenna's marriage to Gage hadn't worked out didn't mean the girl had to spend the rest of her life moping. And no matter how many dates she'd been on recently, that's exactly what Jenna was doing!

She needed a boost. A lift. A little fairy dust to raise her spirits and get her back in the game.

Confident the spinning wheel was adequately covered and hidden behind several large boxes of odds and ends, Charlotte dusted her hands together, patted her brow with the edge of one sleeve, and moved back down the stairs to the doorway that opened directly into her bedroom. She closed and locked it behind her, tucked the key at the back of her underwear drawer, then took a second to glance in the mirror.

Her mop of bright orange hair was still perfectly coiffed, thanks to the industrial amount of hairspray she'd used on it only a few hours before. Her white blouse with its tiny blue flowers was still pristine, not even a smudge of dust from her excursion to the attic on it or her navy blue slacks.

Satisfied with her appearance, she headed downstairs and into the sitting room to collect her handbag and a thick skein of bright purple yarn. Her niece's penchant for knitting sexy, slinky boas to go with just about everything she wore meant that Charlotte had had to spin a light, feathery yarn that Jenna would be likely to start using right away.

It hadn't been easy. Certainly not as quick or straightforward as the thicker, sturdier yarn she'd spun for Ronnie, and which the young woman had ended up using to help teach Dylan—albeit reluctantly—to knit. A competitive challenge that had developed into something much more personal and significant.

Thanks to Charlotte's covert matchmaking efforts, of course. Oh, she hadn't picked Dylan for Ronnie or anything as ordinary as that. No, she'd simply handed Ronnie the special yarn and let the enchanted spinning wheel's powers do their thing.

Which was exactly what she planned to do with this ball of yarn. The rest would be up to Fate and magic . . . and hopefully Jenna's willingness to experience love again.

At the sound of a vehicle pulling into the drive, Charlotte grabbed her things and hurried to the front door in time to see her niece climbing out of her sunflower yellow VW beetle. Falling in line with Jenna's somewhat quirky personality, large magnets in the shape of white and yellow daisies decorated the doors and hood of the adorable vehicle.

Flowers weren't Jenna's only mode of decorating her beloved bug, though. At Easter, she used a nose, tail, and ears to make the car look like a bunny rabbit; at Halloween, a broom and the back end of a witch's robe would appear as though sticking out of the rear hatch; at Christmas, it was antlers and a bright red Rudolph nose.

Charlotte loved to see Jenna's happy yellow beetle

coming up the drive, never knowing what amusing guise the little VW would be wearing.

Today, Jenna herself was dressed in dark blue jeans that flared at the calf and sparkled at the thighs and pockets with a mixture of rhinestones and silver studs. Her blouse was sage green and cut in a tank-top style, made of some soft, flowing, almost diaphanous material that was so popular these days. Never mind that one could almost see a girl's bits and pieces and skimpy brassieres underneath.

And as usual, Jenna also had a boa wrapped loosely around her neck in blending hues of green, yellow, and brown that perfectly matched her top.

"Hello, dear!" Charlotte called as she pushed through the front screen door and bustled down from the porch.

Jenna smiled and raised a hand to wave before reaching into the back seat for her overnight bag.

"You ready to go?" Jenna asked as Charlotte crossed the yard to greet her.

Charlotte's head bobbed up and down. "The station wagon and U-haul are both stuffed to the gills. As soon as you're settled, I'll be on my way."

"If you're in a hurry to get going, don't let me hold you up," Jenna said. She slammed the car door behind her and turned to face her aunt, rainbow-striped valise in one hand. "I know my way around, and some of the girls are coming over tomorrow night to keep me company."

"Oh, good! And you know where everything is, right? Even in the barn?"

Jenna's lips curved indulgently. "Don't worry, Aunt Charlotte, your babies are safe with me. I'll take good care of them, I promise."

A small weight lifted from Charlotte's chest. "Of course you will. I'm sorry, it's just that I don't leave them very often, and I'm too used to taking care of them all by myself, I guess."

"Except when I come over to help you out, which is how I know all of their names, their little quirks, and where everything is that they could possibly need."

Jenna leaned in and Charlotte hugged her back, then let her niece herd her toward her late-model station wagon. It was sort of a buzzard barf brown, according to Jenna, with the prerequisite faux wood side panels. A "woody," as they used to say . . . though the last time she'd called it that, her niece's cheeks had turned bubble-gum pink and she'd been quietly informed that "woody" was a term currently reserved for a rather private, highly aroused portion of the male anatomy. Charlotte hadn't referred to her station wagon in that manner since.

Jenna often told her she should trade the outdated rattletrap in—if a dealer was even willing to take it—and find something a little more modern to get around in. But Charlotte liked her wagon. It had plenty of space and got her where she needed to go, which was all she required of her mode of transportation these days.

Vinyl seat squeaking as she climbed behind the wheel, Charlotte deposited her purse on the passenger side floor before fitting the key into the ignition.

"Oh, I nearly forgot." She hadn't, of course, but the more spontaneous her gift seemed, the better.

Taking the skein of purple yarn from her lap, she held it out to Jenna. "I made this for you. Thought it might give you something to do while I'm away and you're in that big old house all by yourself."

Jenna took the yarn, running a few of the fringe-like strands between her fingers. "It's beautiful, thank you. Purple is one of my favorite colors."

She leaned in to press a kiss to her aunt's cheek, then straightened and pushed the door closed.

"Drive carefully," she said through the open window. "And good luck with the show. I hope you sell out of everything."

"Me, too, dear. Of course, if that happens, I'll just have to start all over again."

One corner of her niece's mouth quirked up in a grin. "Yes, but you love every minute of it."

"You know I do," Charlotte returned with a grin of her own. She cranked the engine and waited for the low throb to vibrate along the car's long metal frame all the way to her posterior. "All right, then, I'm off. You take care, and if you need anything . . . Well, I don't have a cell phone, so if you need anything, you're going to have to run to someone else. But I will call as often as I can to check in."

"I'll be fine. And so will the alpacas. You just go and have fun."

With a nod, Charlotte put the car in gear and rolled slowly out of her drive. She eased the wagon and U-haul onto the dirt road, kicking up dust and waving into her rearview mirror at Jenna, who stood where she'd left her, enchanted yarn clasped tightly in one hand.

Charlotte hoped for a lot of things for this trip. Safe traveling, high-volume sales of her hand-spun yarns and knit goods . . . but most of all, she hoped for a very special man to appear in her niece's life. One who would take the shadows from her eyes and make her smile—really smile—the way she hadn't since her separation from Gage.

It was a lot to ask of one tiny skein of yarn.

But the spinning wheel had worked its magic before, and Charlotte was confident it would do so again.